"You were fated to come here."

Annja thought she showed no reaction but the monk chuckled.

"Oh, I know that yo[...] Annja Creed. Any m[...] Despite the secret b[...] too polite to tell a fa[...] believe he is, as you might say, full of it.

"You believe that only you, and those who think as you do, see the true face of reality. I can only shake my head sadly and hope that someday you might see that this universe of shining gears and ratchets you have constructed to believe in is itself merely a glittering toy, an illusion by which you hide the truth from your eyes."

She started to say something. Whether to dispute him or make some polite evasion, she didn't know. But he held up a chubby finger.

"No need exists for us to debate. My universe, like your unseeing, unfeeling, uncaring machine, shall carry on regardless of whether either of us believes or disbelieves. I only caution you for your sake—do not be too hasty to disbelieve in the help that comes to you in your direst need. You can explain it away later. What is vital to your quest, and possibly your survival, is that you not fight it."

She nodded. "I'll do my best."

Titles in this series:

ROGUE Angel

Alex Archer

SEEKER'S CURSE

A GOLD EAGLE BOOK FROM

W🌐RLDWIDE®

TORONTO • NEW YORK • LONDON
AMSTERDAM • PARIS • SYDNEY • HAMBURG
STOCKHOLM • ATHENS • TOKYO • MILAN
MADRID • WARSAW • BUDAPEST • AUCKLAND

Recycling programs
for this product may
not exist in your area.

First edition July 2009

ISBN-13: 978-0-373-62137-8

SEEKER'S CURSE

Special thanks and acknowledgment to
Victor Milán for his contribution to this work.

Printed in U.S.A.

The
LEGEND

...THE ENGLISH COMMANDER TOOK
JOAN'S SWORD AND RAISED IT HIGH.

The broadsword, plain and unadorned,
gleamed in the firelight. He put the tip against
the ground and his foot at the center of the blade.
The broadsword shattered, fragments falling
into the mud. The crowd surged forward,
peasant and soldier, and snatched the shards
from the trampled mud. The commander tossed
the hilt deep into the crowd.
Smoke almost obscured Joan, but she continued
praying till the end, until finally the flames climbed
her body and she sagged against the restraints.

Joan of Arc died that fateful day in France,
but her legend and sword are reborn....

1

The building fronts were whitewashed in name only. They had long since taken on a dingy cast.

Or maybe that was just Annja Creed's frame of mind.

She wore a gray business suit over a pale lavender blouse and high-heeled shoes that were impractical and uncomfortable on the cobbled streets. With her head held high and shoulders thrown back she looked, she hoped, every inch the typical successful American businesswoman.

But the angles of Kastoria, strewed all up and down picturesque hills on a peninsula that undulated into a lake, conspired against her. The unfamiliar balancing act of walking in heels, which made her back ache and sent pain stabbing up her lower legs at every step, threatened to twist an ankle or send her tumbling down the lane.

As picturesque a little Greek Macedonian town as Kastoria was, Annja felt as if she could smell tension like a tang of wood smoke in the air. Panel trucks blared horns at men trundling crates across the crowded street on handcarts. The way people shouted and gestured at each other made Annja hunch her shoulders in unhappy anticipation that knives would come out at any minute.

And all that was *before* she reached her scheduled rendezvous with a gang of ethnic-Albanian artifact smugglers out of Kosovo.

Along with the diesel fumes and harsh tobacco smoke a chemical smell loaded down what should have been crisp air filtered through the pines on the surrounding hills. Annja passed a stack of cages where long slender animals paced nervously or stood with slightly arched backs and stared at her with beady black eyes. They were minks, destined to play a role in the fur trade, which was still the town's main commerce and Annja reckoned also must account for the unidentified stink, since presumably the furs were subjected to some kind of chemical treatment.

She kept her head turning right to left, hoping she looked arrogant rather than furtive or paranoid. Furtive *and* paranoid would have been accurate. She was looking for a weathered dark blue sign with yellow lettering. Which of course she wouldn't be able to read because it was in Greek. But supposedly that wouldn't matter; it was only a landmark.

How the Japan Buddhist Federation had turned up the contact she didn't know and hadn't asked. She doubted they'd tell her. They'd hired her, for a very nice sum, to investigate why artifacts from Nepalese Buddhist shrines had begun to appear on the black market in Europe, particularly the Balkans. If she had to guess, she suspected certain of their members posed as collectors none too concerned about the provenance of the items in their collections, so long as they were convinced of their genuine antiquity— and value. They were certainly heeled well enough to pull off the pose.

Fearless pigeons bobbed, pecked and burbled everywhere, as disdainful of her uncertain progress as they were of the prospects of destruction beneath the wheels of the trucks and humpbacked little cars and overloaded handcarts. They went about their single-minded business until the last possible moment and a heartbeat or two beyond. Then they scurried or fluttered up from the path of onrushing doom and settled down again a few feet away as if nothing important had happened.

As promised, she spotted the sign on her right, near the base of the hill. A block farther down, the narrow lane opened onto a road that ran around the lake's shore. Shacks and kiosks stood along the water. A few boats bobbed at rickety wharfs. The lake water was very blue but the waves were getting pointy and even flashing a little white in the sun as the breeze strengthened. Some heavy clouds were starting to crowd the sky overhead. It looked as if a storm front was moving down from the Balkans.

Appropriate, she thought.

The sign was a surprisingly deep blue; the weathering showed not in fading so much as severe cracking. In yellow above the Greek writing was an outline of a young woman who appeared to be pouring something from an amphora. Given the location it could be the waters of the lake as easily as the local wine.

At the bottom of the sign the word *Taverna* was written. Not that she had much doubt as to the nature of the business going on behind the gray stone facade. Stocky old men with sailor's caps, gray beards and heavy sweaters stood around the stone stoop smoking. They glared at her as she marched past, whether in suspicion or religious disapproval of assertive foreign womanhood she couldn't tell.

Play the part, she told herself. What've you got to be afraid of? Other than walking alone into the middle of a gang of Muslim Kosovar bandits who are doubtless armed to the teeth.

Thinking those reassuring thoughts, she turned right onto the narrow street just past the tavern's raw stone corner.

The rooftops leaned together as if eventually they'd just meet in the middle in a sort of happenstance arch. They cut off the sunlight like peaks in a high mountain valley, plunging the cobbles below into gloom. Air that had been cool turned chill.

The street didn't meet the other at ninety degrees, but rather took off at an angle up the same hill she'd just walked so precariously down. Great, she thought. Now I get to climb in these stupid heels.

But it wasn't far. Half a block up a pack of men loitered in front of a building where the whitewash had started coming off in sheets, revealing lumpy gray stucco beneath. A blue fog of harsh Turkish cigarette smoke hung over them.

In their sweaters and long black coats and dark beard stubble they were just the sort of group of loitering males Annja would normally give a wide berth to. Unattached males in a clump tended to spell trouble in every time and clime. These toughs looked older than your usual street gang, mostly thirties and up. That didn't much reassure her, though. It likely meant they had a much more advanced thug skill set than adolescent hoods.

The tall nervous-looking man who stepped out to meet her wore a black leather greatcoat over a dark turtleneck sweater. He had a handlebar mustache backed by a three-day beard sprouting from his round face. The roundness was deceptive; he was lanky beneath the coat. Disconcertingly his left eye was milky, dead, beside his beak nose.

"You are Amanda Carter?" he asked in thickly accented English.

Annja followed the old WWII spy rule of using

aliases with her own initials. It made them easier to remember and reduced the risk of some overlooked personal item tripping her up. She didn't exactly have a lot of monogrammed possessions, but you could never be too sure at the stakes she was playing for. Besides, she felt the name was easy for nonnative English speakers to pronounce—and more important, remember—as well as having the Waspy ring appropriate to her current cover story.

"Yes," she said, remembering to be clipped and haughty. As wound up inside as she was it wasn't hard to do. The pack had split and men began to drift up and down the street toward her. The members tended to keep their hands inside their voluminous coats. She was well aware they were positioning themselves to provide security against intrusion, accidental or otherwise. She also recognized a classic predatory move. Hemming in the prey and cutting off escape.

Remember, she told herself, you have something they want—access to abundant American cash.

"You are Enver Bajraktari?" she asked.

"Yes," he said. He indicated over his shoulder. "And this my associate, Duka."

Bajraktari cast a large shadow. Duka loomed like a mountain of bone and gristle over his boss's right shoulder. He had thick black hair greased back from a face and mouth like a jack-o'-lantern carved from scar tissue. His eyes were dark crescents and his smile wide, revealing a jagged jumble of brown teeth. Annja made herself not stare at this disastrous failure of modern dentistry.

Because it suited her persona, and absurdly made her feel slightly better, she held up the black briefcase she had been carrying before her chest like a shield.

"Do you have the items we discussed?" she asked.

Bajraktari held out a hand. It was a surprisingly large hand, with long slender fingers. It was the sort of hand old-time pulp-mystery writers usually described as belonging to pianists and stranglers. Annja doubted the man played much Mozart.

In the big palm lay a figure cast in the shape of an elephant with trunk raised to forehead. It was either gold or gold washed. Although Annja was no authority on South Asian artifacts, it certainly looked authentic.

"You like." His tone suggested a command, not a question or come-on.

"Maybe," she said. "I trust you have more?"

Bajraktari looked at her with his one dark eye. "Come," he said.

He turned and stalked into an oblong of blackness in the ratty building behind him. To Annja's relief Duka followed him straightaway, bending his knees considerably to get through the door. His shoulders squeezed against the frame.

The other goons in view now stood seven or eight yards away toward both ends of the block. She had the option to follow or not.

She followed.

Inside was dim. It was cool to the edge of chill. A musty smell hit her in the face. Dust, mold, general antiquity and—

Pigeon droppings streaked down the sides of water-warped crates and decaying cardboard boxes and big vases Annja hoped weren't ancient amphorae. They were caked in lumpy pale sedimentary layers on every horizontal surface and at the edges of walkways across the hardwood-plank floor of the warehouse. As her vision adjusted she saw it was a warehouse filled with unsteady-looking shelves laden with boxes and objects of uncertain nature.

Following her sketchy hosts, Annja advanced into the crowded interior. It wasn't cave-black; a grayish illumination came from somewhere, like fog. Everything that wasn't horizontal and caked in droppings, it seemed, was draped with cobwebs.

The narrow aisle ahead of Annja was blocked almost entirely by the mountainous mass of Duka, who progressed by leaning side to side, endangering the groaning, sagging shelves at every step, and teetering forward, as if he lacked knees or his legs were very short. Bajraktari was completely hidden by his massive underling.

Annja wondered how the huge henchman did it. She had to focus on walking down the very center of the wooden floor, with her shoulders unaccustomedly hunched forward to keep them from brushing anything, which might cover her in dust, inspire something awful to leap out at her or simply bring a whole overburdened rack of shelving down upon her head. Her shoulders, although broad for a woman even of her height, were nothing to Duka's. Yet he managed to avoid mishap.

At the end of ten yards or so a space opened, seven or eight yards on either side. In the middle stood a large crate covered with some kind of dark cloth. A single lightbulb in a not very reflective reflector cone hung from a cord that led up into blackness so complete it might have gone on forever into the heart of infinite night. It spilled a yellow illumination upon the objects arranged on the cloth-covered surface.

Annja's breath stuck in her throat. They were artifacts: statues, plates, bowls, coins. All gleaming bright gold. A mound of the stuff. A foot-high seated Buddha presided jovially over the lot.

"Samples," Bajraktari said.

If it was all real—meaning both authentically ancient and actual solid gold, not just gold-washed lead, a trick the ancients were perfectly hip to—Annja was looking at upward of one hundred thousand dollars in plunder in the value of the metal alone. If you took into account the historic value, its price became incalculable.

Annja strode forward. As it happened that fit the role she was playing, but that had been driven right out of her mind by the sight. All she could think of now was confirming that she confronted evidence of a truly massive crime against archaeology. And circumstances suggested this was only the tip of the iceberg.

Reaching the makeshift display table, she snatched up the nearest item. Any evidence as to context was long lost already, especially if the loot had been polished, as appeared likely. Her finger oils weren't going to damage the gleaming artifact if it was gold.

Annja stared down at the thing she held. It was a slightly irregular disk—a coin, imprint eroded by its passage through many previous hands. And time. She could almost feel the years adding to its not in-substantial weight. It showed the blurred image of the head of a youthful-looking, somewhat plump man.

To her amazement the letters stamped in it, faded though they were, were unmistakably Greek.

She turned to Bajraktari, who stood to her left with his shadow, Duka, looming as always behind him. "What's a Greek coin doing here?" she demanded. "I thought these artifacts were Nepali."

Instead of responding directly to her question, Bajraktari raised his head and said something sharp in Albanian. Annja sensed movement behind her.

Hard hands clamped like vises on her upper arms.

2

"What the hell do you think you're doing, Bajrak-tari?" Annja demanded. She became aware of a grayed-out oblong glow farther back in the ware-house heights—a time-and-pigeon-grimed skylight. "Don't you know who you're dealing with?"

She knew even as the words left her mouth that she wasn't going to like the answer.

Bajraktari smiled. "There has been a change of plan," he said.

"Says who?" she demanded.

His coal-smudge brows twitched toward one another. "Do not try my patience, woman," he said. "For in the end you are only a woman."

It occurred to her this was not a good time to de-bate feminism. She settled for an angry toss of her head and a glare. "We had a deal," she said.

He nodded. "So we did. But all things are subject to negotiation in this world, are they not?"

"I represent a very important figure in American business."

"Just so. All Americans are rich. If your boss is rich by American standards, he must be really rolling in it, no?"

Annja's lips compressed to a line. She could see where this was going.

"It occurred to us, therefore, that Allah had delivered into our hands a most wonderful opportunity. If your employer would pay handsomely once for our artifacts, then would he not pay handsomely twice for the treasure, as well as for the return of his very lovely assistant?"

"You're making a mistake," Annja said.

Bajraktari said something in Albanian. Around him, unseeable in shadow, his men laughed.

"It shall be as Allah wills," the pack leader said. "If you are a religious woman, you should pray that it is not your employer who makes the worse mistake."

Annja glared at him. She felt the men holding her shift their weight to drag her away. She drew in a deep breath. And prayed forgiveness for the grave sin she was about to commit against archaeology.

Then she kicked the relic-topped crate for all she was worth.

Annja had extensive training in martial arts, Asian and Western. She had hundreds of hours of practice and no little practical experience at using those techniques. And she was far stronger than most women her size.

The crate, though loaded down with tens of pounds of golden wonders, was empty. It rolled right over. Glittering priceless objects flew everywhere.

Shrill voices yipped. Men flew from the shadows like bats, clutching at the lovely tumbling golden things. The hard hands on Annja's arms relaxed their grip.

Driving with her long strong legs and turning her hips, Annja wrenched her right arm free. She continued her pivot to slam a shovel hook with the heel of her right palm into the ribs of the man who held her left arm. The strike delivered force straight along the bones of the forearm; it was little less powerful than a closed-fist punch and presented a fraction of the danger of breaking your own hand.

A squeaking grunt blew out the man's lips and he doubled over. He released her.

Annja was already spinning back. Her elbow smash caught the man on her right on the point of his bristle-bearded chin. She'd been aiming for his nose. The miss was fortuitous. His teeth clashed loudly together. As she followed through, his eyes rolled up in his head and he toppled straight over backward like a chainsawed tree. He wouldn't be unconscious, she knew, and from personal experience she knew *knocked out* almost always meant stunned, not out cold.

She sensed movement rushing on her from the

left. Again she spun counterclockwise to meet the man whose ribs she'd cracked. Roaring with pain-induced fury, he bore down on her with arms outflung to catch her and crush her in a bear hug.

She drove her right hand into his solar plexus and heard a crunching sound.

Bajraktari reached into his coat and came out holding a handgun. His stiffened arm rose straight up over his head.

Annja was already diving away as Bajraktari fired. She briefly considered summoning the mystical sword she'd inherited from Joan of Arc but, useful and lethal as it was, it wouldn't stop bullets. She tucked a shoulder and rolled neatly into an aisle.

A whole row of heavy clay pots on a shelf to her left exploded as Bajraktari hauled the weapon down and triggered another shot. Pale pink dust enveloped her as flying potsherds raked her calves. Annja kicked off her shoes straightaway. She hated it in movies when women tried to flee or fight in heels. It was as absurd as it was unnecessary. And anyway, it was a relief to lose the accursed things.

She got her stocking feet beneath her, pushed up with her hands and launched herself down the aisle like a sprinter off the blocks. Bajraktari didn't have a clear shot at her back but she wanted to get out of the narrow passage before somebody did.

She was still coughing and blinking dust from her eyes. It caked in her unfamiliar mascara, blurring everything beyond. The figure that abruptly blocked the lane ten feet ahead of her was no more than a shadow.

There weren't a lot of things the shadow could be. Except for a gangster. Almost certainly aiming a gun at her. She launched herself into a forward running dive, throwing her arms out to keep from doing a skidding face plant and hoping she wouldn't break anything.

Gunfire erupted like thunder behind her. At the same time she felt the pulsing concussion of a nearby muzzle-blast, powerful and full-auto. A dragon's-breath of muzzle-flame swept over her as she hit the ground.

She skinned both palms and did a sort of belly flop on the wood floor. In front of her she saw motion. The smuggler who had popped up in front of her was collapsing like a suit of clothes falling from a hanger. She knew in an instant what had happened—he and his fellow gang member behind her had neatly cross-fired each other when she dropped unexpectedly out of their line of fire.

Ignoring the pain from raw splinter-snagged palms, she swarmed over the man in a sort of sprawling crawl and flung herself toward the exposed stone of the wall dimly visible ahead of her. A corridor maybe six feet wide ran between the wall and the shelves. She slid across it.

She heard a startled exclamation. A man stood almost on top of her. Had she come out of the aisle facedown he would've been to her left. Instead she had tucked her head and rolled onto her right side to avoid slamming headfirst into the wall. She still caught enough of a rap at the base of her cranium, slightly cushioned by the twist she'd wound her hair into, to shoot a pulse of yellow light through her brain.

Annja had always prided herself on her ability to keep her presence of mind even in blood crisis. With her eyes dazzled from within, her ears ringing from nearby gunshots and her stomach roiling with terror and nausea induced by the crack on the head, she brought her knees up to her belly and shot both long legs out in a kick that struck the smuggler's shins and shot the pins right out from under him.

He fell across her with a guttural exclamation that had to be a curse. She gave him a hard elbow to the left ear, writhed out from under him and found herself on her feet without any clear idea as to the process that had gotten her there.

It didn't matter. As the man reached for her she knew she had no options. She closed her eyes and saw her sword clearly. When she opened them, the weapon was in her hand. The sword gleamed dully in the smoky light. She reversed it and plunged it down between the man's shoulder blades. It bound, not wanting to withdraw. She let it go and it vanished back to the other where.

The echoes of angry shouts and random shots flew around the rafters. The horde of pigeons that had been rousted by the enormous uproar now fluttered around in the shadowed eaves like smoke trying to escape a burning building. Annja started to run. If I follow the walls, she reasoned, eventually I'll find a way out of here.

Shapes appeared ahead of her. She pushed off the wall with her right hand as she spun, adding momentum as she tried to dart into another aisle. A burst of full-auto gunfire ripped the air behind her.

Becoming aware that the rack of shelves to her right ran only about ten feet before another one began, Annja stopped and grabbed the uprights farther from the outer wall. She prayed that whatever was stored on them, too dust caked and cobwebbed for her to identify in the light and urgency, weren't priceless relics. Or if they were, that they weren't fragile.

Adrenaline gave her extra strength. With a couple of quick shakes the whole thing came toppling down across the aisle just as a couple of pursuers appeared. One of them threw up an arm before disappearing with a wail of despair beneath several hundred pounds of plundered antiquities and massive shelves. The other vanished behind a solid wall of dust, his path blocked by the shelves now propped at an angle across the narrow passage.

Annja ran on. A man dashed into the aisle ahead of her. Without time to think she swept her arm along the shelf beside her at a foot or so below her shoulder level. Another big dust cloud swirled out; at least one large pot flew through the clouded air right at the smuggler's head even as he raised a Kalashnikov assault rifle.

He fired a burst straight up into the rafters, causing a brief shower of bloody feathers to fall on him as he warded off the pot with an upflung left elbow. Annja's peripheral vision caught another pot lying on its side right in front of her just before she stepped on it, twisted her ankle and went down. Instead she rushed it with a swift soccer kick. It shot up at an angle and caught the gunman by evil chance, square in the crotch.

He started to jackknife. The sword appeared in Annja's hand. She slashed down right to left, met brief resistance and raised a quick spray, black in the gloom. The man dropped onto his face to rise no more.

She vaulted the body and found herself back in the middle of the cleared space. Golden debris littered the floor. And facing her across twenty-five feet of fallen antiquity stood Bajraktari, his good eye and his bad wide.

He smiled and raised his gun two-handed. "Prisoner!" he exclaimed.

Above her Annja heard a crash, the tinkle of falling glass. Something sailed over the terrorist leader's head to bounce with several dwindling thuds on the floorboards between them.

It looked like a short length of pipe with holes drilled in the sides and big hex nuts screwed onto either end. As it happened Annja knew at once what it was, having seen them demonstrated by some of her friends in Special Forces once upon a time. It was a U.S.-made M-84 stun grenade, commonly known as a flash-bang.

By reflex Annja had turned away, covering her face in her arms and just dropping. Bajraktari, she noted in the instant before she shielded her eyes, just stood there gaping at the grenade. He didn't seem to recognize it. Then again, relatively few people who saw them in use close up and personal like that lived to recall the experience.

The blinding flash neither blinded nor stunned Annja, although she was temporarily deafened by the blast, which was beyond loud and hit her body like a big bat.

Survival urged her to pop right up again and run. Already feeling the effects of stimulus overload, her body was slow to respond. She got up to one knee with a high-pitched tone singing through her skull, aural aftermath of the shattering noise, and looked around. Maybe I'm a little stunned after all, she thought.

The tableau took her breath away. Sunlight of a sort, grayish and feeble by the standards of the outside world but almost dazzling in this dim hell, poured through a busted skylight. Men in black masks and bulky black suits slid down ropes from the gaping hole. One of them fired a machine pistol one-handed. The walls and rafters danced with muzzle-flames in all directions.

With the attackers, almost certainly Greek police

or army special forces, and the Kosovars blazing enthusiastically away at each other, and dust and smoke everywhere, and pigeons flapping through the mayhem in frantic attempts to find their way out, the disoriented Annja felt for a dizzy instant as if she was starring in her own personal movie.

She glimpsed a big black-clad arm reach around Bajraktari's neck from the rear, dragging the thoroughly dazzled gang leader back into shadow. Duka was doing his bodyguardly duty. Then two things kick-started her body and her brain back into lightning action. First, the sheer animal desire to survive, the same thing that had the pigeons so agitated. Her scattered wits had coalesced enough to grasp that lingering in the midst of a firefight in a darkened warehouse was no way to stay breathing.

The second was her intellect re-evolving toward human intelligence from about the level of moss. She realized that getting caught either by the smugglers, who would now believe beyond a doubt she had set them up even though it wasn't true, and the authorities, who would know beyond a doubt she was trafficking stolen antiquities with well-armed criminals, which would be little better and possibly worse than catching a stray round.

She knew neither side was going to feel like listening to her explanations.

She darted into the nearest welcoming dark aisle as a random burst took out the lone light bulb hanging over the cleared space, adding to the darkness and confusion. Bad guys abounded, and if the cops had anything on the ball, there were going to be plenty of them, too.

Annja reckoned that increased her chances of escape. Everybody was so busy killing each other and trying not to get killed they likely had little attention to spare for a lone, apparently unarmed woman.

Hold that thought, she told herself, racing for the outer wall. She burst out into the corridor between it and the shelves.

A smuggler stood not twenty feet from her, holding an assault rifle. His eyes went wide when he saw her. He raised the rifle as she started to turn for a desperation dive back into the doubtful sanctuary of the aisle she'd just left.

A black-clad knee came up right between the gunman's wide-braced legs from behind. The impact raised him onto his toes. His rifle came down and to his right and went off, a short burst kicking up long splinters from the floor and blasting another cloud of dust from the shelves.

The leg straightened, then slammed back diagonally across the gunman's right shin, sweeping it out from under him. Pivoting from the hips, the man behind slammed him face first into the floor. Annja felt the impact through the soles of her feet. The smuggler made a quick grab behind him with his left hand. As he went down he clawed the black balaclava off his assailant's head.

For a moment Annja and the counterterror opera-

tor, or whatever he was, stared at each other. He had
a long, dark olive face and his curly hair was sweat
plastered to his skull. His eyes were dark and piercing and very wide at the unexpected sight of a Western woman in tattered business clothes in the middle
of a warehouse takedown in the back of beyond.

Annja's gaze slipped past him and her eyes went
wide. From the corner of her vision she saw a look
of skepticism cross the operator's face: You think I'm
gonna fall for that old trick, lady?

As she opened her mouth to shout a warning, she
knew she would be too late.

Either instinct or her genuine fear saved the operator. Twisting his upper torso, he threw himself
down. As he did he yanked a handgun from his thigh-
tied quick-draw. Two shots flamed out before he
landed on the prone, motionless body of his first opponent.

Behind him a shadow form fell to the floor. Annja
wheeled and ran straight away from them. Coming
up fast on her left she saw a rude oblong of boards
nailed to the wall, as if covering a window. When she
was outside she'd hadn't seen any bars on the windows, and the wood looked rotten.

If it's good wood I am going to break myself, she
thought. Taking a running jump, she threw her shoulder into it.

Rotten was right. The planks disintegrated into
dust and whirling lightweight flotsam. Annja toppled
through the window. For a moment she lay there in

cold rain that had begun to fall sometime during the fiasco in the warehouse.

From her right gunfire blasted. Somehow she got her feet beneath her and came up to a crouch.

A man in a long black coat was turning toward her with an assault rifle in his hands. A similarly clad man lay facedown in a puddle beside him. Annja glimpsed two other fallen figures, both wearing black outfits, masks and no coats, on the cobbles beyond him. Apparently a pair of bolting smugglers had run into a pair of operators trying to prevent escapes. One of the smugglers had gotten lucky.

But only briefly. Annja formed her hand into an open fist. The sword filled it. She slashed him across the shins.

He fell over backward shrieking in agony.

She turned and took off up the hill toward some trees that stood flanking the block's upper end.

3

Squinting in the dim light of a green-visored reading lamp, Annja looked from the huge book spread open on the table before her to the tiny golden disk she had propped against a stack of other volumes for comparison. The world-renowned National Archaeological Museum in Athens made brightly lit, modern reading rooms available to the public. But Annja felt more in the mood for the confines of the special-collections stacks. Especially since she was a little leery of getting too much exposure to the public after her recent adventure.

She couldn't think of a better place to bone up on ancient Greek history than the museum's Alexander S. Onassis Library, named for the shipping tycoon's son who had died in a plane crash. The subject fell far afield of her specialty, the European Renaissance. She knew the basics about Classical Greece, but nothing that seemed useful in explaining how Classical-era Greek coins could conceivably turn up amid plunder from a looted Buddhist shrine in Nepal.

Actually she could research ancient Greece at any library anywhere, more or less, and turn up plenty of material. But libraries or museum collections always gave Annja a certain sense of serenity. She loved the feel and look and smell of books. Especially old books—much of her more orthodox work involved original manuscripts in sixteenth-century French or Portuguese. And here in the Onassis Library she found abundant material in English, French and Italian, as well as a discreetly helpful staff, most of whom spoke English.

After the warehouse dust-up she had left Greece in a hurry. She then re-entered under her own name, bearing her own academic credentials. Besides which, everyone was happy to oblige the famous American TV star. Even if the show was on a cable network and her role was to play token skeptic, basically the academic foil to the comely Kristie Chatham on *Chasing History's Monsters*.

While Greece was not a large country by North American standards, Athens felt comfortingly distant from Macedonia. Events in Kastoria had rattled her pretty severely. Not the Kosovars' treachery—two days later she was still chastising herself for not having anticipated it in the first place.

Nor did the fact she had killed several of them

bother her too much. She realized that with her possession of Joan's sword came a whole different reality. She wasn't happy about it but she was becoming quite accustomed to killing people in self-defense. She supposed her mentality was like that of a cop or soldier. Someone had to fight the bad guys even if that meant lethal encounters.

Nor was Annja overwrought about her narrow escape from what had turned into a pitched battle in the old warehouse. Narrow escapes had become commonplace in her life since she had gotten tangled up with Roux and Garin and the sword. They weren't the sort of thing you got used to, exactly. But if she went to pieces every time one happened she'd just be a total wreck and never get anything done.

What bothered her was the brush with authority. Aside from the chance of harming an innocent person, which she couldn't stand, tangling with law enforcement carried the risk of bringing her to official attention. That could prove disastrous. Even deadly.

She sighed. The books weren't yielding any helpful hints of connections between ancient Greece and Nepal. None of the ones she'd pored through so far so much as mentioned Nepal. It just wasn't a place you thought of in conjunction with Greece. Rome, Persia, Turkey, Egypt—but Nepal? Sure, they occupied the same continental landmass, and not even its extremities. But it was a big landmass.

A hand suddenly reached past Annja into the yellow spill of light. Strong-looking fingers plucked up the coin, turned it obverse and reverse in the light of the reading lamp. The hand engulfed it and withdrew.

"It is ancient Macedonian," a baritone voice said in Greek-accented English. "It bears the likeness of Alexander the Great, Ms. Creed."

Heart in throat, she turned. And found herself looking into a pair of piercing dark eyes.

She seemed to just sort of swirl right into them. Her stomach did a slow roll. She heard a buzzing in her ears.

It was the special operator she had seen in the Kastoria warehouse.

Though her body felt frozen she took in details. Up close he was even more breathtakingly handsome than he had been in the smoky, dusty, ill-lit warehouse. Curly black hair framed a face at once rugged and youthful, with a strong aquiline nose. His rangy athletic form was clad in a light gray houndstooth jacket over what seemed to be a dark gray shirt with an open collar.

"I am Sergeant Pantheras Katramados," he said. "I am with EKAM, special forces of the Hellenic police. And you are under arrest for trafficking in illicit antiquities."

"I haven't done any such thing," Annja said, fighting to keep her composure.

"You were seen in the company of the notorious antiquities smuggler Enver Bajraktari and his gang during a warehouse raid in Kastoria, in northern

Greece," he said. He smiled grimly. "Not to put too fine an edge on it, *I* was the one who saw you. And then there's this."

She turned in her chair as he held up the coin. It glinted in the lamplight. "You are in possession of a stolen artifact. That may prove the least of your difficulties from a legal standpoint."

Questions crowded in her mind, jostling each other along with protestations of outraged innocence. Well, she *felt* outraged, and knew that in any meaningful sense she was innocent. Whether she could convince the handsome sergeant of the fact was a different issue.

What popped out first was, "How did you identify me?"

He raised an eyebrow at her. "You will not attempt to convince me it is a case of mistaken identity?"

She shook her head. "On the contrary. I want to impress you with my good faith so you'll listen to what I have to say."

"You looked familiar," he said. "Later it struck me I had come face to face with the famous Annja Creed, of the American television program *Chasing History's Monsters*."

He grinned. "I've always been something of a fan," he said. "I am an archaeologist, too, as it happens."

She sighed. Under other circumstances her heart would be fluttering at the announcement by this gorgeous young man that he was a fan of hers.

Instead she felt as if she teetered on a tightrope,

with flames to one side and spikes on the other. On the one hand she feared disclosure—discovery. Getting arrested and publicly tried, even if acquitted, would attract attention that might make doing her work—her real work, both as an archaeologist and as the not-altogether-willing successor to Joan of Arc—impossible. A conviction would certainly sink her, both with the television show and as an academically respected archaeologist.

On the other hand was the dread that the Greek national cops might just disappear her. They hadn't always had the best reputation where torture was concerned. There was always a chance that this smiling man's employers might simply stash her away somewhere until she told them what they wanted to hear.

She figured her only chance of making it across that chasm was to convince handsome Sergeant Katramados that she was more use to him and his bosses at large than in a cell somewhere.

All this flashed through her mind in a desperate instant. "All right," she said. "Don't take me in yet. I'll tell you what I know. Then you can decide what action to take."

He looked doubtful. "You're not going to bluster?" he asked, his tone gently humorous. "Not threaten me with lawyers and the U.S. Embassy?"

She shook her head. "To be candid with you, Sergeant, I think the goodwill I'd give up by playing it that way is more important than any of those other things."

"You are probably wise," he said, "to trust neither our judicial system nor your ambassador. But let me advise you not to try to bolt on me. You seem to be very fleet. I could not afford to take it easy on you if you did so."

"I won't," she promised.

"Very well. Let us go somewhere private and you can tell me everything."

"Now," HE SAID, settling in on a backward-turned chair. "What is it you wish to say to me, Ms. Creed?"

Annja would've thought the largely deserted reading room of the library was as private as it got. But with a word to a passing assistant, backed up by a flash of his credentials, Sergeant Katramados had gotten exclusive use of a small room with chairs, a table and lockable doors that was probably used for meetings and classes.

Now the doors were locked. It was just the two of them.

"You must understand you hold no strong position here," the officer said gravely. "We have no record of Annja Creed entering Greece legally at the time of the Kastoria raid. And with my own eyes I saw you meeting with former Kosovo Liberation Army members affiliated with al-Qaeda."

He crossed his arms on the chair back and regarded her for a moment. "Along with being familiar with your TV work, I hear rumors that you are known to quietly take on certain commissions outside the orbit of conventional academic archaeological fieldwork."

Outrage overcame Annja's fears. "I would *never* do anything unethical from an archaeological standpoint."

"Your name has been connected to certain suspect parties. Before Bajraktari."

"To preserve archaeological treasures—or human lives—I'd deal with the Devil himself," she said.

That got a brief laugh.

"Sometimes one must indeed do so," he said.

Annja drew a deep breath. "I was hired by the Japan Buddhist Federation," she said, "to survey and preserve Buddhist shrines in Nepal."

The truth, she had decided, was her best weapon under the circumstances. Or her best chance.

While Sergeant Pantheras Katramados had started out stern, if scrupulously polite, what struck Annja as a natural affability began to shine through. She also felt a definite chemistry between them. She doubted he would let it affect his judgment. Nor would she. But she couldn't deny it.

So she told him the truth, with just a few select omissions. Such as anything to do with her mentor Roux. And most especially the sword.

"Is that the best story you can come up with?" he asked her.

She shrugged. "It's the truth. Truth doesn't always make the best story. Or even the most plausible sounding one."

"You might claim to be working undercover as a reporter investigating the international trade in plundered antiquities for your program," he pointed out.

Look, you're confusing me, she wanted to say. Whose side are you on, anyway?

"I could. But my best chance of walking out of here as anything but a prisoner is to stay on your good side. If you catch me in a lie, I don't think you'll feel like cutting me any slack."

He grinned. "You're right."

She knew the Japan Buddhist Federation hadn't passed on the Bajraktari lead to police yet because they wanted to follow up on it first. Annja was fine with that. She had nothing against the police, although she lacked the reflex trust of anything in a uniform so many people displayed.

In general Annja felt more concerned about what was good and right than what was legal. Or not.

Sergeant Katramados knit his fingers together and rubbed his chin and lower lip absentmindedly with a thumb.

"You were either very brave or very foolish, Ms. Creed," he said, "to put yourself in such a situation."

She scowled and shook her head. "I guess on evidence it turned out to be foolish. Much as I hate to admit it, it never occurred to me they might decide to grab me for ransom."

"Kidnapping is a growth industry in the Balkans these days."

"Evidently I should have done a bit more research on the modern era."

"You were lucky to escape with your life."

She frowned slightly. "I'm resourceful," she said, "and I'm totally determined to be nobody's victim."

He cocked a brow again. She shrugged.

"And sure, I was lucky. Especially when you and your friends came busting through the skylight," she admitted.

"Speaking of the warehouse battle," he said, "some mysteries exist which I hope you might be able to clarify for me."

The subtext that it could help her case remained unspoken, though unmistakable. She gave him points for not saying it aloud, though.

"Which ones?" she asked.

"One of the bodies bore severe stabbing or slashing wounds. Have you any idea how that came about in the midst of a gun battle?"

"Some of the gang members wore knives, I noticed," Annja said. "They might've fallen out, blaming each other for betrayal. Or perhaps the attack provided the pretext to work out internal gang politics, personal rivalries, even take revenge. Who knows, with violent criminal types?"

"Kosovar and Albanian gangs tend to be both violent and unpredictable, it's true," he said, looking and sounding as if he didn't like the taste in his mouth. "But these wounds were inflicted by a weapon with a very long blade. Not pocket knives or even belt knives."

She smiled and shrugged. "Surely you don't suspect me of packing a concealed sword? I wasn't even wearing a coat."

He looked at her, his long handsome face unreadable in the questionable dim light. Long strong fingers drummed the tabletop briefly.

"No," he said. "I suppose not. It would seem impractical at best."

He showed his teeth in a grin. It was an infectious smile. Annja was too savvy to let it put her off her guard.

She felt a certain smugness over the sword ploy. When you said it flat out like that, it sounded so completely absurd that it would weaken any suspicions he harbored about the dead men's wounds. She hoped, anyway.

"So, what are you researching here?" he asked.

She shrugged. "Classical Greece isn't really my area. I'm trying to refresh my knowledge. Particularly I'm looking for anything that can help me figure out why Greek coins are turning up in plunder from a Buddhist shrine in Nepal."

"Macedonian," he corrected.

"Macedonian. Right. You mentioned that. Might that have something to do with it?"

He stood up and smiled at her. "I'll let you pursue that on your own," he said.

"This means I'm not arrested, yes?"

"For the moment." He frowned pensively. "It might be better to take you in," he said, "strictly for your own good. Our informant inside the gang tells us that Bajraktari blames you for setting them up. He intends to take vengeance. It is a major reason I'm inclined to believe you."

Annja swallowed. "Might the gangs have spies of their own in the Hellenic police?"

He shrugged. "Such infiltration is a problem," he said. "Our particular task force consists only of hand-picked and proven men and women—it's part of the reason we exist. But we lack the resources to provide you a safehouse. You would have to go to jail."

There's a happy prospect, she thought. "Meaning you'd have to get cooperation from other Hellenic police. And you can't take for granted they haven't been compromised."

He spread his big, strong hands. She recognized the typical stand-up cop's dilemma. On the one hand he hated to criticize a fellow law-enforcement officer, especially within his own department. On the other, he was too perceptive and honest not to know there were dirty cops in his house.

"I have not said it," he said, confirming her suspicion.

It cut against her grain to roll over completely. "So, what's a door-busting commando type doing in a library in Athens?" she asked.

Katramados laughed. "The same thing as you—studying. I did serve in EKAM for a time as a commando, as I did in the Hellenic army's special forces. Now I work primarily as an investigator with an organized-crime unit of the national police, dedicated to suppressing the trade in illegal antiquities. Though, as you know, I still take active part in certain raids."

"I noticed."

"As it happens, along with a knack for detective work I have a lifelong love of Hellenic archaeology. Especially as pertains to my native Macedonia. The force finds it useful to pay for me to get my degree."

His smile turned a bit shy. "One day I hope to lead the fight against antiquities thieves. I admit, that's quite a leap from my current lowly status."

I'll bet you're a fast-tracker, Annja thought, despite the humble act. Although to be fair she had to admit it didn't really seem to be an act.

"What now?" she asked.

"It would appear you owe me a debt for saving you from terrorist thugs, Ms. Creed."

She frowned. "I had things under control."

"Perhaps," he said.

She shrugged. She didn't want to go too far down that road, either. "Okay. I admit I got in over my head in Kastoria. But that's a reason I try to fly under the radar. It's just not possible for an archaeologist affiliated with a university or other big institution to do those things. But they have to be done."

"So much is true," the young police commando said. "But again, please keep in mind the kind of risks you run."

"They're seldom far from my mind. I promise."

"Then I shall leave you to your research. I accept your story. For now. But I shall keep an eye on you, Annja Creed."

4

"So," Annja said through the steam rising from her cup of intense Turkish-style coffee, "I remember from my history that Alexander the Great made it all the way in to India. But somehow I never quite associated that with Nepal."

Pan Katramados nodded gravely. "He conquered much of northern India. I doubt he specifically set out to take Nepal. It mostly came as part of the package."

He grinned. He did that readily enough, Annja was finding out. She grinned back.

Traffic beeped and jingled on the street running around the flank of Strefi Hill in north Athens's Exarcheia district, not far from the archaeological museum. The air was cool and smelled as much of the evergreens that thickly forested the crown and far side of the hill as much as it did of traffic and roasting coffee beans. The morning spring sun, though, warmed any surface it reached fairly quickly. Annja found herself alternately moving into the sun when it got too cool under the table's umbrella, then back into the shade when she grew uncomfortably warm.

Her companion looked around.

"Why the head-on-a-swivel bit?" she asked. "Concerned about Bajraktari?"

"Always," Pan said. "But it's mostly habit. This district is a notorious haven for drug dealers and anarchists."

"Really?" Annja asked.

"It's possible that police intelligence exaggerates the amount of drug dealing," he said, "to allow for more actions against dissidents."

Annja sipped her coffee and considered what Pan was saying. The whole point of EKAM—the special antiquities unit of the Hellenic police antiterrorist unit—was that the Hellenic Police in general had been penetrated by criminal spies, particularly for the brutal, well-armed and organized Balkan gangs. And here he was admitting behavior among his fellows that was ethically questionable at best.

It clearly caused pain to a good man who believed, as police were generally taught, that all law-breaking was wrong and that criminals were irremediably bad.

"So," Pan said, visibly dragging his thoughts back to more pleasant pathways, "how go your researches into our Macedonian history?"

"I'm definitely getting up to speed on Alexander. And his father," Annja said.

"Ah. King Philippos the One-Eyed. His son did enough to earn his name of Megas Alexandros. But the son gets credit for much his father did."

"So I gather. I did know Alexander beat the army of King Poros. It turns out that part of Nepal was included in the conquered kingdom. Which would seem to explain how coins bearing Alexander's likeness turned up in treasure stolen from Nepal."

"But not necessarily why," Pan said.

"That's the sticking point. I'm going to have to go to Nepal to find the whole of that reason, I know. Then again, that's what I was hired to do in the first place."

"How long will you remain in Greece?"

"That implies I'll be allowed to leave."

"At this point the government knows nothing prejudicial to allowing you to do so," he said, deadpan. As mobile as his long, olive features were, that in itself was significant. "For my part, as a professional matter I shall be glad to have you take your investigation to Nepal and out of the danger the gangsters pose to you. Provided that you send back any pertinent information you turn up. Sadly, our budget is too limited to allow any of our investigators to make the trip on the basis of the evidence we've gathered so far."

"I promised I would," she said simply. She had no intention of telling him *everything* she found in the troubled mountain republic—most wouldn't be any business of his or his task force. But anything pertaining to the still-mysterious link between Albanian gangs and the land tucked up high in the planet's mightiest mountain range, she'd be happy to pass on to him.

Over the past few days they had bumped into each other more than coincidence could likely account for. Their dealings had rapidly become casual and even friendly. She knew she wasn't totally out from under suspicion, but she had the impression the sergeant was giving her more attention than his job required.

"So, Pan," she said, holding her cup with both hands. "You seem to have more than an academic interest in Macedonian history."

"I do," he said, grinning and bobbing his head like an embarrassed schoolboy. "I come from Macedonia. I grew up in a poor mountain village in northern Thessaloníki province, in central Macedonia. I herded goats as a boy."

"It must have been hard."

He shrugged his right shoulder in what she already recognized as a characteristic gesture. "My refuge from hardship and boredom was recalling the tales the old country folk still tell, of the ancient glories of Macedonia under Philip and Alexander. I used to daydream about them while herding goats."

He laughed. "In my mind I built for myself a whole biography as a Macedonian soldier," he said, growing more animated. "I—he—fought first under Philip and then his son as a shield-bearing infantry-man. He rose to officer rank. Over many battles he so distinguished himself he was elevated to Alexander's personal bodyguard, the Argyraspids, or Silver Shields. Eventually he rose to the rank of general of the Agema, the Royal Foot Guards."

He broke off. Annja was leaning forward, entranced.

"So how does the story end?" she asked.

Pan sighed and shook his head. "That I never saw," he said.

"I hope he lived happily ever after."

Pan chuckled softly. "I do, too."

"So what happened next?" she said. "To you, I mean. Modern Pan."

"I grew up strong and agile," he said. "Constantly climbing rocks in pursuit of straying goats may have had something to do with that. Also I loved to wrestle with the other boys, even though I was smaller."

Annja blinked at him. While he wasn't abnormally large, no one would ever describe him as small. "They must have raised them big in your village," she said, laughing.

He shrugged. "It's a Balkan thing. Some of us grow to be quite large indeed. I am still considered somewhat undersized by my family and old neighbors." He grinned. "But I did have a growth spurt in adolescence."

"So let me guess what came next," she said. "You joined the army to get out from among the goats."

"It is a common story, is it not? I did well on their tests. On all their tests—as a boy I also loved to read. Especially tales of far places and adventure. History, of course, mythology, fiction. And mostly anything other than staring at goats and scrub oak all day. I used to get in trouble with my father and uncles for reading on the job. Although goat herding does not exactly demand constant attention.

"So I joined our army when I was sixteen to escape the goats and my uncles with their too-quick fists. I lied about my age. What can I say? I enjoyed it. The training I found easy. The regimentation—well, it beat the goats. I was quickly promoted. And being a strong lad with much more lust for adventure than good sense, after the necessary five years I volunteered for the special forces, and was sent to Afghanistan. I was there for a couple of years until I was shot by a sniper on the Pakistani border. I came home to recover."

He shrugged. "I left the army. Tried going to school. But I quickly found that unsatisfying. I am afraid I'd become a kind of adrenaline junkie. Since I could not afford to become a mountain climber or amateur parachutist I joined the police force. And there is my story."

He sat back, lost in thought for a moment.

"I sometimes wonder," he said, "how well the wise men who rule, the heads of state, really *know* history. Even Alexander never really tamed that land. Megas Alexandros, history's greatest conqueror."

Annja would've argued for Ghengis Khan, herself. But somehow getting embroiled in a debate with a Macedonian hillman, a warrior-scholar raised on daydreams of his ancestors' martial glory, about whether his hero was top of the world-conquest food chain, did not seem like a good idea. Especially a man who could still cause her to vanish into some clammy, reeking cell and never come out.

"Sometimes at night, listening to the winds howl between the terribly high cliffs of the Khyber, it seems you hear the voices of all the soldiers who fell there. Thousands upon thousands of them. But too many of our enlightened modern types cannot hear them."

He drew in a deep breath and drummed his fingertips decisively on the table. "But I talk out of turn. The soldier should keep from politics. We Greeks know that too well. It is not only the leftists who say it, although perhaps they say it too smugly. And besides, nothing is more boring than an old soldier's tales."

Annja smiled. "Boring is one thing you aren't, Pantheras Katramados," she said.

She sipped her coffee. He was an intriguing man, no question. He could be a fascinating one. But he was still a potential adversary, and in any event his orbit was one Annja the wandering star would not stay in for long. Fascination was a luxury she couldn't afford at this stage in her life.

She set her cup down decisively and checked her watch. "Not that it hasn't been pleasant, but I've hung out here long enough. I need to get back to the museum—those moldering old books are calling to me."

He raised a brow. "Are you still staying in Exarcheia?" he asked.

She guessed that was a rhetorical question. European Union law required hostelries to examine foreign guests' passports, and to report all foreign guests to police agencies. And EKAM probably had ways to keep track of her anyway. She hadn't found any GPS tracker-bugs stuck in her clothing or possessions. She was pretty well-seasoned when it came to that sort of thing. But she still suspected that the Hellenic police special forces could lay hands on her if and when they cared to.

"I'm staying at a little pension. It's convenient to the museum. Cheap, too. But only relative to everything else in Athens. I figured with the National Technical University right nearby there'd be kind of a student-ghetto discount going on."

They both stood. "Watch yourself," he said.

"Because of the drug dealers?" she asked. "Or the anarchists?"

"Both pose real problems," he said. "Most of the anarchists are harmless, really, despite what some of my fellow officers believe. But beware; some of them are violent thrill seekers. But they are not what really concerns me. As you know."

"Bajraktari," Annja said.

"Of course. He is relentless and resourceful—a lot of these former guerrilla fighters are. As well as utterly ruthless. And he has…certain resources."

"I'll be careful, Pan," she said. "And I really should be done here in a day or two. I'm just trying to get as much information as I can."

POISED LIKE A GAZELLE on the edge of a clearing looking out for cheetahs, Annja waited for a break in the noisy metal jostle of midday traffic. She was returning across the Exarcheia plaza to the museum from the café where she'd had lunch. Pale green leaf buds sprouted from the branches of scrawny trees. Pigeons bobbed and bubbled on the pavement, oblivious to scurrying pedestrian feet. The Aegean sun flashing off glass and chrome was hot on her face and dazzling even through her sunglasses.

Her break came when a white panel truck cut off a faded blue-and-white Citroën. She trotted briskly forward. As she neared the opposite side of the street she heard brakes squeal and horns blaring. It startled her enough that she turned her head to glance over her shoulder.

A boxy little ancient Audi compact, its paint faded to leprous gray and rusting through in big patches like scabs, had cut in to the curb close behind her. The fat round shape of an RPG warhead pointed at her from the rear passenger window. White smoke rushed out around it. Garish yellow flame lit the car's interior.

The high-explosives-stuffed metal onion sprang toward Annja's face.

5

Annja hurled herself to the right. Thirty feet to her left the rocket grenade cracked off against the corner of a building. The floor-level window, almost totally obscured with hand bills, exploded in big shards of glass and scraps of colorful flaming paper.

She hit the pavement, skinned the palms of her hands, got a shoulder down, and rolled over and over.

Demonic shrieking rose over the plaza, which had abruptly gone so quiet Annja momentarily thought the blast's vicious crack had deafened her. She rolled on her side into the gutter and looked back.

Yellow flames completely filled the little car and rolled out the windows in big gushes. The front passenger's door was open. A blazing figure had staggered out into the street, waving wings of flame.

A man threw a jacket over his head and bodychecked him to the ground.

Picking herself up to a crouch Annja looked quickly around. People were standing and gaping. Some were screaming, while others ran in various directions. People thronged around the unfortunate victims of the blast's overkill, trying to tend to them.

The Audi's gas tank exploded and a gout of orange flame shot out from beneath it in all directions, driving back would-be rescuers. At least two people were still inside the car, the driver and the shooter. Annja wasn't sure it would be any favor to extract them—if they were even still alive in that crematory.

The crew in the Audi must be newbies, Annja thought, looking to make their bones with Bajraktari's gang. She figured they'd decided to show initiative and really impress their bosses by making a splashy hit on her. No doubt the survivors would find they had succeeded. Their bosses would have the unbreakable impression they were idiots.

Even aside from the little problem of the flaming rocket's backblast—which never caused a bit of problem in the movies—the RPG was a pretty goofy weapon for a targeted hit on an individual anyway. Scanning her surroundings for signs of attack from a different direction, Annja felt a flash of bemusement. Where along the way did I become an expert in the specs and subtleties of deployment of the rocket-propelled grenade launcher?

Nobody was paying Annja any attention as she got upright, a little creakily. She was going to have a nasty bruise on her hip, and her skin almost crawled with the need to pick out the grit and wash the foul gutter goo off her skinned hands. There was no way for anyone to see she had been the rocket's target. She was just another unfortunate passerby who was lucky enough to possess good reflexes.

But the comforting anonymity didn't last. Through the shouting, milling throng she spotted two men in long black greatcoats, open and flapping about their trouser legs, hard faces scruffily unshaved even by the standards of Greek anarchists. The none-too-subtle way they held their hands in their coats and swiveled their heads before their burning crow-dark eyes fixed on Annja showed that, as she feared, the hapless crew in the car had backup. And more seasoned backup, by the looks of it.

She headed down the street that led away from the plaza, toward the Acropolis hill and downtown Athens. She made herself walk, though at a good pace with her long legs. She wasn't concerned about attracting the gangsters' attention—they had spotted their prey already. She just didn't want anyone else to associate her with them, nor to have any reason to remember her at all.

Fortunately the crowd had plenty of distractions. Pedestrians wounded by the rocket blast were being tended. The Audi was wholly engulfed in flames and burning with a noise like a gale blowing down a narrow street, attracting a lot of gawkers. A knot of men surrounded the would-be assassin who had escaped the inferno. They had completely covered him in coats, smothering the flames. Now they jostled each other to kick the unmoving figure, leaving open the question of whether they had saved him from burning to death out of Samaritanism or simply the desire to kill him themselves.

The only people paying attention to Annja, it seemed, were her personal hunters.

The few other people Annja saw were hurrying toward the plaza to see what the excitement was about. She broke into a run. An alley opened to her left. She turned into it.

Once off the street she accelerated into a full-on sprint.

The alley reeked of fish, vegetables and coffee grounds decomposing into the black greasy muck that slimed its floor and made footing tricky.

She reached the end of the short block and dodged left again. This street was narrow and deserted.

She waited. In a moment she heard the footsteps pounding along the alley.

She knew the very last thing on their minds was that their quarry, a mere woman, a soft, weak, Western infidel at that, would do anything but flee like a frightened rabbit until she collapsed of exhaustion.

As the footfalls grew louder she closed her eyes and summoned her sword from the other where. A tall dark figure flashed into view. She swung for the fences.

The edge of the sword was extremely sharp. Annja twisted with her hips and put everything she had into the cut. Subtle technique was not an issue here.

The blade caught the running man at the Adam's apple. In a flash he was tumbling into a loose-limbed sprawl.

His partner came a few steps behind. He tried to brake himself. Annja pivoted around the rough stone corner of the wall and, still grasping the hilt with both hands, plunged the sword into his belly to the cross-shaped hilt.

Her pursuer's mouth and eyes flew wide.

Annja stepped to her left. She released the sword. It vanished. Blood spurted from the assassin's wounds as he fell.

Annja walked away with hands in her jacket pockets as if nothing had happened.

She hoped no one had witnessed the events. But experience had taught her that didn't necessarily matter. Telling skeptical and generally short-fused police they had seen a female American tourist pull a broadsword out of nowhere and kill two gun-armed terrorists, then made the lengthy weapon utterly vanish wasn't a good move.

Cops the world around had ways of dealing with people who told stories like that. None of them was pleasant. And Greek cops weren't renowned for their restraint or regard for human rights.

Annja's heart raced. So did her mind. She was trying to sort out what had just happened—or what lay *behind* what just happened, and what that meant for her future survival.

Clearly, Enver Bajraktari was highly vexed with Annja.

It was possible, she thought, the carload of newbies had been sacrifices. Pawns chosen to noisily and splashily die, attracting the attention of everyone, most especially their intended victim, to give the real kill team a clear shot at her.

It was a good plan, too, she had to admit. It would've worked if Annja's recent life experiences hadn't given her the awareness and paranoid suspicion of an alley cat.

She came to a wider street, filled with tourists and locals far enough from the Exarcheia plaza not to have noticed the commotion yet, although sirens had started to go off and a pillar of black smoked undulated up into the sky. Those events were remote enough that most of them shrugged and went about their business.

Gratefully, Annja joined them.

6

"There was some excitement down in Exarcheia today," Pan Katramados said across a spoonful of soup he was raising to his lips. The candle in its bronze bowl in the middle of the table underlit his face in such a way as to make him look quite ferocious. It contrasted crazily with his mild conversational tone. But it served to remind Annja he was a highly trained and seasoned special-forces warrior, and that nobody sane wanted to see him angry.

"Yes," Annja said. "I saw reports on CNN in my room this afternoon. It looked awful."

They were in a small uncrowded restaurant in Piraeus. The food was superb and the view, of lights twinkling on the water and white boats bobbing at anchor in the harbor, was lovely.

Pan grimaced and shook his head. "Well, perhaps. And perhaps not so awful. Some bystanders were hurt, and property destroyed, which is to be regretted. Yet the passersby were not badly injured, and are recovering nicely in hospital."

"The news said four people were killed," Annja said.

"Indeed," Pan said, nodding. "Four terrorists."

"Terrorists?"

Again he nodded. "Albanians. Or, rather, ethnic Albanians from Kosovo. Two were burned beyond recognition, and the other two fatalities carried papers falsely identifying them as Krasnovar Serbs from Croatia. But we have an injured survivor under guard in hospital, with third-degree burns over fifty percent of his body and badly broken ribs. He is expected to survive to face trial. He has confessed. It appears he was the racketeer and was unwise enough to fire his launcher inside a small imported sedan, apparently in ignorance that the rocket exhaust produced a substantial fiery backblast."

"That's a terrible thing to go through," she said. "Not that they didn't have it coming, I guess. And from the way you're looking at me—"

He laughed softly. "Can't I just enjoy looking at you?"

"Do you?" she asked, surprised.

"What man would not?"

"Well—a man who was mainly interested in looking at me wouldn't look at me in that particular way. At least I hope not," she said.

"I suppose not."

"So they were Bajraktari's men?"

He nodded.

"I don't suppose any of them happened to be Bajraktari? Or Duka?" she asked.

"Don't you know?"

"Don't I know? How on earth should I?"

"Well, to start with, you know full well Enver Bajraktari is a cagey fox. Would he let anybody on an operation he commanded in person do anything so foolish as to fire an RPG inside a car? Unless he meant to produce a diversion to allow the real killers to strike."

Annja struggled to keep her face impassive. Fortunately she had had lots of practice. "The real killers?" she asked.

"We suspect the other two dead men were the real hit team. We found them several blocks away."

"I thought you had a confession," Annja said with a sinking sensation.

Pan shrugged. "The burn victim has confessed to taking part in a terrorist attack. He claims it was merely to strike a blow for independence of all ethnic Albanians from the former Yugoslavia. That seems unlikely. Bajraktari isn't the sort to indulge in violence for mere political posturing. He takes his violence far too seriously for that."

"And the others?" Annja asked.

"Our suspect disclaims all knowledge of them." Pan sipped his ouzo. "He may be telling the truth. In fact, he may be telling the whole truth. As he knows it."

Annja knew otherwise, but she wasn't going to tell him how.

"But it smells like an assassination. The two dead men had Skorpion machine pistols in their hands. Nasty pieces of work. You know them?"

She realized she was nodding. "I've read about them. I have to admit I'm mildly interested in firearms."

Comfortable as she was coming to feel in his presence, she knew she had to tread carefully. She didn't dare play dumb with him—he knew her background too well for that. She'd already shown Pan ample evidence she knew how to react in combat simply by getting out of that Kastoria warehouse alive. So she reckoned being up-front about a familiarity with guns would make him least suspicious.

"The two on foot would seem to have been closing in on a target," Pan said.

"What happened to them?"

"They were killed by someone wielding a weapon with a long, double-edged, sharp blade. Exceedingly sharp. One of them was almost decapitated at a single blow. Although the position in which his body was found indicated he was running, which would add his own momentum to the force of his blow, that is…unusual, to say the least."

"Didn't you find similar wounds in the warehouse?" It's coming out anyway, she thought.

He sat back from her, turning slightly sideways in his chair and crossing one long lean leg over the other. "Exactly."

She took a bite of her stuffed grape leaves. "I guess they went after the wrong person."

Pan's chuckle had an edge like broken glass. "It would certainly appear so. The other man was stabbed clean through the torso. Our medical examiner says both entrance and exit wounds had the cleanest edges of any stab wounds he had ever encountered."

"Seriously," Annja said faintly, laying down her fork. She hoped he'd think such a detailed post-mortem made her feel appropriately squeamish.

His eyes were intense as a falcon's as they gazed at her. "The most obvious person for Bajraktari to expend such effort to target," he said, "is you, Annja. And you were at the warehouse."

She laughed weakly. "Somebody else must've been, too," she said. "Or do I look like Conan the Barbarian to you?"

He laughed. "You are an exceedingly strong and fit woman," he said after a moment. "And you clearly know how to handle yourself in dangerous situations. But no—" he shook his head "—I can't see a woman delivering a decapitating blow. Call me a male chauvinist if you will. And there is of course the astonishing fact that the weapon, which the medical examiner judged must have been nothing less than a broadsword, is unwieldy and most inconvenient to carry. Much less conceal. Especially on a frame as spare as yours."

"Are you saying I'm skinny?"

He held up his hands defensively and laughed. "I

didn't say that. I just mean you'd have to be built like
an ox and dressed in a tent to have a hope to hide such
a weapon."

"That's not my style," she said.

"Of course not." He shook his head. "It's a mystery.
It preys on my mind. Yet rationally it cannot concern
you. So let's put it aside and enjoy our meal, yes?"

"Yes," she said. "I have news, anyway. I found
something fantastic today."

He turned forward and leaned closer. "And what
is that?"

"At the museum I found a remarkable story in a
Medieval Latin translation of a Byzantine manuscript. It told of how Alexander faced increasing dis-
content from his Macedonian soldiers, worn out by
marching so far and fighting so much. His treasury
was getting low. Then from an informant he learned
of a cave shrine high up in the mountains of Nepal
that contained a vast treasure. He sent a general from
his bodyguards with a small handpicked force to
seize it. And guess what?"

"I'm all ears."

"The general's name was Pantheras. Isn't that
strange?"

Pan went still. Then he leaned back slowly until
his face was shadowed in the darkness of the restaurant. Outside a patrol boat putted across the harbor,
probing left and right with a blue-white spotlight.

"So how did the mission turn out?" he asked after
a moment of silence.

"I don't know. The fragment ended there."

She could see a smile play over his lips. "That's too bad," he said.

AS THEY WALKED along the base of the brightly lit hill their arms had become interlinked. Annja felt disinclined to disengage, somehow.

"I've started to have the dreams again," Pan said. "You know, the ones from my childhood. About actually *being* an ancient Macedonian general."

"I can see why it might come out again now, with the ancient Macedonia-Nepal connection coming to the fore. Although it's still an interesting coincidence, given what I found out about that earlier Pantheras today," Annja said.

"Interesting. Yes."

They walked a while along an old stone retaining wall. The traffic was sparse. Flute music played from somewhere.

"I have to leave soon," Annja said. "I hope you and your superiors are all right with that."

"Well, much as I might regret the fact of your going, our investigations have turned up no evidence your involvement in the case is other than you have described. Which is perhaps unwise enough in its nature that I should be rather relieved to see you go."

"Really? You'll regret my going away?"

"Well…you make life *interesting*, let us say." He laughed softly.

She laughed, too. But she felt an unexpected pang

that she would soon have to say goodbye to the handsome police officer.

Pantheras Katramados was clearly as strong in character as in body, but without the blustering machismo so common in Mediterranean cultures. Rather he had the confidence that comes from being truly competent and knowing it, overlaid with wry good humor. His interests were as broad and deep as Annja's own, and his wit as quick. They found much to talk about. Much to laugh about. He reminded her, in many ways, of her dear friend Bart McGilley.

"Where will you go now?" he asked.

"Nepal. It's where my real job begins." She had been getting polite e-mails from the Japan Buddhist Federation hoping she would soon be able to go to Nepal. Apparently the political situation there was rapidly deteriorating. Whether full-scale civil war was in the offing Annja couldn't tell from the news online, but lawlessness was clearly rising in the countryside.

He stopped and turned to face her. "Don't let your guard down."

"Bajraktari won't have any reason to suspect where I've gone," she said.

"He has contacts in Nepal, quite obviously," Pan said. "Don't get complacent."

Annja grinned. "Thanks. But I think I can promise you, that's one thing I'm *not*."

He took her in his arms and kissed her. Almost despite herself she responded.

Too soon he broke away. His face looked troubled.

"Was it that bad?" she asked shakily.

"As an experience? Certainly not," he said. "As a thing for a policeman on a case to do—perhaps."

He turned and walked quickly away. She made no move to follow. She felt a combination of sadness and relief.

And she couldn't help wondering how much of his interest in her was really romantic—and how much was special-forces cop?

7

"Lumbini is a foremost shrine of Buddhism," said the smiling man in the saffron robe. He walked beside Annja along a paved path next to a square pool sunk into worn gray stone. "Here Siddhartha Gautama was born to Queen Mayadeva. The fig tree you see before us closely resembles the one under which he later received enlightenment, thus becoming the Buddha."

His smile widened. "Or rather, the most famous Buddha. Others have come before and since."

"Really?" Annja said.

"Oh, yes."

The morning sky was bright blue, with a wash of thin white clouds away off to the west over northern India. In south Nepal the sun shone unimpeded from the east. It was surprisingly warm. The long sleeves and pants she wore out of respect for her host weren't optimally comfortable.

Away to the north, blue with distance, the low wall of the Himalayas rose from the horizon. Annja felt a minor thrill at knowing she'd soon be among those legendary stratosphere-scraping peaks.

The lama Omprakash was a stout man whose round body seemed to taper directly to the shaved crown of his head. Though his broad face was unlined he claimed to be in his eighties.

"I thought the Buddha was born in India," Annja said. The sacred site lay just across the Indian border, although Annja had reached it by flying into Kathmandu in the east of the country, then taking a feeder flight on an alarming Russian-built two-prop plane to Sunauli, the town nearest Lumbini. A taxi had brought her the rest of the way. Though high up near the foothills of the Himalayas, the surroundings were a wide, well-forested river valley just greening into spring. The valley of the Upper Ganges, in fact.

"The distinctions were not so clearly drawn in those days," Omprakash said. His name, he told her, meant "Sacred Light." "Certainly this land was claimed by the great Maurya king, Ashoka. Some believe it was he who brought the doctrine of Buddhism to Nepal. Great proselytizer that he was, that is not so. He did make a pilgrimage here in 249 B.C., after he had reclaimed north India from the successors of Alexander of Macedonia."

Ah, she thought, that name. She didn't press. She

was here to listen. It was easy enough. Omprakash was a pleasant old gentleman who spoke beautiful English, with a liquid Hindi accent and a perpetual twinkle in his anthracite eyes. The Japan Buddhist Federation had sent her specifically to speak to the rotund monk. She badly needed background. This was way off the map of her previous studies and experience. She had decided to let the old man tell her whatever he wanted, and try to soak it up as best she could.

"King Ashoka did erect here a sandstone pillar to signify the great spiritual significance of the spot," Omprakash said.

"I take it it's that one there?" Annja said, pointing across the pool past the temple.

"The very one!" the monk exclaimed, beaming as if he had built it.

"But my good friends in Tokyo desired that I should tell you a particular tale," Omprakash said. "It is said that shortly after Gautama's death one of his disciples decided to exalt the Enlightened One in the heights of the world. Obviously, we find these most conveniently nearby. Traveling alone, north from Lumbini, he climbed the Himalayas in what is now the Dhawalgiri Zone, until a dream revealed the location of a cave.

"In accordance with his vision the lama consecrated there a shrine. He even contrived to get a gold Buddha statue weighing hundreds of kilos up to it. Some say this was by magic. I myself prefer to believe he employed the power of *devotion,* in himself and his disciples. And who is not to say that is not real magic?"

He laughed again.

"For centuries truly dedicated Buddhists made the difficult pilgrimage to the high, remote shrine to leave tributes of gold or silver or jewelry to signify their rejection of Maya, the world of illusion. Gradually a treasure trove accumulated. It was already immense when the Macedonian invaders came two centuries later."

Annja caught her breath. Could this be the treasure the Byzantine fragment recorded, in search of which Alexander sent one of his most trusted generals? Unless immense ancient treasure troves lay thick in the Himalayas, it seemed a pretty good bet.

"But precisely because the unenlightened might be tempted to plunder it, binding themselves more tightly to the wheel of karma by their greed, the mountain shrine's location was kept most secret. The shrine could only be found by a quest—something more arduous than simply a climb to a great height. The pilgrim was required to pass through a sequence of shrines and lamaseries, proving sincerity and spiritual worth at every stage to the lamas. And possibly to less earthly guardians, as well."

He stopped beneath a tree and turned to face her.

"This is your path, Annja Creed," he said, still smiling. "It is the road you must follow to find that which you seek. You, and one who is to come later. As has been foretold."

Annja kept her face set in a mild smile. Although she didn't believe in destiny or prophecy, she didn't want to antagonize a man she hoped would give her more information.

He radiates serenity, she thought. There's no questioning that his beliefs give him that.

"I see you are skeptical," Omprakash said. His smile didn't falter. He couldn't, in fact, have sounded more pleased if she'd explicitly accepted his every word as gospel, or converted to Buddhism on the spot.

"I'm…sorry," she said.

He laughed. "Please, don't be. All traditions are equally sublime. Even agnosticism and atheism. Your path to enlightenment can only be your own."

"All right." She smiled back. "Then I'll go ahead and confess I am skeptical of the existence of a single fantastic treasure."

"Yet the Japan Buddhist Federation has hired you to find it."

"They never actually said anything about it. I did read a Byzantine fragment that mentioned such a treasure," she said.

"Perhaps they had their reasons for wishing you to find out on your own. If you wish you may correspond with them. You need not take my word. I won't be offended—I don't claim to be immune from error."

"That's okay," she said. She was annoyed at the JBF for holding out on her. "They may not even know about it. But you're absolutely right—if it exists, it's part of my job to find it and see that it's properly preserved like any other shrine. And I'll do my level best to find it."

Omprakash nodded. "I believe in your integrity, Ms. Creed. You will not accept if I speak of auras, although your own best researchers years ago discovered means of tracking individuals by their unique personal electromagnetic fields. A phenomenon which I surely find difficult to tell from auras. Out of respect for your beliefs, I will point to a lifetime spent learning to read people."

"Thanks." She unbuttoned one of the cargo pockets of her khaki trousers and took out a plastic bag containing the coin she had taken from the warehouse in Kastoria. To her surprise Pan had given it back to her and allowed her to keep it. She might find it useful in shutting down the artifact-smuggling operation at the source, which would serve both their ends.

She presented the bagged coin to the lama. "This was found in Thessaloníki, in Greek Macedonia."

"Hardly surprising, inasmuch as it appears to bear the likeness of Alexander," he said.

"It was being sold by a notorious and highly dangerous antiquities-smuggling gang as part of a trove looted from here in Nepal. I saw other artifacts of clearly Buddhist origin, although I admit I don't know enough to determine whether they were Nepalese. Archaeologists with the Hellenic police antismuggling task force authenticated them, however."

"You are wondering," Omprakash said, handing the coin back, "if it came from the Highest Shrine, as tradition calls it. Or legend, if that gives you greater comfort. As to that, I cannot say. But far more likely is that it came from a lesser shrine."

His smile widened. "You see, no impious hands can ever defile the Highest Shrine, Ms. Creed. Some guardian will always arise to defend it."

More mysticism, she thought. Since he no doubt sensed her disbelief again, she didn't have to worry she might show lack of courage in her own convictions if she didn't say it out loud.

"Well, just in case," she said, "I'll do my best to locate this Highest Shrine and ensure its proper preservation. If, ah, my hands turn out to be pure enough."

"That will be determined in the course of your quest."

She had nothing to say to that.

"A final bit of advice, Annja Creed, before I impart the information necessary for you to proceed," her host said. "Your progress will depend upon your actions and the state of your soul, regardless of whether or not you believe. Please be aware that your skepticism can put barriers in your path."

"It's part of me, Lama. And I choose to walk the rational path," she said.

He nodded. "Does that require you to form preconceptions and prejudices?"

"Well…no. The opposite, I like to think."

"Just so. All I ask, and urge, is that you keep an open mind."

"I can do that," she said. Can't I?

8

The monk's advice sent her north to Baglung, chief town of Baglung District in the Dhawalgiri Zone. A garishly painted bus took her from Lumbini into almost the center of the long, striplike country. It also took her up, along precipitous narrow switchbacks.

Baglung sprawled along a wide ledge at the base of a big hill. Its blocky white multi-storied structures, roofs pitched high to shed the massive yearly snowfall, spilled out onto a couple of naturally terraced sandstone buttes thrusting out over the river valley below. The land around was scrub and stands of small trees, pitching quickly up into more hills, dusted with snow, with the stark blue-and-white mass of the real mountains looming beyond.

To the north a gigantic white mountain, shaped vaguely like a tooth, dominated the skyline.

When Annja got off the bus her legs were a bit unsteady with remnant adrenaline. Some of those last hairpin turns had been hair-raising. Shouldering her pack, she hiked to the police headquarters to check in.

It wasn't hard to find—an old British colony, heavily influenced by India and increasingly by the U.S., Nepal depended almost entirely on tourism to keep its economy rolling. So even in this remote place English-language signs abounded alongside the curvy local writing.

The cop shop was a three-story building with a roof of dove-gray slate. The Baglung contingent of the armed police force were glum and wary little men in brown berets, light gray shirts, darker gray trousers with white-and-orange stripes down the legs, black belts and boots. Their holsters held modern Glock autopistols, Model 19s with high-capacity 9 mm magazines.

To Annja's surprise each Glock was counterbalanced by what looked like a forward-curved short sword on the other hip. These had to be the Nepalese *kukris,* made famous by their Gurkha mercenary troops. They still carried them in modern-day assignments in Afghanistan and elsewhere. Annja hadn't expected to see police officers toting huge fighting knives, though.

She filled out the usual reams of paperwork. She was all aboveboard, prepared to brandish her documents from the JBF, as well as the letter of recommendation the well-respected Lama Omprakash had provided her in Lumbini.

The police didn't care. Without so much as glancing at her archaeological bona fides the officer referred her to the Baglung District commissioner for antiquities, a man named Chatura.

Somewhat to her surprise the district antiquities office lay outside of town proper, on a rocky little rise surrounded by dwarfish, wind-gnarled evergreens. Hiking up to it, Annja found herself running short of breath despite the fact it was an easy walk, even lugging the bulky backpack that constituted her entire luggage for this expedition. She knew it was the altitude, of course. Baglung was something upward of 6500 feet. Nothing serious—yet.

But *serious* was coming. She glanced at the white-clad mountain, which, though distant, loomed over the town.

The stout, almost fortified appearance of the antiquities office startled her. It was a one-story stone blockhouse with narrow slit windows set high off the ground. Its position gave it a commanding view in three directions. The hill behind was steep enough to make it tricky for attackers to negotiate, and mostly bare of cover. It must, she realized, have been a colonial police outpost at one time.

The whitewash on the stones looked fairly recent to her archaeologist's eye. That made the gray dimples of bullet impacts in it even more recent.

"Well," she muttered to herself, standing outside

the scarred red wooden door, "they warned me civil disorder was on the rise here." Although it looked to her as if somebody had behaved in a most uncivil manner toward the blockhouse's occupants.

Hoping that the antiquities department had only moved in recently—say, after all the gun battles— Annja stepped inside. Small copper bells hanging from the knob by a leather strap tinkled as she shut the door behind her. She entered a small room with a couple of chairs and a big metal desk. She shrugged off her big pack and let it down to the bare concrete floor.

Though large and solid enough to suggest it could be pretty bulletproof—to Annja's relief, she couldn't seen any actual evidence it had taken gunfire—the desk wasn't the dominating design element in the room. That honor belonged to the gigantic portraits hung on the rear wall, flanking and indeed somewhat dwarfing a map of Baglung District.

One of the portraits sported the unmistakable huge head and wide grim face of Mao Tse-tung. The man in the other picture, this one a photo, was leaner and wore spectacles, but was equally humorless. The man was still pretty sturdy, with a seamed square face sagging into middle age behind glasses and a large mustache.

She was so engrossed staring at the portrait she barely heard the door in the back open and someone come into the room.

"This is Prachanda," a voice said in English. "He

whose clarity of vision lights the way forward to a progressive future for all nations, not just Nepal."

"Really?" Annja said. "I'm pretty apolitical myself."

"Not to be political is to be political," the man said sternly. "I am Chatura, district commissioner of the Antiquities Division of the Ministry of Culture, Tourism and Civil Aviation for Baglung. And you must be the American archaeologist I was informed had arrived."

"Uh, yes. My name is Annja. Annja Creed." She proffered the thick bundle of papers she'd accrued since entering the country.

Chatura accepted them with a sour expression. He leafed through them, scowling.

"You will investigate shrines, then?"

"And catalog them for proper preservation, yes." Once again, telling as much of the truth as possible seemed her best path.

Chatura's mouth pinched beneath his nose. "So you will celebrate and propagate the pernicious superstitions which have held humanity back for so long," he said. "The Great Steersman had the correct idea with his Great Proletarian Cultural Revolution, purging such baggage and breaking the chains of the past."

Annja didn't like where the conversation was headed. "But these shrines are priceless relics," she couldn't help saying. "Common heritage of all humankind."

The little bureaucrat sneered. "A common burden

on mankind," he said. "And you have come bringing your Western decadence and your oh-so-corrupting American dollars. Which do not buy so much corruption as once they did, do they?"

She shrugged. Her shoulders were knotting with tension. She had a hard time reining in her anger. But she knew it was vital she do so. She wouldn't be helping her employers or Nepalese archaeology—or her bank account, as Roux would no doubt rush to point out—if she was deported before so much as glimpsing a single shrine, with the exception of Lumbini, which was somewhat tacky and in any event the opposite of lost.

A small man with a round belly and hair cropped close to his round head, the district commissioner didn't exactly look like an intrepid former guerrilla, Annja thought. He must be some old Party hack, not a front-line fighter. Instead of being rewarded for long years of drudgework he's been stuck off in this nowhere job in a blockhouse outside a hick district capital, where the people with real power won't have him underfoot. No wonder he's bitter.

As if to confirm her diagnosis, he sighed and tossed the sheaf of official documents onto the desk. "It is the policy of the *central government*," he said with contemptuous emphasis, "that the ministry coddle and empower foreigners who seek to meddle in our country, in the name of a past filled with oppression and slavery. In the interests of the proletariat our general secretary sees fit that we obey such edicts.

And so my hands are tied. I must permit your survey. You will of course tender me a full report of its results."

"Of course," Annja agreed, know full well this was not a man to be trusted.

"But be aware, Ms. Creed," Chatura said. "If you engage in any counterrevolutionary activity the consequences shall be swift, sure and severe. I shall be watching you."

He smirked. "I shall watch you very closely indeed."

9

"Annja," a man called from twenty yards downslope of her. "Look there."

It was late afternoon in the remote country northwest of Baglung, near the fringes of the Dhorpatan Hunting Preserve, which clung to the base of the Dhaulagiri Himal subrange of the Himalayas. A light overcast covered most of the sky. The wind rustled in the dry brush around them. Some kind of bird was persistently whistling, unseen nearby.

Crouched down next to a jumble of head-sized granite rocks with tufts of tan grass sprouting from the cracks, trying to figure out whether the formation was natural or had been piled by human hands—indicating a possible hidden shrine—Annja straightened and turned. Her chief guide and outfitter, Prasad Ale

Magar, was pointing a baggy-sleeved arm back down the rocky valley.

A small knot of men were hiking up the sloping valley perhaps five hundred yards behind and below them. Annja grabbed her binoculars. She held them to her eyes and adjusted the focal length.

"They carry rifles," Prasad said. He was short, like most of the Nepali Annja had encountered, wiry and bowlegged, with a face seamed by long exposure to the sun. He was on the long side of middle age, late fifties or sixties. Or so she judged—his hair, cropped close to his head, was the color of cold rolled steel. But the years hadn't much diminished his sight.

His unaided vision confirmed what Annja's binoculars were telling her. She counted perhaps half a dozen men. At least three carried long-arms. One of them, to Annja's surprise, was unmistakably a long black M-16. She knew the American-made weapon was standard issue to the Nepali armed forces.

She pointed that out to her guide. "Should I feel reassured?" she asked. "I wouldn't think Maoist guerrillas would carry a Western-made weapon, would they?"

"Like everyone else, the guerrillas must make do as best they can," said Lal, Prasad's nephew and chief helper. He straightened from chopping some brush away from a possible opening in the rockpile and wiped sweat from his brow with the back of his hand.

He was a pleasant young man with a shock of heavy blue-black hair and a kind of sad downturn at the outside of both his eyes that didn't seem mirrored in his manner or his grin, which was frequent.

Annja's third local helper, a cousin of Prasad's named Bahadur, set his pick down and stood up to wait and watch.

"Will they give us trouble?" Annja asked. Lal had a rifle himself, an old bolt-action British Enfield .303 propped against a rock. As friendly and helpful as the family had been they had not even asked if their carrying weapons would bother their employer.

It might've bothered most tourists but it didn't bother her. She was a firm believer in self-defense. Especially in a part of the world where insurrection and banditry, wherever you drew the line between them, were on the rise.

Prasad shrugged. "Armed strangers can always bring trouble. We can only wait and see."

Still showing no outward sign of having noticed the team, the strangers vanished behind a shoulder of land to Annja's right.

Prasad said something in the local language.

Lal nodded. Without another word he picked up his Enfield and scrambled up the rock-strewed slope above them. In a moment he was out of sight like a prairie dog down its hole.

Annja noticed the older man watching her with a guarded smile. She guessed he wanted to know whether she wished to try eluding the armed party or not. She noted his body language—he stood centered, legs slightly flexed, almost a wrestler's posture of readiness for anything. It was his basic posture. He showed no trace of nervousness or any desire to flee.

She nodded. Experience had stamped into her pretty deeply a rule about expeditions in the outback anywhere—vet potential local assistants and employees rigorously, and if they proved worth taking on, trust them implicitly. Even, or perhaps especially, when their advice or actions ran contrary to Western wisdom.

Annja had seen too many expeditions hit the rocks—from being flooded out by unexpectedly early monsoons to capture and being held for ransom by grumpy armed formations—by ignoring what the local helpers said.

Without presuming to speak, Prasad was telling her that there was no point in trying to hide.

"So what do we do?" she asked him.

His smile widened slightly. Clearly it pleased him his employer was proving reasonable. But his eyes continued to scan their backtrail where the mysterious men had disappeared.

"As I have said," he said. "We wait. See. Be prepared for what the next turn of the wheel brings."

"Meaning if we've seen them they've seen us, right?"

He laughed. "Truly you are wise beyond your years, Annja Creed."

She sat on a big rock near the base of the outcrop of gray stone she'd been working. She might as well conserve breath and energy for whatever came next. Though geologically already in the Lesser Himalayas, they weren't high up by Nepali standards, maybe eight thousand feet. Annja still had to remember to take frequent breaks.

Prasad and Bahadur stood on a relatively level patch of ground a few feet below her. They lit cigarettes and puffed stolidly away. Prasad stood. Bahadur squatted beside him.

They waited. As she often did Annja grew aware of the presence of the mighty main peak, Dhaulagiri I. Even with her back to it Annja could *feel* it like a living presence, ominous, overpowering.

A harsh voice suddenly hailed them from the slope of a rise to her right. Six men appeared and began to scramble down the scrubby slope toward them. If I saw all of them they haven't left any kind of reserve in hiding, she thought.

As the party approached she stood and called out. "Hi. Can we help you?"

Being polite and respectful, she reckoned, gave them the best chance of avoiding a nasty confrontation.

The newcomers swaggered up smoking and joking, as Annja's military friends would put it. They acted careless, in the sense that they apparently saw nothing here to care about. Her team showed no visible firearms. Prasad and Bahadur wore big knives.

While they were clearly related to the *kukri,* the men used them so casually in the most brutally utilitarian contexts, as machetes, axes or even pry bars, that Annja presumed they were tools rather than weapons. Although that didn't mean they couldn't do damage.

One man stepped forward. A black leather belt, faded and cracked but looking like some kind of official issue, circled his rather capacious waist. A burly revolver rode in a holster on his right hip. Though the closed flap concealed most of it, Annja made it for a double-action Webley, the signature sidearm of British colonialism. As the Enfield had so long been its signature long-arm.

He spoke to Prasad.

Annja was able to make out the meaning of one phrase. "My name is Agrabat."

Two men with long-arms flanked him. To his left was a big man who looked like an overstuffed hassock with tufts of horsehair stuffing sticking out from random locations. He held a single-shot break-action shotgun. The stock had weathered to driftwood gray. The forestock was split down the middle and attached to the long barrel with windings of tarnished copper wire. It looked like a 12-gauge. Annja judged that if he triggered that sucker off, it was even odds whether it would burst in his hands. That didn't make it any less dangerous to her and her friends.

On Agrabat's right a shorter, leaner man with an M-16 was shifting his weight constantly from one boot with the sole held on by electrician's tape to the other. Despite the growth on his lupine jaws, which had gone beyond stubble to a sort of patchy black mat without rising to the status of a real beard, he looked like a kid.

The leader spoke self-importantly. Prasad listened intently and nodded. The other three newcomers carried drawn *kukri*-like knives but no other weapons. Annja guessed Agrabat's sidearm, traditionally allowed only to officers, was his badge of authority.

"He says that they are tourist police," Prasad said when Agrabat finished. "He says he has heard we might be conducting unlicensed explorations."

"Where's his hat?" Annja asked. On her way to Nepal she had done a little of her customary Internet research into the law-enforcement structure of her destination. She knew a few things about the tourist police, who were associated with Commissioner Chatura's ministry.

Deadpan, Prasad relayed the question. The bearish man with the shotgun growled. Agrabat laughed.

"We are undercover," he said through Prasad.

"But there's no tourist police detachment in Baglung," she pointed out. "And also, aren't you supposed to be chosen for your command of English?"

She thought she saw Prasad's right eyebrow twitch up about a hundredth of an inch. She smiled at him. She already suspected this would not end well. Certainly these men were no more police than she was.

Shrugging scarcely less microscopically, he turned and conveyed her words to Agrabat.

"Bah," he said. "Enough delay. If you have the proper authorization, produce it at once!" he ordered.

Annja was ready for that. Specifically she was prepared for the common trick, used by the ill intentioned on both nominal sides of the law, of grabbing her papers and refusing to give them back. Before ever setting forth from Baglung she had made Prasad hunt down for her perhaps the only copy machine in the town not in some official office. Well, actually, she thought it *was* in some official office, but it was after hours and another cousin let them in the back. She had made multiple copies of all her documentation. It constituted their single heaviest item of luggage.

Agrabat accepted her authorization from the armed police and the ministry. He studied them with a deepening scowl.

"He might have better luck with that if he turned them right side up," Annja said. Then, hastily added, "Don't translate that."

Agrabat dashed the papers to the ground. "Don't try to hide it!" he shouted, spewing spittle. Fortunately Annja was ten feet away and out of range. "You're hunting treasure!"

Uh-oh, she thought as Prasad translated. She wondered if Prasad had spoken too freely with his extended family.

"Not the kind you're thinking of," Annja replied calmly. "We are cataloging shrines for eventual preservation by the Ministry of Culture, Tourism and Civil Aviation."

"You find treasure!"

"No," she said.

In a week of tramping the uplands, basically the enormous widespread skirts of the mountain, her little team had turned up numerous shrines—in rock cairns, tumbledown wooden lean-tos, in caves. Some really did seem to have been lost; she wasn't sure she would have characterized any as hidden. Aside from statues of the Buddha, mostly running to gold-painted plaster of paris castings, they contained nothing that even the most avaricious optimist could call treasure.

More to the point, none were of particular antiquity. In a few cases it was hard to tell. But since this was a survey, not an excavation, all Annja could do was inspect the sites, photograph them on her digital camera, log them in her GPS and move on.

None of that was what Agrabat wanted to hear. "You lie!" he barked.

His men were getting tense, although neither the bear with the shotgun nor the nervous kid with the M-16 was pointing his gun at anyone yet. Annja sensed it was a matter of time. And not much time.

"Wait," she said, holding up a hand and making a sort of smoothing-down gesture. Even with Lal and his old Enfield as an ace in the hole they were outnumbered and outgunned. And that was only if Lal hadn't prudently just kept scampering up the hill and off across the landscape, leaving his mother's brother, his cousin and their outland employer to whatever the wheel of fortune had in store for them.

"We have little of value," she said. "We've found no treasure. We're not looking for any. We're merely looking for artifacts."

The last sentence was barely out of her mouth before she realized her mistake. Nor was there any calling it back. With his excellent command of English Prasad translated her words almost as quickly as she said them.

It was as if a shift in the light struck a glitter from Agrabat's obsidian eyes. His beard rounded in a smile around his gap-toothed mouth.

"So," he said. "You find *artifacts,* then." Clearly he knew about the relics trade, where even a piece of outright junk, a broken tool or pottery shard, could command big money in the international market if it was old enough.

Annja shook her head. "Nothing valuable yet. I told you, we're not collectors—"

Agrabat barked something to his men. "Get ready," Prasad murmured unnecessarily.

Agrabat's expression softened. "You lie," he said again. This time he said it calmly, almost conversationally. That was a bad sign. It meant he had settled upon a course of action. And was utterly confident the outcome would go as he anticipated.

"We will see," he said. "We will take what we want in the name of the people. And maybe—"

His smile widened and his eyes ran down Annja's body like clammy hands. "Maybe we shall enjoy ourselves some, too."

He unsnapped his holster flap. To left and right his gunmen raised their weapons. His other men drew their knives with chilling deliberation.

10

The blast of a rifle fired from close by struck the back of Annja's head, almost deafening her, stirred her hair like rough fingers and slapped the back of her shirt like a glad-handing drunk.

A small round hole, blue-tinged, appeared in the center of the M-16 kid's forehead. The young man toppled straight backward as the gunshot echoed down the valley. The long black rifle fell from his hand.

At the same moment Bahadur's arm whipped up from his side. A chunk of rock bigger than his fist flew up to smack the shotgunner between his eyes. The burly shotgunner dropped his weapon and went to his knees, bawling like a branded calf and clutching his face. Blood squeezed out between the knuckles of his grimy hands.

Annja was already moving. Prasad had already sprung upon Agrabat and wrestled him for control of the still holstered Webley. Bahadur whipped out his big ungainly utility knife, shouted and lunged to engage the man on the right in blade-to-blade battle.

That left Annja facing two bandits. Though she was a head taller than either, their eyes gleamed at the prospect of coming to grips with her. She knew well not to underestimate the strength of these men, the way they'd underestimated her.

She only hoped her allies were too engrossed in defending themselves to watch her too closely.

The nearer goon, to Annja's right, didn't even draw his blade. He just grinned with jumbled brown teeth and reached for her. She threw a shin kick up at the fork of his baggy trousers that lifted him onto his toes. He squealed in pain.

For a moment she thought she'd get away with not invoking her sword and all the potentially unanswerable questions it raised. But her opponent made another grab for her. He was wide open when she flattened his nose into his face with a forward right elbow smash that knocked him clean off his feet.

His pal came lunging from the left with his knife cocked back over his shoulder and a mad look in his eyes.

But Annja knew combat body mechanics on the reflex level. No matter how fast he was, the power shot he was readying took time to deliver. She didn't give him that time. Instead she half turned away, raising her left knee, then pistoned her heel out in a side kick. She heard ribs crack with a sound like snapping kindling as her kick flung the knife man backward down the slope.

Strong arms enfolded her from behind in a bear hug. She felt hot breath down her neck as a powerful stink of accumulated filth enveloped her in an almost visible cloud. She had committed a cardinal sin of combat—forgotten a potential foe.

It had to be the shotgunner. Bahadur's rock to the face had tripped his switches momentarily with the twin shocks of surprise and serious pain. Now he was back in the fight.

Annja's legs flailed as he lifted her feet off the ground. Accidentally or by evil intent he swung her around to face the man whose nose she had smashed with her elbow. He was grinning through a half mask of his own blood, a *kukri* glittering in his hand. He drew his arm back to plunge the huge blade into her stomach. The forward-curved knives weren't really optimized for stabbing. But it would make an awful mess of her.

She whipped her head back. The back of her skull slammed into the already injured face of the big bandit behind her. He grunted. His grip relaxed.

Annja whipped up both her arms. That broke the hug. She wheeled sharply right, cupping her left hand over her right fist to add extra force to a horizontal elbow smash into the side of her opponent's head. He fell away from her.

But the knife-man was lunging for her. From the corner of her eye she saw a third bandit, the one whose ribs she cracked, was also on his feet and headed her way, knife in hand and eyes filled with rage.

She formed her right hand into a half fist and reached with her will.

Instantly the reassuring heft and solidity of her sword's hilt filled her palm. Even as he raised his hand to strike, the charging knife man's eyes flew wide at the lightning apparition of the blade in Annja's hand. She slashed him downward across the chest. Blood spurted as he dropped to his knees, then pitched on his face.

She spun toward the bandit with the broken nose, intent on paying her back for his pain. Before she could counter his clumsy swing a shot cracked like thunder from the rocks above. Dust flew from the bandit's chest. He grunted and collapsed as if his bones had dissolved inside him.

Annja turned to her right. As she did she saw Agrabat falling backward with blood streaming from his head and skinny Prasad, no longer bespectacled, following through the death stroke he had dealt his opponent.

Looming behind him, a *kukri* held blade down by two grubby, bloodstained hands, was the bearish man who had originally wielded the shotgun, his face a bloody mask of rage and diabolical triumphant glee.

He was too far for Annja to reach. As Prasad sensed the danger and began to turn, too late, Annja's eye lit on the wired-together shotgun lying unfired ten feet from her.

Making the sword disappear, she swooped on the gun. Without time for finesse or care she stuck it out in front of her held in her right hand like a giant unwieldy pistol. The bandit was barely a dozen feet away. Annja knew in that distance the shot column from the long barrel would only expand slightly beyond the size of the bore, just under three-quarters of an inch. But she had to aim high along the long barrel to be sure of missing her guide.

Wincing in anticipation of pain and the weapon's possible explosion in her face, Annja fired. The weapon roared, kicking itself free of her grip, nearly spraining her wrist and gashing her trigger finger with the trigger guard. Blood and cloth unraveled from the bandit's left forearm.

He bellowed and staggered back a step. He still kept a grip on the hilt of his knife.

But he'd moved enough that Lal could shoot without endangering his uncle. The bandit spun with the third gunshot and went down.

Annja was swinging her stinging right hand in the air and wishing she'd used her left. Prasad looked up the slope and waved to his nephew. Then he turned to his employer.

"Are you injured, Annja Creed?"

"My hand's felt better. With luck it isn't broken."

He bent down and picked up his glasses from where they had fallen. Miraculously they remained intact. He put them on his nose and blinked through the round lenses at her.

"You are bleeding," he said.

"Not as bad as Bahadur." She pointed past Prasad with her chin to where his cousin squatted on the ground beside the body of his foe, who lay face-down and unmoving. Bahadur's face was pinched and sallow. He clutched his left arm. The sleeve from biceps down was red and dripping.

"Help get him fixed up. I'll see if I can handle this myself," she said. She had long since learned to be pretty adept with her left hand.

She dared hope—faintly—none of her companions had seen the Sword for the furious action. Their own death-battles had occupied Prasad and Bahadur. Annja knew how that tended to wind the vision down to a narrow tunnel focused on the foe. But Lal had been sniping, perched up ahead with a godlike view of the whole action, probably from seventy-five feet or less away. What had *he* seen?

After checking to make sure that all the downed men were going to stay that way, Prasad knelt beside Bahadur. Annja found a large rock near her backpack and sat down. She was shaking as she dug in a side pocket for her first-aid kit. She felt chilled, knew she was probably pale. Her fingers trembled and her joints felt like overboiled pasta.

And none of it was from fear. Nor revulsion. And

least of all from remorse. But rather from the after-effects of the massive adrenaline dump invoked by fighting for her life, inevitable and unavoidable as hitting the floor after rolling out of bed.

Lal came down the slope. He held his stubby little Enfield at midpoint balance. He had evidently hung out up in his hideout perch to make sure the bandits hadn't had any pals following behind. He spared no more than a glance to the fallen men. He had seen his uncle make sure of them. That was enough for him.

The young guide was giving Annja a curious eye. Her lips compressed. Her mind started sorting through the possible rationalizations knowing they could only sound as unconvincing to this intelligent young man as they sounded to her.

As rapidly and efficiently as a seasoned cook chopping vegetables, Prasad was slicing untainted parts of Bahadur's clothing into strips.

"So those are real *kukris,*" she called to him. "I thought they were just utility knives."

"*Just* utility knives?" He laughed as he wound a makeshift bandage over a hastily folded compress. Annja hadn't gotten a close look at Bahadur's wound, nor was she eager to, but she was pretty sure his opponent had gotten a lick in on him that had laid the arm open to the bone.

"It is all things, Annja Creed. It does whatever we call upon it to do. When we wish to chop firewood, it is an ax. If we must drive nails, it is hammer. When we fight, it is the finest weapon in the world."

She smiled and nodded, brushing away a wisp of hair that had strayed from the tight ponytail she normally wore in the field.

"You seem to be reacting well," Lal said. His head was tilted to the right and he had a strange appraising light to his eyes. "You handled yourself very well."

"For a tourist, you mean? I've had to learn to take care of myself since I was a kid. And I got lucky," she said.

She didn't want to insult the intelligence of these men—they had, after all, put their lives on the line for her against terrible odds, never suspecting she might be capable of taking a useful hand in the fight, far less a decisive one. But a little of the self-effacing act couldn't hurt. She still hoped to defuse those questions she saw sparking behind Lal's eyes.

And she knew she *had* been lucky, even though it didn't feel like it as she bandaged her torn finger. As one of her countless martial-arts instructors had told her, "When two tigers fight, one dies, and the other is wounded." So far Annja had been lucky enough never to take a truly incapacitating injury. She knew that couldn't last forever.

"You fought well, too," she said, trying to nudge the conversation away from her. "Are all Nepali guides so handy in a fight?"

Lal shrugged. "When they are Gurkha."

She looked at him sharply. "You?"

"I served with the Indian army and the Royal Singapore Police," he said. "My uncle fought with the British in Belize and the Falklands."

"I thought you were Magar," she said.

"We are," Prasad said. "Gurkha come from many Nepali peoples."

"My cousin did not serve abroad." Lal—not so young as he looked, apparently—went on. "But he, like my uncle and me, fought with the army against the Communists." His voice took on an unaccustomed edge.

His expression turned troubled. "I watched the fight for a clear target," he told her. Her heart sank. Here it comes. "Something strange happened. I thought—"

Straightening, Prasad said something to the younger man. His voice snapped with a tone Annja had not heard the slight, self-effacing man use before. Prasad had never raised his voice.

Lal muttered something in return. He sounded defensive to Annja, but she didn't really know the inflections of their language.

Lal turned to her, pressed palms together and bowed. It seemed to be in nature of a salute—unusual, as it was normally used as an all-purpose hello or goodbye.

"You fought as well as anyone I have seen, Ms. Creed," Lal said. "I salute you."

"Thanks," she said. She'd always reckoned that was the best way to react to a compliment. Plus it could be a conversation-killer. And she *really* wanted this one dead.

A flying subject change never hurt. "What about those men?" she asked, waving at the bodies. Apparently all six were dead, which comforted her. She had a prickly certainty in her belly that if any had been merely wounded her companions would have finished them off without compunction. That would put her in a place, legally and ethically, she didn't really want to go.

"What do we do about the bodies?" she asked.

Lal glanced at his uncle, who had helped Bahadur to his feet and got him to sit on a rock to gather strength. Annja felt momentary concern about circulation being cut off in his wounded arm by the tight wrappings Prasad had applied. Then again, it was a long walk to any kind of real medical assistance, and if Bahadur bled out on the way nothing else would matter much. Besides, it was clear the veteran Prasad had definitely done this before.

Prasad shrugged. "The ground here is hard," he said, "so we should start digging before the sun gets much lower."

He smiled. "Fortunately, there are plenty of loose rocks to help us cover them."

After a quick check to make sure the hilt was clean she picked up a *kukri* that its former owner wasn't going to be needing again. "These are shovels, too, I'm guessing?"

Prasad and his nephew exchanged surprised looks. "When they must be," Prasad said. "But you—"

She smiled a taut little smile. "I'm an archaeologist, remember?" she said. "I *know* how to dig. And the daylight won't last forever."

11

A soft knocking at Annja's door awoke her.

As was her habit she came fully awake. It was a trick she'd had to learn. By reflex she reached to her cell phone. Pressing a button at random lit its face to show her it was a little after two in the morning.

A lamp stood on the bedside table. She didn't turn it on. Power service had been spotty since the troubles restarted. Anyway, turning on a light inside would alert whoever was in the hallway she was inside and awake.

Better a would-be evildoer think her either helpless or absent, rather than prepared to defend herself with ruthless ferocity. Cautiously she slipped bare legs out from under heavy blankets still smelling heavily of the original sheep, piled on her lumpy but cozy bed in the Baglung inn she had made her main base of operations.

Something slid beneath the door. Annja frowned. An envelope?

The sword appeared in her hand. The stitches a doctor in a Baglung clinic had sewn in her right forefinger and the bandages the nurse wound around it didn't render the hand useless, as Annja feared they might, although her grip on the hilt was less positive than she liked. The savage kick of the 12-gauge monkey gun hadn't broken anything, or even sprained her hand. It had bruised, twisted and torn it some. A random starlight gleam straying in through drawn shutters skittered reassuringly up her blade's length as she crept noiselessly to the door.

Breathing shallowly through her mouth, Annja listened closely. Late night in Baglung was dead silent unless the wind blew—and it always did, chill and heartless from the mountains, booming at the windows, rattling the shutters, moaning like the damned beneath the eaves of the sharply pitched roofs. It was an eerie, soul-sucking sound. Her night visitor made no noises she could hear above the wind.

At last she slipped the chain as quietly as she could, turned the knob and peered out.

The hallway was dimly lit by what seemed like a five-watt bulb in a black iron sconce. It was enough light to show no one lurking there. Whoever had pushed the envelope under her door had slipped away as mysteriously. She let the sword go, back into the other where, farther than the end of the universe and never more than a thought away.

She ducked hurriedly back into the room, locked the door and reset the chain. Not that it would resist a stout kick or, if the door was cracked open, a good shoulder. But she knew from living in the thieves' den that was New York that there was a certain benefit in culling the amateurs. It was like window screens and flies—if you didn't take the trouble to screen out all but the wiliest, you got nothing done but swatting.

She turned on the table lamp.

She studied the mystery missive from several feet. It looked like a regular white envelope, the kind a hotel might leave in the drawer of the writing table along with some stationery for the convenience of its guests. This cobbled-together little inn offered no such amenities.

After a lengthy moment during which she failed to develop X-ray vision, Annja sighed. She felt much put-upon. I need sleep, dammit, she thought bitterly. In the morning they were headed up to the heights, inside the Dhorpatan Hunting Preserve. There would be much trudging, and little oxygen to breathe.

I doubt the bomb squad's going to want to turn out in this wind at oh-dark-thirty, she thought, on the off chance Baglung has a bomb squad. Besides, she felt a moral certainty that if she successfully summoned demolitions specialists she'd wind up with what turned out to be a soggy note from the night porter.

Trying to suppress dark thoughts of exotic contact poisons as way too pulp novel, she walked over, bent down and picked up the envelope.

It wasn't sealed. Inside was a scrap of blue-lined paper that had obviously been torn from a pocket notebook. On it a couple of lines of the script used in Nepal had been handwritten in purple ink.

Annja stared at it. Momentarily she drew a blank. Am I being threatened by somebody who's not so bright? she wondered. Am I the victim of a wrong address?

It struck her as entirely plausible that this might be a totally innocent message, intended for someone who actually read Gorkhali, that it had been pushed under the wrong door.

She sighed again. Her initial sense of alarm had almost entirely faded. In its place was a wool-blanket itch of curiosity.

Yeah, she thought, and if I get somebody up to translate at this hour, it'll be a laundry list meant for the guy across the hall, and I'll look like a total fool.

Reluctantly she set it on the bedside table, lay down and turned out the light. One useful trick she'd learned was how to blank her mind, with the help of deep abdominal breathing exercises. If she *didn't* have that skill she'd never get any sleep, considering the sort of life she led.

Inside of three breaths she was asleep.

IN THE MORNING Annja drank coffee that, even well whitened with cream, grabbed her by the scruff and shook her back into place. She ate big chunks of fresh, tough-crusted bread for breakfast.

"Annja Creed?"

She looked up. Prasad and Lal stood outlined in the doorway, blinking dubiously at the gloom. She smiled and greeted them. They advanced into the tourist-friendly café as if it were enemy territory. Clearly they felt as out of place as they looked.

"How's Bahadur?" she asked when they sat, a bit reluctantly, at her invitation. They refused refreshment. Annja and some French tourists, now bickering in Lyonnais accents, were the only customers in the place.

Prasad smiled. "He rests at his mother's house in the hills," he said. "He should recover soon."

The arm wound, which turned out to be more ugly than serious, had been stitched up at the same clinic that tended Annja's finger.

She smiled. "I'm glad."

"You seem troubled," Prasad said. He smiled at her. But his eyes were more penetrating than she cared for behind his thick round glasses. It was still hard to think of this skinny self-effacing man as a battle-hardened Gurkha veteran. Even though she'd seen him leap into action like a tiger from the Dhorpatan woods.

Annja described her nighttime adventure. Prasad and Lal looked at each other. They said nothing—aloud. She had the impression a whole extensive conversation took place in indecipherable and, to her, mostly undetectable body language, right before her eyes.

"May I see the letter?" Prasad asked mildly, turning back to her.

She already had it out. She slid it across the white tablecloth to him. He flattened it carefully with both hands and bent to read it.

She expected anger, outrage, perhaps even fear. Instead a look of wonder spread across his rather delicate features. He turned and spoke to his sister's son in what she could only think of as tones of awe.

They both looked at her with eyes agleam. "You are invited to the Lamasery of the Woods," her guide said. "You have passed the first test."

12

A battered white Land Cruiser hauled them wheezing up the flank of the Dhaulagiri Himal to Dhorpatan village, north and west of Baglung. There they picked up two new porters, called Sherpas after the eastern Nepali ethnic group, from Prasad's extended family.

The day was clear, the sky a dazzling blue, with just a few fluffy clouds flirting with the peaks of the great mountains, as they headed out on foot into the hunting preserve. Annja couldn't help but notice they did not check in with the game park's administration in the small, picturesque village.

She supposed it was obvious they weren't hunting game, even though Lal carried his inevitable Enfield, and a similar battered old bolt-action rifle was slung over the shoulder of one of the Sherpas, whose names Annja had never quite caught.

They crossed a rounded wooden footbridge arcing over a stream, and set out along a very well-trodden path into the hills. The air was crisp. Birds flashed gaudy colors in the branches and sang eerie songs. The trees were evergreen, but some of the scrub was leafing out. The air had an astringent scent from the trees, as well as the weight and chill edge of the perpetual snows of the peaks.

Their destination, Annja's guides had not yet disclosed.

"I have heard of this Agrabat," Prasad said as they hiked between gnarly-trunked rhododendrons with sprays of evergreen leaves like spearheads. They had not yet begun to flower.

He and his nephew usually conversed in English out of courtesy to their employer. Of course, it made their occasional exchanges in their native tongue seem more purposeful and possibly alarming. Less so when they spoke to the porters, who seemed not to know English.

"He does not come from a bad family. But they fell on hard times."

"Hard times fall on all of us, Uncle. We don't all become bandits," Lal said.

"No, indeed. Yet when you are as old as I, you might find yourself not so quick to judge others. It is easier to feel compassion when one's blood has cooled from the fires of youth."

His nephew was scandalized. "You killed him."

Prasad shrugged his narrow shoulders. "That is different. That was a matter of defending myself—

and our employer. But it does not mean I would presume to judge him."

Annja's mind wandered. She couldn't help worrying about the note's reference to her passing a test. She'd killed two men and played a pretty direct role in getting another killed. She thought of Buddhism as an intrinsically peaceful religion.

She wrenched her attention back to the present—the cool fresh air smelling of chilled distant stone, the sun warm on her face, the burble of water over the smooth-pebbled bottom of the brook that wound for a time alongside their path.

"The way he talked," she said. "Agrabat, I mean. Were they really Maoists?"

Prasad laughed softly. "Not likely. Bandits have long been a problem here. Even during the war we spent as much time hunting them as we did fighting the Communist guerrillas."

"There's a distinction?" she asked.

Lal laughed. "The guerrillas tend to be better organized." She couldn't help noticing the use of the present tense. "Although it's not always easy to tell. Sometimes the bandits pretend to be Communists. And the Communists are seldom reluctant to plunder. 'Expropriation,' they call it. But Agrabat and his lot were clearly just vicious fools."

Annja was edging around a subject that had bothered her since the encounter with Agrabat, reluctant to confront it internally or externally. But now it seemed she couldn't avoid it any longer.

"How do you think they found out about us?" she asked. "If Agrabat was such a low-level bandit, how did he know what we were doing?"

The only logical conclusion seemed to be that someone had blabbed. The question was frankly making her worried about trusting Prasad and Lal. She could trust no one, Roux always assured her with a sort of world-weary glee that he loved to affect when unloading an unpleasantly weighty time-gleaned truth on his reluctant protégée. Yet she *had* to trust people to help her. No one could do everything by herself.

Even at her most paranoid Annja couldn't quite twist things around so that Prasad, Lal and Bahadur— who would rest at home for at least a week to recover from his injuries—could be in cahoots with the late bandits.

Lal laughed. "Do you think we can take a single step without the people of the country knowing? This land seems unsettled to people who don't know it. But our folk live everywhere, and see everywhere."

"This land is us," Prasad said. "We are this land. Its stone makes our bones—our flesh makes its earth. The peasants know we walk it the way you know a mosquito walks on your arm."

"But what made Agrabat think we might be hunting treasure?" She *was,* in fact, even though not for the conventional reasons. It struck her she hadn't confided that to Prasad and Lal, either. That only deepened the mystery of how an opportunistic bandit would know.

"In these hard days," Prasad said, "the people assume all expeditions hunt ancient treasure."

"It's a poor country, Ms. Creed," Lal said. "Now maybe more than ever, with the war starting up again and the global economy coming apart."

"Then what about the real Maoists? What do they think we're up to? I mean—Commissioner Chatura's one of them, isn't he?"

"He is a Party man," Prasad said. "Never a warrior. An organizer, he was. Administrator."

"Schemer," Lal supplied.

"Are the Maoist guerrillas active in the area again?" Annja asked.

"Still," Lal said. He seemed more comfortable contradicting their employer than his uncle, although his manner had never been anything but friendly and respectful. It had gotten more so since they fought together by the lost hillside shrine. "They never went away—never demobilized. Much less laid down their guns. As yet there's no open fighting in the district. Who knows how long that will last?"

Annja had a sinking feeling. "You think they might be interested in us?"

Prasad shook his head. "Not *think,* missy," he said. "Not think. Know. Major Jagannatha is an old leopard and a wily one."

"Major Jagannatha?" she said. That doesn't sound

good, she thought. She had no idea who he was but she knew what the word meant.

"He's another former Gurkha. Many of the guerrillas are, too."

Annja nodded. The *jagannatha* was an immense cart used to haul an outsized idol of a Hindu god on religious festival days. The British colonizers had believed, or claimed to, that people flung themselves under the big wheels to allow themselves to be crushed as sacrifices. Modern Indians dismissed that angrily as racist twaddle, although Annja suspected that, given the nature of crowds and how crowded Indian cities had been throughout known history, people getting inadvertently run over was anything but rare.

"He sounds like a dangerous man," she said. "Let's hope we don't meet him."

"We will pray," Prasad said seriously.

"At the least," Lal said with a lopsided grin, "it can't hurt."

THEY HIKED STEEP HILLS and narrow valleys, thickly forested. Climbing higher, they had left the rhododendron forests behind and come into a region of dark, shaggy conifers. Prasad identified them as hemlocks.

Annja had noticed that, while Lal deferred to his elder relative when explanations were called for, and Prasad duly supplied them, most times Prasad said little while Lal chatted. Meanwhile the two Sherpas conversed happily in Gorkhali. It made Annja's lower back ache just to look at the packs they carried, but to them, clearly, this was literally just a walk in the park. Her respect for their sturdiness of body and spirit increased.

She found these woods spooky. They were more like the ancient German forests that had so unnerved the Romans than anything Annja ever associated with Nepal. The photos and videos she'd seen of the country were all snowy peaks and Sherpas. Not dense, dark woods. Not that the White Mountain wasn't making its presence felt. Even when she couldn't see it Annja felt it threatening to topple on her.

Daylight in the mountains was fleeting at best. In these claustrophobic valleys the sun dropped from sight and the shadows began to thicken into twilight not terribly long after midday.

"Where are we going?" Annja asked, not for the first time.

She didn't really want to be caught out in the woods at night. She wasn't afraid of wild animals or even bad men, although knowing Major Jagannatha might be taking an interest in her could get to be a concern pretty quickly. Mainly she was sure it wouldn't be very comfortable in a forest that daylight barely brushed at this time of year. Particularly once the wind began to whistle through the valleys, down from the eternal ice fields of the greatest mountain range on Earth.

"We go where we are summoned," Prasad said, as always politely, yet with a certain brisk finality that told her it was all she was going to get. Some guide, a snarky part of her said. But in truth he was doing what he was paid to—guiding her.

He just wouldn't say where.

Particle by particle the shadows condensed around them into dusk. Though the sky overhead remained a brilliant blue, the few cirrus clouds only beginning to blush with the pink of sunset, down here among the rustling hemlock boughs it was getting to be dark. The hiking party came around the side of a steep ridge and Annja glimpsed a warm orange glow ahead.

"Is that where we're headed?" she asked.

"Yes," Prasad said.

The porters began to mutter in their native tongue. They seemed nervous, although they continued to forge on stolidly beneath packs that looked as big as they were. Not briskly but relentlessly, as if they could keep this pace up all night and all day tomorrow, and for all Annja knew, all week.

Her own lean-muscled legs were beginning to ache. Her feet were sore and she felt a little flutter in her quadriceps from the constant climbing along scanty trails. And I thought I was in shape, she thought ruefully.

The glow vanished beyond a twist of the trail. Prasad and Lal picked up the pace. The rising sense of mystery actually invigorated Annja. And the change of pace itself provided a welcome break from the steady upward trudge of the past couple of hours.

The trail wound around another bend and they saw before them a tall wooden structure, with a steeply pitched roof of wooden shakes and sweeping eaves. Torches burned to either side of the entrance, casting a wavering glow across a door painted red with gilded dragon figures twining up it.

Annja's first thought was that it was an inn or maybe a hunting lodge. But Prasad said, as if in invocation, "The Lamasery of the Woods."

13

"Go on, Annja Creed," Prasad said, gesturing with a knobbed and weathered hand. "You are expected."

"What about you?" she asked.

"We will be provided for. You must go inside."

"Alone?"

"One always walks the path alone."

Trying to look bolder than she felt, Annja approached the door. The dirt of the path, packed and well swept, crunched softly beneath the soles of her shoes. As she mounted the warped wooden steps the torches made soft popping and rushing sounds. The wind, rising, whistled in the flaring eaves and made the dark hemlock branches swoop and sigh.

Annja knocked on the door. Nothing happened. She turned back to look at her companions. The porters had shed their packs and squatted beside them, featureless shadows against gloom. Lal showed pale teeth in a smile Annja thought was supposed to be encouraging. Prasad simply stood, unmoving as a stone, gazing at her. The round lenses of his glasses were unreadable disks of reflected flame.

She turned back to the door. She gazed at the two dragons carved on it, sinuous bodies intertwined like a DNA double helix. They seemed to writhe in the torchlight.

She put a tentative hand to the heavy black iron latch. It opened. The big door creaked inward on its hinges. She cringed.

"Hello," she called. The word seemed to echo softly into the darkness. Knowing firsthand how actively Buddhist monks could express their resentment at unwanted intrusions, she stuck her head reluctantly inside.

All she could see was that a narrow corridor moved away from her. Little copper dishes of oil, or yak butter, held burning wicks. They glowed yellow but without actually casting much light. It was only the slight gleams from massive roof beams and polished floorboards that gave Annja any hint of the dimensions and solidity of the corridor.

The little lamps flickered alarmingly in the breeze she was letting in. She was going to have to make up her mind quickly. If she let the wicks blow out she did *not* want to try groping her way into the monastery in suffocating darkness.

She took a deep breath, stepped into the lamasery and closed the door behind her. It shut with a final-sounding thump and clatter of the latch.

Somewhere in her pack she carried a small flashlight. She didn't fumble for it now. She felt nervous, uninvited. She did not want to literally highlight her invasion of this holy sanctum by blasting bright artificial light into it.

Someone wanted you to come here, she told herself. If the monks wanted to keep strangers out, they could always lock their doors.

Cautiously she advanced.

Could it be a trap? she wondered. If Prasad or Lal wanted her dead, or secretly worked for someone who wanted her dead, they'd had plenty of opportunities to make her disappear in the time she'd spent combing central Nepal with them. Maybe there were villagers, farmers and hill herdsfolk everywhere, unseen by foreign eyes. But there were so many narrow crevasses and caves hidden among rocks it couldn't be that hard to stash a body without anyone knowing.

No. Whatever this was, it wasn't a trap meant to kill her. At least not at *first*. That raised the hairs at the nape of her neck. She knew there really were worse things than death that could happen to you. She'd encountered way too many of them in the past few years.

The wind whistled in the space above her head.

The wooden walls creaked and thumped uneasily. Beneath her feet the floorboards squeaked. The place sure sounded deserted. Possibly for centuries.

But someone had put those torches outside the door and lit them. Not too long ago, either. The same went for the lamps.

"Hello," she said again. "My name is Annja Creed. I don't want to go anywhere I'm not supposed to be."

A groan came from down the hall. She flinched. She almost formed her right hand to summon the sword.

She saw a hint of motion. It was deliberate enough not to feel threatening. She walked forward.

When she was about halfway down the corridor, as far as she could tell, she made out a vertical slit of gray in the darkness in front of her. It suggested a door had opened a crack.

She ran her fingers along the dark-painted wall to her right. Its texture felt rough. She detected expressed cross beams and posts. She got the impression there might be doors in one or both walls. She couldn't tell for sure.

The door ahead seemed to beckon her. She shrugged and walked forward.

At the door she paused. "Hello," she called out. Then louder, "Hello? Anybody here?"

The rustle of the wind and the creaking of the wooden structure around her was her only answer.

She stepped through. The dim gold gleam of a pair

of bowl lamps illuminated another doorway. The dark wood door was open.

Annja went to it, pushed open the door. Inside was a chamber about twelve feet square. A circle of the bronze or copper bowls had been set out in the middle of it, with a diameter of perhaps nine feet. At its center waited remarkable objects. She glimpsed other items laid against the far wall, indistinct in the gloom outside the circle of tiny yellow flames.

The objects within the circle held her attention. To the right lay what appeared to be a book, hefty, its pages warped and cover blackened and cracked with age and perusal. On the left a pile of golden coins glittered.

At the edge of the circle she paused. She wasn't sure why. She knew circles often served as ritual barriers. I don't believe in any of that, she chided herself, so why the hesitation?

Leaving the matter hanging for the moment, she sidled around the circle to the far wall. A rolled pallet lay there. Shrugging, she squirmed out of her pack straps. She let the bag down softly to the floor beside the pallet and sighed and stretched with relief. It was awfully heavy, and her shoulders were sore from bearing the weight. Getting free of the straps always made her feel better; she didn't care for confinement of any kind.

Taking a deep breath, Annja stepped into the circle and knelt facing the door. It had shut without a sound. She put it from her mind.

It *felt* as if she were alone in the lamasery. But it had to be occupied and the occupants were choosing to remain unseen.

At least there's four walls and a roof, she thought, as the wind began to howl and a curl of cold air seemed to pass through her jacket and muscles and bone to her marrow like a chill scythe. She wondered what kind of accommodations Prasad and the others would find to pass the night. She hoped they'd be comfortable. If anyone can find decent shelter it's got to be Prasad, she thought.

Sitting back on her heels with hands on thighs she studied the curious display before her by the yellow lamplight. Then her breath caught in her throat as if she'd swallowed a burr.

Lying atop the small pile of golden glittery disks was one showing the unmistakable head of Alexander the Great. Eyes wide, she reached for it.

She stopped with her fingers hovering just above it. For a moment her hand looked like a pale spider, its underside turned scarcely less golden than the ancient Macedonian coins by the light of burning butter.

She sucked in a deep breath. Reluctantly she withdrew her hand and studied the two displays.

"Someone went to a lot of trouble to set up this whole tableau," she told herself aloud. She no longer felt as if speech was a violation of sanctity.

"It has to be a test," she said. "So I guess I better pass it."

Looked at in that light it seemed fairly obvious. Simplistic, even. Material desires versus longing for enlightenment. "Easy for you to say now," she told herself, "after your first response was to go grabbing like a magpie for the nice shiny gold thing."

She didn't know whether her invisible audience would understand her words. She took for granted she had one now. The lamas wanted to see how their test subject performed, after all. She didn't care what they might make of her words. Either she'd passed the test or was hopelessly adrift.

She carefully lifted her pack over the lamps and dug around. From an outer pocket came a digital camera.

"If you lamas don't want me doing this," she said, focusing and snapping a picture of the pile of coins, "feel free to speak right up. Or ask me before I leave to erase the images from the card. I'll do that if you want."

Only the wind's buffeting answered her. She moved around the pile of coins, taking pictures from various angles. She took care not to upset any of the butter bowls. She also did her best to expose the ancient book to the flash as little as possible. It was unlikely the brief glare would damage it, but especially given what she intended next, she wanted to minimize the risk.

When at last she'd taken sufficient shots of the coins, concentrating on the Alexander piece, she wrote everything down in her spiral-bound note-book. Then she turned her attention to the book.

To avoid contaminating the binding or pages with finger oils she pulled on thin latex gloves from her bag.

She pulled over a couple of bowl lamps, being careful not to spill them, for light to work by. The book's cover was bound in thin, very fine-grained hide, blackened by age and probably finger grease. In fact the grain was so fine it made her shudder. Then again, she reminded herself, this wouldn't be the first old tome bound in human skin you've han-dled.

Cautiously she opened the book. She was unsure what to expect. So she felt neither surprise nor dis-appointment to see she couldn't read any of it. Even if the writing had been transliterated into Latin char-acters it was almost certainly a tongue she didn't know. She wished she could transcribe some of it, so that she could get it to a translator and find at least a clue as to what this was all about. And why it had been presented to her with such showmanship by the brothers of the Lamasery of the Woods. But she didn't dare use her flash for fear of degrading the brit-tle paper.

Despite her lack of comprehension the sinuous characters seemed to entice her eyes, draw them in and then along as with the flow of a stream. She scanned the first page, then turned it and worked her way down the next.

A strange sense of peace suffused her. Her mind

a meditative blank, she paged through the ancient volume. She lost track of time, of location, of the sounds of the wind and the squeak of wooden joints. She lost all sense of self in the waterlike rippling of unknowable words. It was as if the dancing letters conveyed some message directly to her subconscious without passing through her conscious mind.

She found herself at the end. Closing the book, she sat back. She became aware of ferocious aches in her thighs and lower back.

"Just how long did I spend at that?" she wondered aloud.

Instead of checking the time on her cell phone she stood and stretched. That helped, but her feet prickled as blood flowed back into them, and her joints still felt stiff. She returned the butter lamps to their original position in the circle. Then, working around lamps and relics, she performed some yoga poses.

As well as gently unkinking her joints and muscles, the moves allowed her to slip into a familiar meditative space. She was aware without forming thoughts that this was different from the trance state in which she had read through the whole book without understanding a single character. It was as if she was somehow processing.

For all her skepticism about the mystical, Annja had learned to respect the power of the human subconscious. In fact she attributed much of what some people called extrasensory perception to the subconscious processing normal sensory inputs of which the conscious mind was unaware. She perceived that something of the sort was happening and she was content to let it.

When she finished she realized she smelled smoke. Looking around quickly in alarm, she saw a brazier of glowing coals and several covered porcelain bowls had been placed just inside the door.

"Is that really a good idea?" she asked aloud, but softly. "This whole place is wood." The bowl lamps didn't worry her much. The wood was dense and tough. She doubted a spill of cool-burning butter would make the floor take light. But a brazier full of hot coals...

"The lamas have run this place a long time," she reminded herself aloud, "and they've got no electricity, much less natural gas. If they haven't burned the lamasery down by now, what're the odds of them doing it tonight?"

Then again, how often did they host long-legged Western adventuresses who might inadvertently kick the brazier over in her sleep? Oh, well, she thought. That's why they call it adventure.

She discovered she was intensely hungry. She brought the bowls and then the brazier, holding on by a pair of wooden handles, over to the wall outside the circle of lamps. She opened the bowls to find steamed rice and beans. The standard daily Nepali fare.

She ate, finding the food anything but bland as it might appear. It wasn't just hunger that added flavor to food, she'd found. It was also *strangeness*.

And this was high strangeness indeed.

When she replaced the intricately painted lids on the bowls they were all empty. Almost at once she felt her eyelids sag. A strange lassitude overcame her.

Not so strange, she assured herself. It's been a day. And she was far from used to the altitude yet.

Yet she was used to far greater exertions, physical and mental. Or so she thought. She found herself barely able to unroll the bedding and slip inside before her eyes fell shut.

IN THE MORNING SHE FOUND the brazier glowing red with renewed coals. White sunlight slanted down from windows up beneath the rafters she hadn't known were there before. The coins, the book and the butter lamps were gone.

She smelled food. More legumes and rice awaited her in bowls, steaming hot. To the side was tea, flavored with rancid yak butter.

Oh, well. She was ravenous again.

As she ate Annja tried to parse out exactly what had happened to her. As she finished the meal she decided she had no idea. But the monks had staged a truly elaborate show on her behalf.

"I guess," she said, standing up and stretching, "I'll have to wait to find out."

To her surprise she felt well rested and not at all sore, given she'd passed the night on a hard plank floor with only a thin pad beneath her.

The door opened suddenly. She froze.

A monk appeared. He wore yellow robes. His shaved head was painted with dots and lines in white. He smiled shyly, pressed palms together and bowed to her.

Recovering, she returned the greeting.

He presented her with an envelope. It was a normal-appearing manila envelope about six inches by eight, with the metal clasp fastened. She accepted it with a thank-you and a brow creased in puzzlement.

With clumsy fingers she fumbled to open the clasp. She put her lack of dexterity down to the room's chill. Even though the brazier had been replenished during the night it basically, so far as she could tell, prevented frost from forming on the walls, icicles dripping from the heavy rafters and Annja from freezing into a woman-shaped plank. And not much more. Her breath still produced dragon puffs of condensation.

Finally she got the flap open and looked inside. She gasped. It contained a scrap of paper, almost orange with age and dried to brittleness. She could clearly see that the writing on it, faded to a faint violet, was in Greek characters.

She looked up. She was alone in the room. The door was closed. She felt an eerie sense the lama had never been real at all.

Nonsense, she told herself. This paper is real enough.

Feeling a stab of annoyance at the monks for such cavalierly improper treatment of a clearly invaluable document, she fumbled in a cargo pocket for a plastic bag, friend to specimen takers and evidence techs around the world. When she had the paper sealed safely away she replaced it in the envelope.

She hesitated. She wasn't about to entrust the frail scrap to a pocket. Much less fold it to fit. She wanted to keep it immobilized and protected. One classic field-expedient method was to close it in the middle of a big book, preferably hardcover. But she was traveling much too lightly to carry anything that weighed that much and used up so much precious pack space.

Kneeling, she placed the envelope carefully on the dark floor boards. Then she opened her pack and pulled out her computer. The manila envelope fit handily between the screen and the keyboard. The clasp wouldn't quite catch but a couple of strips of the tape she carried as another frequently handy item secured the top well enough to satisfy her. Being stuffed in the pack would help hold the lid shut.

After zipping the computer back into her backpack she donned her heavy jacket, shouldered her pack and stood. Clearly it was time to go.

In daytime the lamasery corridors remained dim. The friendly glow of butter lamps burning in their niches showed her the way out.

Brilliant morning sunshine made her blink. Chill air hit her in the face like a bucket of ice water.

She barely noticed. Because sitting on a rock not twenty yards from her, with one long leg cocked over another and swinging idly, was Pantheras Katramados.

14

At the sound of the little copper bells, Baglung District Commissioner Chatura sighed, set down his tea on his Spartan, scrupulously ordered desk and rose. He walked through the room divider and stepped into the waiting room.

What he saw brought him up short. The two figures looming there crowded the room all by themselves. Clearly foreign, each topped him by at least a head. One was lean and lupine; the other was so wide, especially in his heavily padded jacket, he resembled one of the legendary ape-human monsters, the so-called *bonmanche* or yeti, which the absurdly superstitious had recently begun reporting seeing again around Dhaulagiri.

Chatura grunted. "Come on, then," he said in

English. He turned briskly about and made himself strut back into his office as if neither surprised nor concerned.

Inside he seethed.

ANNJA CREED RAN to embrace Pan. His strong arms felt good around her. His long wiry presence was a reassuring solidity in the warm sunlight, after the unreality of the night before.

The embrace broke. Annja stepped back. "What the hell are you doing here?" she demanded.

He laughed. "I'm happy to see you, too, Annja. I hope you're pleasantly surprised."

Behind him Prasad, Lal and the two Sherpas sat smoking and chatting. Their cousin Bahadur sat with them, his wounded arm in a sling.

"Well," she said, "yes. But I'm still surprised."

Pan nodded. He wore a padded jacket in green and yellow over a pair of well-worn blue jeans and hiking boots. He was also wearing a holster beneath his left arm.

"I suppose I owe you an explanation, Annja," he said.

"I don't know about *owe*," she said. "But it'd be nice if you gave me one anyway."

"The special antiquities task force has decided to extend their investigation of the Bajraktari artifact-smuggling ring to Nepal," he said. "For some reason they chose me for the job."

He grinned as he spoke. For all his modest manner

he knew as well as she did how uniquely qualified he was for this mission.

His presence still seemed odd. "I didn't think they had the budget for this kind of junket," she said.

"Not on the basis of what we knew at the time you left," he said. His voice had deepened and his face had hardened. It was as if a cloud had passed before the sun. "But we have received new intelligence. Enver Bajraktari, his henchman, Duka, and a number of his gunmen have come to Nepal. Specifically to hunt you down."

Annja pressed her lips to a line. "How did they know I was here?"

He winced. "Apparently their spies have penetrated the Greek military or law-enforcement community more deeply than we even feared. None of the task force's members has been corrupted—I think. Unfortunately, we are required to pass certain information on. Both laterally and up the chain of command."

"You think they might've got to some of your bosses?" Annja asked in alarm.

"Anything is possible, I'm afraid. But it could also be that no one in the Hellenic police deliberately shared this information with the gangsters. Somebody boasting in a taverna, a police bureaucrat trying to impress his mistress... And our government shares much information with other governments. Especially where international terrorism might come into play. The leak may have originated elsewhere entirely."

"So that's what brings you to Nepal," Annja said, sounding lighter than she felt. "But how did you happen to wind up *here,* at this allegedly hidden lamasery in the middle of a Brothers Grimm forest?"

He smiled, although she could see in his dark, expressive eyes that the implications of what he had told her worried him. Me, too, she thought.

"On my own initiative—and telling no one else— I contacted the Japan Buddha Federation and explained to them that you were in great danger."

Annja smiled at him. "So now you've got an international reputation as a fighter of antiquities trafficking?"

He shrugged. "In a minor way, perhaps. The Buddhists satisfied themselves of my bona fides. They provided me contacts that led me to Baglung and this gentleman."

He gestured. "Bahadur," Annja said, nodding and smiling at the Nepali. He grinned back.

"Despite his help," Pan said, "I've searched for you for several days. It may sound paranoid, but I got the distinct feeling I was being *tested* somehow."

"I have the same feeling," she said. "And I suspect we're both right. Take a look at this."

She handed him the scrap of paper and explained succinctly how she got it. She saw no reason to hold anything back.

Pan's only response to her bizarre account was to raise his eyebrows and nod. He did not project skepticism. She wondered what he'd experienced himself since arriving in the mountain kingdom.

He turned his attention to the plastic bag in his

hand. Instantly his body language changed to resemble a hunting dog pointing out a pheasant in a nearby bush. He didn't quiver with excitement, but did transition from relaxation to a taut, though not rigid, readiness.

"It's in the Macedonian dialect of ancient Greek," he said. "It's a transcription."

"I figured. I'd guess it's several hundred years old. Certainly not 2300 years old. So it can't be original. You can read it, yes?"

Absently he nodded. "Oh, yes," he said. "The lamas must have copied it. Perhaps again and again. Most probably, few of the transcribers could have read it, although no doubt they translated it somewhere along the line."

He raised his head to stare hard at the lamasery. Unlike many Buddhist monasteries and temples Annja had seen in Asia, it wasn't gaily painted, aside from the splendid scarlet-lacquer-and-gilt door. Instead it was dark, whether painted or weathered that way. It showed unmistakable signs of having endured the turns of many harsh mountain seasons. Built of planks and posts and shakes of the native wood, presumably the very hemlocks that surrounded it up close, its steeply pitched roof and rough walls seemed a natural outgrowth of the forest itself.

Annja guessed Pan was holding a raging internal debate about pounding on the dragon door and demanding to be shown the rest of the manuscript the scrap came from. The archaeologist won out over the cop in him. He chose not to try throwing his weight around. She thought that wise, since his effective weight was an unknown quantity in the wilds of an alien land. In fact she could almost see him reach the same conclusion she had—this was what they were meant to have, so it had to satisfy them. For now.

"So what is it?" Annja said, rather irrationally angling to peer over his shoulder, trying to see through the dazzling highlights the bright mountain sun raised on the plastic bag. She still wouldn't be able to read the paper even if she could see it.

"I can't believe it!" he exclaimed. "This is a transcription of what purports to be a journal written by my ancient namesake. General Pantheras himself."

"You're kidding!"

Pan's grin was enormous. "It's true. Or at least, that's what it says. Listen to this—

> The yellow-robed monks seem to know of my quest. Although it is to despoil them of their tribute to their own chief god or seer, they do not resist, but smile and nod and assure me that my feet are on the proper path to the greatest treasure of all. Their easy acquiescence gives me greater pause than the fiercest resistance— which, after all, I expected to encounter.
>
> Perhaps they intend to direct me deep into the jaws of a trap. If so, my duty to my king requires that I continue along my road.

"And where does that go?" Annja asked, feeling excitement sizzle in her veins.

Pan raised his head and extended his arm to point to the angular white head of Dhaulagiri peak, looming above the steep wooded hills that surrounded the lamasery and the valley.

THE MEN SEEMED TO FILL the district commissioner's tiny office to overflowing. Like the waiting area it was dominated by giant color portraits of Chairmen Mao and Prachanda. The battered metal desk with chipped green enamel was bare except for a notepad, several pencils lined up beside it, and an empty in-box and a teacup. Chatura's chair was the same as the two his visitors occupied—wooden, with no arms and an uncompromisingly upright back. To one side a brass teapot bubbled on a hot plate atop a low bookcase stuffed with books of regulations and bound official documents.

"No, I don't want tea," Enver Bajraktari said in English. "It tastes like shit."

"I am sure you'd know well," the commissioner said in Gorkhali.

"What was that?"

"Nothing," Chatura said in English with a thin smile. "A native benediction."

"Huh," said the flamboyantly mustached Kosovar with the dead milk-white eye. His bodyguard loomed like the shadow of a mountain behind him, thick arms folded over his chest. "Well. We bring you news from far places, comrade. Good news and bad."

Chatura did not bother to try suppressing his distaste at being called *comrade*.

He refused to ask the question which, even in Nepal, popular culture made practically obligatory.

After a moment Bajraktari gave in. "I shall tell you the bad news first, my friend," he said. "First, a meddling American woman named Annja Creed caused us to lose our last shipment to the Greek police. The good news is that the witch has come to Nepal."

"How is it good news that this meddlesome Western woman has come here?" Chatura demanded. He didn't see fit to mention he was well aware of the fact. He was too disappointed and angry at Bajraktari's first information. He had a substantial investment in that shipment.

The foreigner grinned. "Because she's on the trail of the greatest treasure trove in the Himalayas—the lost treasure of the Highest Shrine. All we have to do is follow her and she'll lead us to unimaginable wealth. She's here, is she not?"

Chatura conceded the fact with a slow nod. His scowl had if anything set harder.

"She is," he said. "And I have already put Jagan-natha on her trail."

Bajraktari nodded. "Well, that's a good thing, isn't it? You have told me of this man. He is a bulldog who will not lose the witch, nor give up the trail."

"You don't understand. Although he is the regional commander of front-line revolutionary fighters, he is not objectively Marxist. He does not understand certain realities," Chatura said.

The Kosovar cocked a brow at him. "I thought the major fought well in your revolution," he said. "Not to mention successfully."

Chatura made a low growling noise in his throat. Did this ridiculous gawky, hirsute barbarian dare to mock him for his less active role in the civil war? Bajraktari was a fool who had no understanding that without a proper theoretical foundation mere action was useless. It was men like himself, Chatura, who had done the real work of bringing the socialist revolution to this state. And small thanks he had received...

Chatura shook his head. Surely the foreign devil had no notion of what Chatura had done in the war. He was merely gibbering like the ape he was.

"The major is a hammer-headed fool," Chatura said. "He is likely to persist until he kills this Creed woman or drives her away. And then we shall never claim the treasure for the proletarian revolution."

Bajraktari showed him a humorless grin full of teeth stained brown by strong tobacco and uncertain dental hygiene. "Then you'd best make sure he doesn't do any such foolish thing," he said. "You are his commissar. Surely he will obey you."

Chatura grunted again. He had better, he told himself.

He rose. "I shall order him to back off and merely observe what the intruder does."

"What about us?" Bajraktari said, sprawling insolently in the chair despite the fact it couldn't have been comfortable. Chatura had chosen the chairs to ensure his visitors were uncomfortable.

"You must return to the village and wait until I call you."

Duka made an ominous sound in his throat like distant thunder over the White Mountain.

"I will send for you when I learn more," Chatura said, steadfastly refusing to be intimidated by these European monkeys. "And now I bid you good day."

15

"This is almost too good to be true," Annja said. "We've got what looks like corroboration that our objective exists. And we're literally following in General Pantheras's footsteps! Can this be real? Is there any chance the document could be a fake?"

Pan laughed. "You think there're many people in these mountains who could write convincingly in the vernacular of ancient Macedonia?" he asked. "There must be fewer than a thousand living in all the world today. It's easier for me to believe it is what it seems."

"Me, too, since you put it that way," Annja said.

They were walking along side by side up a trail covered with hemlock bark. The Nepalis stayed a respectful distance behind.

"You may be doubtful about having me under-foot," Pan said. "I feel the same about outsiders in the line of my everyday work. Please remember, though, that I am also a colleague of yours, if still in training."

He spread his arms wide and grinned at her. "Just think of me as that which every archaeologist most requires in the field—a graduate student!"

She looked at him a moment. "Do you know what you're asking?" she said with mock severity.

"Oh, yes," he said, dark eyes laughing. "You could hardly prove more tyrannical than Dr. Haralabos, under whom I made my first expedition."

"Well," she said, setting hands on hips, "watch me."

"So, please fill me in on what's happened since you arrived here," Pan said.

To hide any hardening of expression or concern in her eyes Annja turned her face as if to look at a black-headed jay that scolded them from a high hemlock branch off to her left. They continued to climb higher. Once again their guides hadn't told her where they were going. But by this point she felt both confident in putting her fate into the capable hands of Prasad and his clan, and needful of doing so. They had yet to locate anything of particular archaeological value. And she sensed that time to rescue the big prize, the Highest Shrine, wore thin.

She sensed Prasad come up closer behind them, as if innocently. She guessed he was interested to learn how much Annja would tell this newcomer.

For all that I trust Pan, she thought, and for all that I'm attracted to him, I'm sure not going to tell him about the encounter with Agrabat. At least in any detail.

He was a good man and a valuable ally, especially with the potential of having a wily and determined enemy like Major Jagannatha on their trail. Yet he was still a cop. He might revert to type at any time. Beyond doubt the gang's dispatch by Annja and her guides had stretched local law to the breaking point. *Concealing* the deaths snapped those laws beyond repair.

So she gave him the redacted version. She alluded to an encounter with bandits but suggested that they had bluffed their way clear. She caught a furrowing of his dark brows, a sideways glance of his dark, liquid eyes. But he said nothing.

He suspects, she thought. But as long as he doesn't know, he probably won't press. As a police officer, especially a special operator as Pan was, he'd most likely sympathize with the way they'd dealt with their attackers. Just so long as he didn't know for sure a major law breach had occurred, he could deal with it.

"So what about more organized opposition?" he asked, allowing the bandit encounter to drop. "You indicated we might be running afoul of the local Maoist guerrillas."

Gratefully she tossed that off to Prasad and Lal. Bahadur had headed back alone to Baglung, leaving behind the two extra Sherpas who had accompanied him with fresh supplies. That brought her little expedition to eight. Enough for a little heft, not enough to get unmanageable.

She would have preferred more firepower than two old bolt-action guns, plus whatever sidearm Pan had brought along. The porters, however, like Lal and his uncle, all carried the big *kukris,* and she had witnessed how fearfully effective those were in close quarters. Still, against even a single assault rifle they could find themselves holding the seriously short end of the stick.

Prasad mostly let Lal fill Pan in on Jagannatha, interjecting as he deemed necessary. As always his words were few and to the point. All the same Annja learned more about the shadowy guerrilla chieftain. He had always been a maverick, it seemed, almost as great a headache to his superiors and fellow commanders as to the government forces.

"He does what he thinks is right," Lal explained. "And his successes—he's very crafty—make rival commanders look bad. They hate him for it, and they're always looking to hurt him."

"You sound as if you respect this man," Pan said.

Lal shrugged.

"The wise warrior respects a worthy foe," Prasad said. "I see you are a man who knows this thing." Pan let that pass without comment.

"He's an honorable man," Lal said grudgingly. "Unlike most guerrillas."

"It makes him the more dangerous," Prasad said.

"Hmm," Pan said. He glanced at Annja. She said nothing. This was a guy thing; she didn't know him well enough to be sure he'd appreciate her actually offering an opinion at this point. Besides, she was intrigued to hear what the former Gurkhas would say without her tainting the discussion with their employer's viewpoint.

"I'd have thought the other," Pan admitted. "That someone who was treacherous and unscrupulous would prove the deadliest enemy."

Prasad grinned. "Might it not be that even so seasoned a warrior as yourself has things yet to learn?" he asked. Though his tone was gentle, almost bantering and cheerful, Annja knew it was tantamount to a major smackdown. Pan's blink a beat later confirmed that he'd caught that, too.

"His men are fanatically loyal to him," Lal said. "Even though he enforces the old Maoist rules of war—which few enough other guerrillas do. Nor do the peasants hate and fear him the way they do most guerrillas. He respects them, their homes and their religion."

"And the people are the water in which guerrilla fish swim," Pan said.

"Yes," Prasad said. "Though few sympathize with the Maoists they let Jagannatha swim where he wishes."

"If the peasants aren't Maoist, do they support the central government, then?" Annja asked. She knew it was perilous to intrude too deeply into local politics, but it could prove important. Anyway, she was curious.

Lal looked at his uncle, who shrugged. "Most just want to be left alone," the young man said. "When I fought overseas, for the British and for the Indians, I learned that it's much the same everywhere. Life on the land is hard for the people everywhere. Political struggles at best make it harder for them to feed themselves and their families. At worst—"

He shrugged. Annja nodded. She knew what the worst could look like. She'd seen some of it herself.

"How do you feel about all this?" she asked.

"We're glad to see reform come to Nepal," Lal said. Prasad's face tightened ever so slightly. She guessed it was a touchy subject for him, that he had a deeply ingrained regard for the monarchy. Yet he didn't contradict his nephew. "The people need more say in their own lives."

"Isn't that what the Maoists are fighting for?" Pan asked.

"So they say," Prasad replied.

"We fight them because we see they'd be worse than what we have, regardless of corruption and abuse," Lal said.

"And Jagannatha?" Annja asked.

"He fights because he fears what the West will do to our country more than what his own side would," Lal said.

THE HEAVY WOODEN DOOR, blue paint cracked and peeling from overlong exposure to the harsh weather of the hillside, opened with a creak of hinges. The inside air that rushed out into the visitor's face felt hot. It was redolent with the smells of human occupancy and cooking.

A family of four was gathered around a heavy table, about to eat their supper. Blunt peasant faces filled with alarm as they turned toward his. "Please forgive the intrusion," the visitor said. "I need to ask you some questions."

"You are Major Jagannatha," the father said as the visitor pushed into the room. A pair of his men followed him. They had Kalashnikovs slung over their backs. Like him they wore heavy fur-lined local jackets and fur caps with long flaps. The major's jacket hung open, revealing his khaki shirt—and the long holster he wore at his belt.

"I am," the visitor said. "I know there are Westerners intruding upon this land. Asking questions, prying secrets. I know that kinsmen of yours guide them. I wish to learn about them."

"So that you can kill our kinfolk?" the youngest man flared. The only female in the room was the mother, who at a slow, insistent hand gesture from her husband laid her serving bowl upon the sturdy wood table and sat down. The speaker was her younger son.

"I have no wish to make war upon any Magar," Jagannatha said, using the name that served both the tribe as a whole and as surname for its members. "I only need to know what the Westerners are up to."

The woman lowered her face and looked at her hands, which intertwined helplessly in her lap. Her husband's face was broad, flat, weathered, reddened by long exposure to sun, wind and chill. The peasant farmer said nothing.

"Will you kill us all if we don't do what you want?" the youth asked.

The major's eyes narrowed to slits in his own dark, grizzle-bearded face. Though a lifelong soldier who had never worked the land, he likewise bore the marks of wind and weather and sun.

"You know who I am," he said.

The father was nervously eyeing the flapped cross-draw holster where Jagannatha carried his unmistakable long-barreled Chinese Type 80 pistol.

"Yes," the farmer said.

"Then you know I follow Mao's rules for revolutionary armies," he said. "I insist that those who follow me do as well."

"He doesn't disrespect the shrines," the mother said, reluctant to put herself forward, but eager to avoid any confrontation with this supremely dangerous man and his human wolves. "He doesn't sneer at us who follow the great Lord Buddha."

"That's true," the father said, nodding slowly. "You don't bother the Hindus, either."

Jagannatha wanted to tell them that he fought for *them*—for the peasants, for the people, for their culture and independence. But he couldn't bring himself to speak the words—they brought on too much self-disgust.

It was what every rapist-brigand of a terrorist and every political officer would say. That Jagannatha *meant it* made little difference.

"I only want information on the foreigners," he said.

The old man looked him in the eye for a moment. He had, Jagannatha knew, never been a soldier. One of the things bitter experience had taught the major was not to look down on these tough mountain peasants on that account. The man may not have fighting skills. But he knew how to endure.

You are just another mountain storm, the farmer's look said. You and your kind. You may smite us as with lightning, or wash us away with a sudden flood. But if we survive, we shall remain and you shall go. If we do not survive our people will remain, as we have for ages. Whereas those like you come and go.

Jagannatha wished he could refute the wisdom in that look.

"We will not give you information that might bring harm to our kin," the father said with finality. Then he sat back and glanced at his wife, who sat with her head bowed, tightly gripping her apron in fear. "Do with us what you will."

Jagannatha rose. "Then I will leave you. I admire your courage, comrade. And your loyalty. Just look deep in your heart and make sure it is not misplaced."

The farmer did not meet his gaze now. It wasn't

from fear, Jagannatha knew, but contempt. The peasant would see loyalty directed toward anything but his family and blood first as misplaced. That was the curse of this tribal land.

Yet it was also its strength.

With a grunt and peremptory head shake Jagannatha ordered his two men out into the rapidly deepening mountain dusk. He stared at the farmer until the man looked at him. He nodded once. Then he followed his men from the hut.

His patrol of twenty men, each armed with an assault rifle, had gone barely a quarter of a mile through the farmer's terraced fields when the sounds of a scuffle came from nearby. Guns came up and safeties switched off—showing just how disciplined Jagannatha's men were despite their ragged demeanor.

The major raised a hand. His men gripped their weapons in tense readiness. No one spoke.

A steep, pebbly ridge ran past them to the right, descending to meet the narrow valley they walked along. In a moment Jagannatha heard crunching and saw one of his scouts with his *kukri* pressed to the skinny neck of the older son of the family they had just left. From the narrow ridge's top the scout gave the boy a shove. He rolled down and landed just in front of the major's boots.

Rifles swung to cover the boy. Jagannatha waved them off.

"Why are you sneaking after us, boy? Are you spying on us?"

"No!" The boy scrambled to his feet. Jagannatha hooked his thumbs through the web belt he wore and rocked back on the heels of his British Army-issue boots. "I want to help you."

"What kind of help can you give us?"

The youth looked around nervously. It seemed he was more afraid one of his kinfolk had followed him and might see what he was about than he was of the heavily armed pack surrounding him. "I can give you information," he said.

A jay stridently abused the guerrillas for their trespass from a scrubby, spiky bush.

"You will give up your kinsfolk, then?" Jagannatha asked.

The youth licked his lips. He wore a Western-style jacket, T-shirt and jeans. "You won't hurt my relatives?"

Jagannatha shook his head. "I can't promise that. If you know my reputation you know I don't kill unless I have to. I shall try not to harm your cousins. If they fight me, though, they take their chances."

The kid squinched his face up in an agony of indecision. Jagannatha stood looking at him unsympathetically.

The youth gave his head a spastic shake. "I don't know much. Only this one thing—a foreign man has joined them. He is tall, clean shaved, dark. He has the look of an eagle. Or so they say."

After a moment, Jagannatha nodded. "That is a good thing to know."

He turned to walk on. The sun had vanished. The rising wind blew cold. Clouds streaked across the sky were turning orange and violet.

The boy reached out and grabbed the major's sleeve. With an alacrity astonishing in a bandy-legged, middle-aged man with something of a paunch, Jagannatha spun and backhanded him to the ground.

To his credit the young man didn't waste time on foolish questions—such as why the major had struck him—nor whining complaints. Instead he pushed up to a sitting position and said, "Let me join you."

"No," Jagannatha said. "Go to school. Learn the skills to make your family and your people strong."

He started to walk on again. The youth leaped to his feet. "You can't just blow me off like this, no matter who you are!" he shouted. "I helped you. You can't just leave me here!"

He tried to run after Jagannatha. The guerrillas thrust him rudely back. One raised a gun to smash the youthful face with the heavy steel-shod butt.

"Enough!" Jagannatha roared, spinning around again. "The child blusters to cover his disappointment. For this you would break his head? Show off your manhood when government bullets crack so low over your heads their passage stings your face like wind-blown ice crystals. Not by offering to descend in a pack and tear apart some foolish pup who yaps and shows his teeth to cover his own embarrassment at being rejected. That impresses no one."

His men hung their heads and fell back. The young man looked little comforted at being left suddenly alone beneath the glowering scrutiny of the major.

"As for you," Jagannatha said softly, "be grateful you asked *me,* and not some other who would be only too eager to enlist your flesh—to shield his own from enemy bullets."

The youth looked blank. "But I want to fight the corrupt government!"

"Do you?" Jagannatha smiled. The young man's face lost whatever color it retained. "Bored with farm life, are you? Then go and join the army."

"What? But you're rebels! I don't understand."

Technically the guerrillas weren't rebels at all, but an armed formation belonging to a party that legally held a major share of power in Nepal. Jagannatha didn't feel like mincing such legalisms with this callow child out here on a windy hillside.

"Learn something. Get training. Get tough. Learn what it means to be a soldier. Get some discipline. Get some real training. If you can, go and fight."

The boy shook his head. "I don't understand," he said again. "If I'm to fight the government, how can I join its army?"

"How better? Half of us were government soldiers once. Let your enemy train you and arm you. Then some night, when you are ready—when you know something worth knowing, including who you are and what you really want—then take your weapon and your pack and slip away to join the revolution. Then you will have something valuable to bring us."

The kid shook his head uncomprehendingly. His mouth hung open.

"It's an old trick," Jagannatha said. "But it's being used right now in Iraq and in Afghanistan, and a dozen other countries. The forces of repression are training and equipping those who will defeat them in the end."

With an air of finality he turned away. His men took their weapons off the youth. The section moved off down the slope, seeming to dissolve into the heavy mauve twilight.

The boy stood and watched them go. Then he turned and scrambled clumsily back toward the comforting yellow glow of his family's hut.

16

The next day the members of the expedition found their first lost treasure shrine.

They were working in a saddle of scrubland between densely forested hills. Snow clumped on the north sides of rocks, hollows and bushes. An outcrop of rock seemed to have crumbled and slumped at the foot of a large boulder.

With nerve-straining care, Annja eased a basketball-size stone out of place. Then she held her breath. She was afraid the whole apparently random rockfall would come sliding down on top of her.

The rocks stayed put.

She raised her flashlight and shone it into the hole exposed by the rock she had removed. A golden fat man beamed back at her from the lotus position.

"Bingo," she said, easing back. She got her camera and took some shots.

The Sherpas all sat on their packs smoking. They talked in quiet voices among themselves. A couple of new ones had joined them from a village in brushy country above the Lamasery of the Woods. One served solely as a local guide.

The notion of sitting and watching while their employers worked seemed to afford them endless amusement. Prasad and his nephew kept watch.

Showing the same well-schooled patience and discipline she'd expect from a grad student, Pan helped her ease other rocks away from the opening of stones cleverly constructed to appear natural.

The shrine was small. Some long-cold joss sticks sat in little porcelain containers flanking the Buddha. A litter of dried flower petals, white and pink, covered offerings in the form of crumpled, faded bills. Beneath them, when Annja shifted them aside, lay gold coins.

Painstakingly they transferred the treasures out to a blue plastic ground cover, photographed them, noted them and examined them one by one. The local porters seemed to grow somewhat tense during this proceeding. Prasad and Lal spoke encouragingly to them. They continued to watch the foreigners like hungry falcons.

To her disappointment none of the coins was particularly old. As far as she could tell from Prasad's reading of inscriptions blurred by the handling of countless fingers, the oldest dated back to about the mid-eighteenth century. They were not even back to her primary period of interest and far from the distant Macedonian occupation. Still, it was definitely the sort of thing she'd been hired to find—originally.

Am I getting tunnel vision? she wondered. Have I become so fixated on the Highest Shrine I'm overlooking sites of lesser value? It was possible, she had to acknowledge to herself. She didn't think she was feeling the lure of gold per se. She had no expectation of being allowed to keep any treasure she came across, nor any intention to do so.

"You know," Pan said, holding a note up to the sun in fingers clad in fine cloth gloves, "I get the feeling this shrine isn't 'lost' at all. Some of these banknotes are quite recent."

"You think it's just hidden, then," Annja said. "Maybe to keep tourists and bandits from cleaning it out?"

"That'd be my guess," he said, placing the note back down on the plastic sheet as carefully as if it were a thousand years old. Annja approved. Good practice was good practice. A good field worker never handled any artifact casually, much less carelessly.

They recorded the coordinates on Annja's GPS. Then they carefully replaced everything in the shrine—using the camera to document that, too—in the reverse order they had taken it out. Carefully, they rebuilt and resealed the happenstance-looking cairn in a way that concealed it from profane eyes.

When everything was duly recorded in images

and cataloged in Annja's computer, they backed it all up to handy thumb drives. To Annja they were a great boon to fieldwork. She had already encountered grad students who didn't remember doing archaeology before the advent of the USB flash drive. They made Annja feel old.

Finishing, they stood and looked around. The local men had visibly relaxed. They nodded to the two foreigners and then paid them no further attention, chatting among themselves in a local dialect. Prasad and Lal openly grinned at their employer.

"It might just be me," Pan said, "but your friends from Baglung have the air about them of men who've just won a bet."

THE BURST OF METAL-JACKETED bullets kicked up puffs of dust and grit four feet in front of Annja.

She threw herself behind a big granite rock to the left of the path. Fortunately they weren't traversing a long open slope with a sheer drop to one side—at the moment. Instead they were in close country, where hills sparsely tufted with brush and winter-brown bunch grass pitched sharply up and down all around them.

She looked around. The rest of her party had gone to ground like prairie dogs at the distinctive thudding of a Kalashnikov. The Sherpas weren't ex-Gurkhas or army vets like Prasad and Lal. But they had either experience of taking cover from gunfire or just a natural aptitude.

Across the path Pan crouched behind a clump of rocks with a wind-gnarled cedar sprouting from its top. He had his pack grounded at his side and his sidearm in his right hand. It was a full-sized Glock, either a 9 mm or a .40 caliber; she couldn't tell at this range. With his left hand he was digging behind his back under his jacket.

His came up with an abbreviated version of the piece he held in his right hand—black, with the unmistakable boxy Glock outlines. He tossed it to Annja.

"Keep it," he called. "I've been meaning to give it to you."

She caught it by reflex. "Anybody hit?" she called out behind her.

"No," Lal called back. Another burst of gunfire snarled from somewhere behind and to Annja's right. These reports were higher pitched. Annja guessed they came from an American-made M-16.

Fearing that she might still be exposed to hidden ambushers, Annja took stock of their surroundings. A mountain brook glittered and tinkled down the slope to her left. Ahead of the expedition a big brow of granite rose maybe four stories high, with bits of brush sprouting from it, and more wind-twisted cedars crowning it. The stream wound past its base. That was almost certainly where the first shots had come from. Even as she looked she saw smoke puff from the gray rock brow as another burst echoed through the valley.

Another higher-pitched snarl ripped from behind her. A despairing cry answered it. Annja's heart slammed as she turned her head quickly to see another bluish wisp of smoke whipped away from the rocky top of the ridge paralleling their line of march.

Their ambushers had caught them in a classic fire sack. But she could see at once they had chosen inexpertly. The ground around her party was too irregular, with too many folds providing dead ground out of the attackers' field of fire, too many clumps of scrub and mounded boulders. The defenders had plenty of cover available, as well as concealment, from every angle.

What they lacked was an easy way out. Annja knew the classic technique for dealing with an ambush was to assault right into it. Fast and hard. Probably the attackers knew it, too; certainly if they were in fact Jagannatha's men. Prasad and Lal had him down as a man who knew his craft, and they knew theirs well enough to tell.

To attack straight up that rock cliff with any speed Annja figured you'd have to be Spider-Man, or at least a champion rock climber. And even to get to the base you'd have to cross open ground with men shooting automatic weapons at you.

A big-bore handgun cracked to Annja's right. She kept her eyes on the cliff, saw dust puff away from the rock near where the last burst had originated. She doubted Pan had hit anyone. But at fifty yards it was a hell of a shot from a handgun fired at an upward angle. It would at least keep the shooters up there from getting too cocky.

The problem was the enemy held the heights. That meant they could shift position unseen by their targets, in perfect safety. While the expedition members could readily find cover against observation or fire from almost any angle, they couldn't be shielded from every direction *simultaneously*. All the bad guys had to do was keep firing off enough rounds to keep their heads down while their buddies scouted for better shots. And when they had those lined up...

Annja checked her Glock's chamber. Then she got up and rabbited up the slope to the right.

Pan shouted something as she flashed past him. She ran bolt upright, hair streaming behind her, trusting speed rather than hunkering down or dodging to get to the temporary shelter she sought. Automatic weapons, several at once in different timbres, roared angrily at her, filling the valley with shuddering thunder. Behind her Annja heard the harder, measured whack of Lal squeezing off aimed shots from his Enfield. Pan, shouting wordlessly, emptied a double-stack magazine at the granite bluff, desperately trying to force the ambushers' heads down.

Annja's goal was a narrow, dry channel that ran down the slope to their right. It was floored with a lot of loose rock, treacherous footing. But if she judged properly she'd be protected from fire from both directions once she reached it.

Bullets struck off a rock in front of her. A ricochet moaned past her ear. She launched herself forward in a dive, remembering to hold her Glock up with her finger outside the trigger guard as she landed on her bent arms in the scree.

She slid, scraping her hands and banging her elbows cruelly. As she crunched to a stop she heard a scream. She raised her head far enough to see the granite cliff. A rifle fell, sling flapping. The figure of a man followed flailing. He fell headfirst into the rock at the foot of the cliff. His drawn-out cry died with him.

"Whoa," Annja breathed. Evidently an incautious ambusher, overcome by buck fever and trying furiously to track the sprinting woman in his battle sights, had risen out of cover. Either Pan or, more likely, Lal had nailed him and he'd toppled forward into the air.

A sudden attack of common sense made her flatten herself as a single shot fired from ahead and above cracked over her head and hit a flat rock a yard away. It didn't much surprise her that nobody had hit her on her desperate dash. Nor that the opening burst of the engagement hadn't hit anybody. The truth was nobody could hit anything full-auto at any distance except by accident or sheer volume of firepower.

The ambushers had made mistakes but were smart

enough to figure that out. An assault rifle, especially a Kalashnikov, wasn't ideal for aimed fire. But if you had the self-discipline to aim and fire single shots, the range was actually pretty short.

Annja crawled fifteen feet up the dry wash. The rocks gouged at her. Fortunately she wore long sleeves rolled down and long pants, or she'd be scraped seriously. As it was, she was going to look as if she'd been dragged through the proverbial knothole backward.

If she lived long enough. That was key. Living until you could *care* how you looked.

She had gotten far enough upslope for serious rock juts to flank her on the left—the direction the granite cliff now lay in relation to her. Tufted dry grass shielded her from the guys high right.

She came up to all fours. She scrabbled up the narrow draw until larger rock outcrops to either side protected her from the sides.

Full-auto volleys cracked off to both sides of her. Despite their advantage in height and firepower the ambushers acted tentative. Nobody wants to get shot, she realized.

Temporarily shielded, Annja scrambled close to the ridge top. She hoped to find a way to work around and catch the snipers on the granite knob unexpectedly from behind. If a straight-up countercharge isn't going to happen, she thought, there's always a sneak attack. She could do sneaky.

Carefully she kept low, beneath the crest of the ridge. To silhouette herself against the painfully blue

Himalayan sky and its light screen of white clouds
would be to make herself the ideal target.

As she worked her way forward toward the cliffs
she almost immediately saw the bent-over backs of
a pair of men wearing bulky fur-trimmed jackets.
One carried an AKM, the other a long black M-16.
Fortunately their attention was fixed totally to their
front as they picked their way to a vantage point
from where they no doubt hoped to catch Pan, still
popping off pesky shots from his Glock, unprotected.
They were completely unaware of her.

Her own Glock was in her right hand as she moved
toward them as fast as she thought she could without
being heard. The noisy firefight helped. She was still
a good twenty-five yards away from the men. A good
shot herself, as well as a skillful combat handgunner,
she carried an unfamiliar weapon with a shortish
barrel. A shot she wouldn't hesitate to take on the
shooting range looked way too long to her here on this
windswept ridge. And with both men carrying rifles,
she couldn't afford to shoot and miss. Both men had
to go down, as close to the same instant as possible.

A firecracker ripple in the air right beside her
made her heart jump practically through the roof of
her skull. It was the sound of bullets, shattering the
air at supersonic speed. She didn't need the reports
of another M-16 firing, arriving a half beat later, to
tell her that someone had fired up at her from behind,
narrowly missing to splash a burst of copper-jacketed
.223-caliber needles off a flat rock nearby.

Annja had exactly zero good options. All she could do was act. She sprang into a full-on run at the men in front of her. All she had was hope that her combat-honed reflexes had chosen one of the alternatives that sucked least.

Loose gravel crunched and slipped beneath her soles. She was practically flying, miraculously managing not to twist an ankle or fall. Either would have finished her.

The closer of the two men was quick to respond. He turned toward her, bringing up his long black gun.

A wild burst cracked over her head, aimed at the clouds and distance-blue peaks far to the north. She pushed the Glock out on the end of her arm, locked the elbow and started cranking off rounds as fast as the handgun would cycle.

A fountain of empties spouted from the Glock's ejector port, twinkling as they turned over and over in the intense mountain sunlight. Fortunately she ran under the glittering arch. No hot brass cylinders seared her face or touched her skin. A couple bounced on her left shoulder; most missed her.

She tried to keep the white dot of the foresight centered in her vision—and centered in the middle of the turning rifleman's torso. She struggled not to yank the piece offline as she worked the long Glock double-action trigger as fast as she could. Her dead run, which she did not dare slow, and the weapon's recoil didn't help.

But she did enough. She actually saw the gunman's round, stubbled face grimace in shock as her bullets hit him. He crumpled. His rifle clattered to the ground.

The gunfire stopped. Her ears rang from her own wild fusillade, but she could still hear the new gunman's shots, as though from a great distance. Now, miraculously, he had quit firing for fear of hitting his comrades.

But her stubby Glock had its heavy steel slide locked back on its light polymer body. She had cranked through the whole 11-round magazine and the chambered round in dropping the first guerrilla. The Kalashnikov man had almost finished pivoting toward her, heavy rifle at his hip.

She dropped the empty Glock, formed her right hand in a fist and reached with her will. She felt the reassuring solidity of her sword's hilt spring from nowhere to fill it.

The man with the AK might have been fast enough to get a shot into her. Regardless of how seasoned a fighter he was, the sight of something simply impossible—a pointed three-foot length of razor steel appearing from nowhere—short-circuited all of his battle reflexes.

He might have been able to fend off the sword with his rifle. But he did the worst thing possible— threw it and his arms up by reflex to protect his face.

That wasn't Annja's target. She thrust home. With almost seductively little resistance the point took him in the sternum. Driven by Annja's whole weight charging full speed, the sword slid right through him, thrusting out the back of his parka. She felt weird vibrations run up her arm as the blade grated alongside his spine.

She released the weapon and put her shoulder down as she ran into him headlong. As tackles went it might not have made the sports center plays of the day, but it served its purpose. They both fell over a low pile of rocks.

What might have been a bone-snapping impact was cushioned by the gunman's body. He was limp as she fell atop him.

A shudder went through her body. Like it or not— and she didn't—since acquiring the sword she had often been forced to experience a very intimate form of killing. But seldom had she felt one of her victims die.

Have hysterics later, she commanded herself, setting her jaw against a surge of bile from her stomach. The Kalashnikov lay by her victim's outflung arm a yard to her left. She snatched it up. Bringing the stock to her shoulder, she came up and around into a crouch.

Apparently the M-16 gunner coming up behind took for granted his comrade would quickly overpower a mere woman—even a woman a head taller than he was. Her body, bulked out by her colorful down jacket, had blocked the sword's apparition from his view. Or his mind had simply refused to process it. He had his gun lowered to a sort of patrol position, slanting before belly and hips, and ambled forward at a bowlegged gait.

His eyes barely had time to begin to widen at the unexpected sight of Annja popping up from behind a rock like a prairie dog. Then the hooded front sight blade of Annja's scavenged AKM came up before her eyes. She hammered a 3-round burst through his chest and he went down.

From behind him another burst clattered. Without seeing the second shooter Annja ducked. He was good enough or lucky enough that bullets spattered the very rock she hid behind. The piercing wails of the tumbling ricochets chilled her soul. Have I just given the guys on the cliff a clear shot at my back? she wondered.

She couldn't worry about that. Any more than she could give in to the fear that yammered like a frightened dog pack in her skull. The immediate threat was the guy shooting at her.

She did something she usually despised. She held the big Kalashnikov up over her head and shot blindly. The 7.62 mm bullets it fired carried more energy than the slimmer, faster M-16 projectiles. But the Russian-designed rifle also weighed about ten pounds loaded, which served to soak up a lot of the recoil. With her upper-body strength she could hold the piece over-head and at least hang on to it while she sprayed the landscape, hoping to force her attacker to duck.

She brought the stock back to her shoulder and came up behind it, just high enough to see and sight over the rock. Either her spray-and-pray had worked or her enemy had just ducked after shooting on general principles. He popped up quickly, though, bolt upright and firing furiously. He was about twenty feet to the right of where she expected him, down the slope toward the narrow valley where the rest of her expedition hunkered down.

Gritting her teeth, she swung the heavy weapon toward him, determined to end this, while there was still a chance the shooters on the cliff—now behind her—were more occupied trading shots with Pan than coming up to blast her in the back at point-blank range.

She saw something dark puff out the right side of the gunman's head, just beneath his fur cap with the earflaps tied over the top. His head jerked and then he simply dropped like an empty suit of clothes slipping from a hanger.

The hearty crack of Lal's Enfield echoed between the valley walls.

Annja threw down the Kalashnikov and slid forward over the rock to snag the sling of the first man's M-16.

She spun quickly, ready to fire. She saw no one. She made herself take time to bust the curved black magazine out of the well. It still had rounds in it. She looked behind her, back along the ridgeline. Nothing. Turning back toward the unseen granite cliffs, she crept forward, keeping low.

Inside of thirty feet the slope steeply dropped away right in front of her. She went to her belly and crawled up to peer through some tuft grass. The gray granite cliff proved to front a bluff thrusting out from the same ridge she was on, which curved out around to Annja's right. She had an unobstructed view of a pair of gunmen crouched in a rocky, brushy perch, still shooting down into the valley at Pan and the others.

Anger filled her. She aimed two-handed over a rock at a fur-capped head and fired. She missed. Maybe the iron sight was off. Or maybe that was an excuse, and she'd pulled off. The enormous adrenaline dump her body had experienced had caught up to her. Annja felt clammy and sweat covered, and her fingers were as thick and clumsy as cold hot dogs.

But her first shot did make her target duck back in terrified surprise. After a second shot, which went even wider off target, both gunmen turned and rabbited out of sight, losing themselves quickly in the scrub.

She continued hunkering there for what seemed an eternity or two, tense behind the black rifle's receiver, stomach churning with nausea and head ringing like a bell. She was trying to guard in all directions at once. Then a shout from back along the ridge made her whip back around, pointing the M-16.

A figure approached with empty hands held high above his head. A very tall figure, dark against the looming white mass of the mountain.

"It's over, Annja," the figure shouted to her. "They pulled back. They are gone."

She threw down the rifle and ran to catch Pan Katramados in a bone-crushing embrace.

17

"He says he hears rumors of other foreigners about," Lal translated as Prasad conversed with a wizened old farmer and his grandson, who led their yak by a brass ring through its nose. The beast took advantage of their temporary halt by dropping its big, shaggy, short-horned head to crop at some khaki bunch grass jutting up from a patch of snow. "They're heavily armed, too. They are rude and make the people uncomfortable. But the word is also out they enjoy the protection of the local Party."

"Sounds as if Bajraktari and company have joined the fun," Pan said.

Annja looked at Lal in alarm. "Does he mean the Maoists? Why would they help ethnic-Albanian gangsters from Kosovo?"

"The Maoist Communist Party of Nepal recalls how Albania was the only other officially Maoist nation on Earth," Lal said. "And that they kept the faith longer than China herself did."

The answer surprised her. She had to remind herself the young man wasn't just bright and well educated; he had also traveled a fair part of the world before returning to his mountainous homeland. It wasn't quite so incongruous for a hill-man guide in a remote country to have a fairly sophisticated knowledge of the outside world as it might seem.

Pan, ever the policeman, had a more cynical take on the subject. "The lure of corruption knows no party bounds," he said. "Any more than national borders."

Through Prasad Annja pressed a few dollars on the elderly peasant. Nepal was one of the world's poorest countries, and the resurging political strife wasn't helping. The man seemed reluctant to accept until she suggested he could buy something for his grandson. The boy, with round brown sun-reddened cheeks and bright obsidian eyes, was clearly his grandfather's special pet; the old man's own eyes twinkled, barely visible within triangular slits in his deeply seamed, copper-colored face. He accepted with bows and profuse thanks.

The yak gave them a reproachful look as he tugged its broad head up and urged it under way through the hemlock forest. Apparently it thought Annja could've kept its master occupied a lot longer than that.

"Sorry," Annja said with a little hand wave at the beast.

They climbed higher. The forest was still around them, except for a slight rustle of wind in the high boughs, the twitter of distant birds, the crunch of snow under their boots. They had come high enough that snow still lay plentifully if patchily on the ground. Annja, who had grown somewhat accustomed to the altitude, found her breath coming a bit short again.

Puffy white clouds concealed the dizzying heights of the White Mountain itself and its attendants to the west, as well as mighty Annapurna to the southeast, which they otherwise might have seen through breaks in the woods. The clouds concerned Annja, who wasn't eager to get hit with a snowstorm. Prasad assured her one wasn't coming soon.

"Still," he said with his quiet smile, "where your path leads you will find snow aplenty."

"Great," Annja said.

The head guide now carried an AKM muzzle down. Annja carried a similarly slung M-16. Another cousin to Lal and Prasad, Pritam, carried the other salvaged M-16. Pan, interestingly to Annja, preferred to tote the other Kalashnikov taken from the four guerrillas who had died on the heights.

They had found the sniper who had fallen off the cliff from where the original ambush had been launched. He was broken across a rock with his rifle next to him. It was another Kalashnikov. Its stock was split but it proved to still fire. One of the locally hired Sherpas who hadn't quit in the wake of the attack and the death of a kinsman, a national army vet whom Lal vouched for, carried it. A few turns of black electrical tape had patched the stock.

As a foreign national carrying an automatic weapon Annja had begun feeling a little dubious about the prospect of being caught by a government patrol. She said so. But Prasad and Lal made light of that concern.

"Government patrols don't come here now," Lal said.

"Technically," Prasad said, "Jagannatha's men are government patrols." That left Annja feeling sobered.

In Nepal it seemed the difference between rebels and police depended on political tides in the capital that shifted literally from minute to minute.

She was intrigued at Pan's response to taking part in killing what might have been called fellow law-enforcement officers. He'd shown no reaction. He was first and foremost a warrior, a soldier, an elite special operator. Cop was his current assignment, not his identity. His ethics on the subject were simple, having apparently been forged in the brutal war in Afghanistan—anybody who shot at him, he killed, and he didn't lose any sleep over the fact that she could tell.

But that didn't mean he was sleeping peacefully. From the way he thrashed and called out in his sleeping bag at night he was having his dreams again. The dreams of that ancient Macedonian general who seemed so much like him. Whether it was that other Pan whose trail they followed, she couldn't say. But he never had any nightmares over killing people who were trying to kill him. Any more than she did.

"How do you know our attackers were this major's men?" Pan asked. His instinct had been to hang around to examine the bodies in detail after the fire-fight. Prasad and Lal had had none of that. One Sherpa had been killed; two others quit on the spot. The Magar guides feared the guerrillas might return with reinforcements.

"It was a professional ambush," Lal said. "The ambushers didn't dump their whole magazines at us instantly the way bandits would. Or even most guer-rillas. But Jagannatha knows his trade."

"How do you know we weren't hit by Jagannatha himself, then?" Pan asked.

"Because we are still alive," Prasad said matter-of-factly.

18

As they walked a precipitous path away from the latest shrine they had uncovered they found a party of peasants waiting silently for them on the rocks above the trail. Annja felt a crawling at the nape of her neck.

It had been the richest shrine found yet. This one was public, or at least not hidden. Another cairn of rocks with a cheap gilded-plaster statue of the Buddha within, presiding over offerings of dyed plastic flowers, joss sticks, crumpled Nepali banknotes and wallet-size photos of those for whom blessings were sought. It was like a hundred small popular shrines she'd seen all around the world, from Mexico to the Philippines.

But a secret compartment in back held a cavity, perhaps a cubic yard in volume, that contained offer-

ings of jewelry, gold and silver, including coins that
dated back a millennium or more, as far as Annja or
Pan could tell. They had carefully documented all in
sight—and left it covered back up, undisturbed.

She felt Pan's big hand descend on her shoulder. She
could feel the power of his gentle squeeze reassuring
her. She patted his gloved hand with hers. It was cold
up on the open slope, the morning breeze brisk.

Prasad and Lal spoke to the waiting peasants in
low tones. They were three young men and an older
one. Though short and not prepossessing at first
glance, the way they held themselves on their bowed
legs suggested the remarkable strength so many
Nepali hill folk possessed.

The peasants were unarmed, except for the big
knives at their belts. Annja had learned better than
to underestimate those. They in turn did not seem in
the least intimidated by the long-arms the party still
openly displayed.

"The last thing we need," Pan said quietly by her
ear, "is to have to fight people trying to protect the
same treasures we are."

She nodded, not taking her eyes from the men. He
had echoed her thoughts exactly.

"We just have to count on Prasad and Lal to keep
that from happening," she said.

He nodded. "I doubt our fates could rest in better
hands."

At last the oldest peasant nodded. His brutally
weathered old face smiled, seeming to become a

series of more or less concentric circles. The younger men laughed, perhaps a trifle nervously.

The elder spoke at length, his manner serious but no longer suspicious. Prasad and Lal listened intently, nodding. Occasionally Prasad asked a question. Lal maintained respectful silence between his elders.

"You go safely," the old man called to Annja and Pan. He waved. The four turned and scrambled up into the snow-clumped rocks and quickly vanished as if swallowed by the rocky hillside.

"Bad news," Prasad said to Annja. "The elder tells us there are more foreigners in the area. They are numerous, a dozen or more. And armed. They go in concert with Party men. They act very arrogant, threatening. That's why the peasants are so wary."

"Bajraktari and his Maoist helpers," Annja said.

Pan looked at Prasad. "These peasants, do they support the government, then, and not the guerrillas?"

"They are poor people, Sergeant," Prasad said. He and his nephew insisted on calling the Macedonian by his rank. "This is hard country, as you can see. Those who live upon it can afford to support no sides— they are only for themselves, and their families. Especially since these Party men are *with* the government. No longer is it easy to tell what the sides even are. But the peasants want no one desecrating their holy places, as the Maoists often do."

He smiled. "Once I explained the nature of

your pilgrimage, they gave you their blessings, and wish you success in your quests, both temporal and spiritual."

Annja and Pan exchanged glances. "I'll take all the good wishes I can get," he said.

"Likewise," Annja said. "Thank you, Prasad, Lal. Once again we'd be lost without you."

"They gave us one more warning," Prasad said. "The *bonmanche* is abroad in the lower reaches of the White Mountain. Its cries have been heard along the Myagdi River, and travelers say they spotted it in the heights above here."

"Bonmanche?" Annja asked.

"It means 'wild man,'" Lal said. "You would call it yeti, I think."

"Ah," Annja said. She flicked a quick glance Pan's way. The very immobility of his long and usually expressive face told her all she needed to know.

Glad to know he doesn't buy into the myths, either, she thought. She was also pleased he had sense enough not to embarrass their guides—and comrades—by openly scoffing. Then again, that squared right up with everything she'd seen of Pan Katramados. He was fundamentally a decent, polite man, even kind, with a quick, keen mind—and sound judgment.

Prasad smiled his ever ready smile. "You are skeptical, my friends. Perhaps you will learn to your satisfaction."

His manner quickly sobered. "The wild man can

be very dangerous. Yet his appearance can also be
most fortunate. It remains to see which his appearance portends for us—good fortune. Or death."

WATER GURGLED GENTLY over big smooth rocks
flanking the Buddha's altar and ran down channels
in the floor. A bare electric bulb hanging from the
dark wooden ceiling lit the chamber. The walls were
whitewashed, whether over stone or brick Annja
couldn't tell.

She sat with Pan on cushions on a stone floor
polished to glassy slickness by generations of bare feet,
drinking tea. The tea was way sweeter than she liked.
On the other hand it completely lacked the traditional
salt and rancid butter. So on balance it tasted fine.

Their host smiled at them and bobbed his head. He
was a tiny, wrinkled monk in a saffron robe. He spoke
barely understandable English. Annja wished Prasad
or Lal had come in to help—discreetly—with translation. But their guides insisted on remaining outside the
monastery on the outskirts of the terraced hill town, so
she had given them and the porters the afternoon off.

"It is an honor that you visit us," the monk told
them.

Trying not to be too obvious, Annja glanced at
Pan. She got the strong sensation he was wondering
the same thing she was. Why?

"We're doing the best we can to help protect
Nepal's ancient Buddhist heritage," she said, taking
a blind stab.

The lama grinned and nodded. "Ah, yes. That, too. It is most important work, and does your souls credit. And now we have something I believe you will wish to see."

He gestured with a hand toward a wooden door on one side of the chamber. As if on command a red-robed acolyte opened it and gravely beckoned them.

Annja rose. Knowing it wasn't precisely correct but strongly suspecting its intent would be understood, she pressed her hands together and bowed toward the lama in yellow. Pan mirrored her actions so closely it might seem they had rehearsed the gesture.

"We thank you for your kindness, sir," she said.

The monk chuckled. "Do not thank me for showing you the next step on your journey," he said, then turned serious, "until you have seen—and felt—where it leads."

He settled into an immobility no less absolute than that of the gilded image behind him. Clearly he had said all he intended to say. Annja didn't bother questioning him any more.

Pan showed her a raised eyebrow. When she shrugged and walked toward the newly opened door he did likewise.

Inside were large cushions and a low reading table. On the table lay several yellowed scraps of what looked like dried animal skin of some sort. Butter-bowl lamps on the tables and arranged in a score of niches around the walls cast a rich if not particularly bright illumination. The red-robed young man bowed and withdrew, closing the door.

For a moment Annja and Pan just stood there. The room was silent but for the bubbling of unseen water that seemed to pervade the entire building. The lamasery was built over a spring fed by the enormous snow mass of the Dhaulagiri Himal. As he took leave of them at the scarlet-painted doors, flanked by stone prayer wheels tall as a man, Prasad had informed them that it was called the Lamasery of the Waters for that very reason.

Annja sat down. Putting on a pair of latex gloves, she examined the scraps. The skin the parchment was made from was thin, pale and fine pored. "I'm not so sure I want to know what this is made of," she confessed.

Pan laughed softly. Both spoke in hushed tones, as if in a library.

"Good thing that's not vital to our mission," he said, seating himself across from her.

With gloved hands he picked up the parchment and squinted at it. After a moment he requested a magnifying glass. Annja took out a retractable piece in a sturdy and much used green leather case and handed it over. He opened and peered through it.

"It's transcribed ancient Greek of the Macedonian dialect, all right," he said. "And it appears to be further journal entries from our friend…the general."

She noted the slight catch in his words and the way he did not speak the ancient Macedonian's name. The dreams seemed to be affecting him more, at least to judge by the way he sometimes woke her in camp at night. Sometimes, though, he smiled blissfully, his long handsome face composed, serene. Perhaps the dreams of his imagined prior life didn't always distress him. He didn't speak of them during the daylight, and she didn't press. She felt like an intruder as it was.

He carefully scanned the scraps for several minutes. Annja sat and meditated, drawing deep abdominal breaths, holding them briefly, letting them go and then remaining with her lungs emptied for several seconds. She found it calmed her and cleared her mind—for whatever might come.

At last Pan began to read aloud.

I feel keenly the suffering of our soldiers, good Macedonian men, a world away from their homeland, caught up in endless war. Although none can match them for bravery, before I set out upon this journey I heard many asking, "Why? Why have we come to leave our bones in this hostile place at the end of the Earth?"

Now as I sit and think, here at this monastery, whose barbarian monks have treated me as courteously as they might a prince of their own land, I can find no reason to give our men. Try as I might.

Not all the inhabitants of this cold and thin-aired land prove so hospitable. The day before we arrived here Patrokles and Diomedes were slain in an ambush. We slew three in return before our attackers vanished as though melting into the rocks and snow. We are men of the hills ourselves, but these are not our hills.

Beyond defending our honor and ourselves as warriors of Macedonia I have not sought to punish the inhabitants of the area. We lack the skill to track them, as our guides at least profess to. Nor can I bring myself to fall upon whatever village we first come across and take retribution. Although they are tiny of stature and cannot speak human language—

Pan paused and looked at Annja. "He means Greek," he said.

"I figured," she replied.

—still they remind me of my own men, my own family and tribe back home. And I think how, if an invader came among us and slew ten of us for each man they had lost to ambush in our country, we should rise up and never rest until we had killed ten more of them for each of ours. Nor, as Pallas Athena is my witness, have I in truth the heart for it. I tire of the endless cruelty we seem to visit everywhere we go. It seems to burst the bonds of military need, and to give the lie to our claims of superior civilization.

He broke off there, frowning.

"What's the matter?" Annja asked. "Did you hit an illegible spot?"

"No. But I grew up idolizing Alexander and his men. These words—written by a man who knew him well—leave a bitter aftertaste in my mouth."

"I don't know what to say."

"You don't need to say anything, Annja. If I let myself be deterred by mere words I'm the worst kind of coward, no matter what physical dangers I may have faced down. I still believe physical bravery is a virtue—I do. But it's also the easier kind."

"I know," she said.

He scratched his temple as if to reset himself, and read on.

Sometimes it seems the land itself resists us, with sudden rockfalls and no less sudden storms. Two days ago a flash flood rose up as out of the very rocks and swept away Herakles and two of our porters crossing a bone-dry wash, dashed them to their deaths on rocks below. And this from a clear sky, with neither speck of cloud nor sound of thunder.

Yet my hosts here, gracious though they be, warn me that the way becomes only more perilous from here. The air grows colder and thinner, the snow and ice thicker. The gods' whims become more capricious in directing the weather. Zeus forgive me, but I cannot say whether our own gods and goddesses hold sway at all in this land so distant from lofty Olympus.

And most sinister of all, it seems, is the Lost Monastery, high up beyond the point at which even the toughest native tree will grow. The very mention of that accursed place caused a half dozen of our porters to desert. The others grew glum, and mutter continually themselves that demons guard it. Yet there, it seems, our quest inevitably leads us.

Ah, well—what treasure worth winning was ever easily gained? So great is this treasure of which my master Alexandros hears, had the dangers not been supernaturally great, it should have been plundered long since.

Reverently Pan placed the last scrap on the table. "Whew," Annja said.

He looked at her. "Whew," he agreed.

THE MARKET TOWN TERRACED into a steep subpeak of the Dhaulagiri Himal teemed with tourists and locals, bright as tropical birds and all talking at once. It was a bright, crisp morning. The inevitable white-and-blue bulk of Dhaulagiri I dominated the scene.

Pan and Annja had checked into a hostel on a lower level and left their packs behind. Despite the sunscreen she'd slathered on before they set out to tour the unusual settlement, the high-altitude sun stung her nose and cheeks. She'd given Prasad and Lal and the Sherpas the rest of the day off. She hoped they'd get a good rest.

The town's multilevel market offered a surprising array of wares. Gold-painted plaster Buddhas from Macao and Taiwan vied with bolts of bright cloth, modern sporting goods, stacked clay pots ranging in size from palm fitting to vessels Annja reckoned she might just fit in, and the inevitable racks of bottled water—apparently a staple of foreign and local mountaineer alike, mostly imported from India and China, as close as Annja could tell by the labels. Up-to-date cell phones and used iPods lay alongside stacks of colorful boxes of tea and biscuits and carefully arranged strands of exquisite turquoise jewelry. Bent low beneath big wicker baskets, men and women of all ages hustled along the avenues between white-washed stone buildings and the vendors' stalls and blankets spread out on the hard gray dirt.

Bins displayed fresh vegetables in a variety Annja hadn't anticipated in such a remote location, not to mention such a vertical one. She saw beans, cabbages, turnips and many she didn't recognize. Apparently the area's farms, terraced like the town, were very productive. Diminutive women with colorful turbans picked through them with expressions that even to Annja, stranger to local conventions of body language, saw were skeptical. Then they and the shopkeepers would screech at each other in mock rage.

In fact the level where Pan and Annja stood bustled with noise, as well as bodies. Chickens squawked from wicker cages. Music blared from overloaded speakers; strange skirling Himalayan and Indian music competed with Western rap and European techno. Annja found herself drifting away from the small tinny speakers hung from garish stalls toward a stone stoop where several people wearing ragged, ill-fitting Western cast-offs played skirling music on instruments like rough-hewed violins with no facing on their hollow bodies and sang in high voices. A middle-aged man would sing a verse. Then two women and a man sang the chorus in a higher pitch.

"What fascinating music," Annja said. "I wonder what they're singing about."

She spoke to Pan, but a small voice piped up right beside her in English. "They are the Gaines," it said, pronouncing the name *gah-eenes*. "They sing songs of old heroes, you know."

In surprise Annja looked down to see a boy of maybe eight or nine standing next to her. He wore a blue plaid flannel shirt that hung clear to the knees of blue jeans that pooled over the tops of faded red athletic shoes with splitting toes.

"Well, thank you," she said. "What's your name?"

"I'm Yuvaraj. What's yours?"

"I'm Annja. This is Sergeant Katramados."

The boy blinked up at Pan. "Are you a soldier?"

"Not anymore," Pan said. He dropped a hand to the boy's head to ruffle his dark close-cropped hair. Then his eyes snapped to focus past Annja's shoulder and he went rigid.

A heavy hand clamped on her left bicep. Startled she looked around.

She found herself looking up into the moon-faced, brown-toothed leer of Duka, Enver Bajrak-tari's giant bodyguard.

Wide-eyed, she glanced back toward Pan. Yuvaraj had vanished into the crowd. Another Kosovar in a black leather coat had Pan gripped from behind.

He had the muzzle of a Skorpion machine pistol pressed up under the angle of the special operator's jaw.

19

"Pan!" Annja exclaimed.

"He cannot help you, I'm afraid," an unfortunately familiar voice said from behind her. She didn't have to turn to know that Bajraktari himself was approaching.

She caught Pan's eye. He winked.

She needed no more. She could smell the overpowering odor of Duka, mostly stale sweat, human grease and harsh Balkan tobacco. In the cool air the heat washed off his body as from an open oven. By accident or design he had come up on her with his left side turned somewhat toward her, blocking the obvious shot at his crotch.

Instead Annja yanked hard with her captive arm. Duka's hand clamped down like a vise. He grinned.

She raised her right knee and kicked hard down and out. Her heel hit the front of the big man's knee on the inside. She felt and heard a pop as his kneecap slid around out of place to the side.

Duka folded like a cheap suit. He lay on the ground clutching his leg and screaming in pain.

From the corner of her eye she saw Pan make his move. His right arm came up fast. The machine pistol's muzzle raked a bloody line up his jaw as he knocked it skyward. Caught flat-footed by the quick, decisive move, the Kosovar hadn't had time to fire.

Pan caught his gun wrist with his left hand, turning hard into him. Using his raised right arm as a fulcrum he locked out the man's elbow. He snapped it with a sound Annja heard even as she took off like a sprinter off the blocks.

She dodged through the throng of chattering locals. She was betting—hoping—that if Bajraktari and his goons didn't have a clear shot at her they wouldn't dare just rake the crowds with gunfire in hopes of thinning them away enough to hit her. I so love having to depend on the good grace and judgment of terrorists, she thought.

A burst of gunfire crashed out. She grimaced, expecting to feel the sting of bullets piercing her back. Instead the bullets cracked over her head. One of the terrorists had noticed she was taller than almost anyone else in the bazaar, and ripped off a shot over the heads of the Nepali townspeople. Fortunately he'd aimed too high.

Can't count on that happening again, she told herself. Spinning right as sharply as she could she ran up the tongue of a parked handcart full of green apples, presumably imported from nearby India with its yearlong growing season. As she reached the box the apples rolled right out from under her feet, dumping her forward. She grabbed the cart's back end, stuck up at an angle, and hauled herself onto it.

The cart overbalanced and dumped her unceremoniously on the other side. Apples cascaded around her and went bouncing in all directions. The apple merchant bounded from behind his table, waving his arms and expostulating vigorously.

Not so many style points for that one, she thought. She picked herself up and started running again. But I wound up where I needed to be.

She now had the apple-seller's ramshackle kiosk, as well as its neighboring booths, between her and the Kosovars. She heard them shout, their voices harsh and alien over the more musical cries from the locals. She heard more shots. Concern for Pan hit her like a stiff jab to the sternum. She absorbed it and ran on.

His wink had told her he was fine and that she should take whatever steps she could to get herself free. At this point she knew the best thing she could do for her friend was to get clear as quickly as possible, so he wouldn't feel he had to battle the whole gang single-handed to cover her escape. If anyone knew how to handle himself when the hammer came down, it was Pan Katramados.

She took a rapid right. At once she saw she'd made the wrong choice—she was running right into a rough stone retaining wall that held up the hillside where the street ended. Another course of houses, with white-painted wooden walls and sun-peeled red trim, ran about eight feet higher up, on a level supported by the wall.

Or maybe I didn't choose wrong, she thought. Right behind her she heard harsh shouts in a language that clearly wasn't any kind of Nepalese.

Drawing a quick breath from her diaphragm, Annja raced straight at the retaining wall. As she reached it she jumped. The crudely dressed stones offered ample hand- and footholds. She stuck like a fly and swarmed quickly up and over.

A burst of gunfire raked the house wall to her right. Flying rock chips stung her hands and cheek.

More full-auto bursts snarled at her. They weren't the deep stutter of a Kalashnikov, well-known and unmistakable to television viewers worldwide. And especially to Annja, who in the past couple of years had made something of a secondary profession of being shot at with AKs. The Kosovars were shooting machine pistols at her. Fortunately, the weapons, true fully automatic handguns, were simply too light to be controllable except for when firing single shots.

Not looking back, she sidestepped rapidly along the irregular lip of rocks that served as the foundation on which the house was perched with her back against the wood wall. She hoped her pursuers wouldn't fire again. Aside from the danger to her, she worried the bullets might punch right through the planks and endanger any occupants of the little house.

Annja heard angry shouts in Albanian, as alien to this land as to Annja's ears. They didn't seem directed at her.

The village of terraces, over nine thousand feet up the Dhaulagiri Himal, was a trade crossroads for this part of western Nepal. Its inns offered convenient bases for those who wished to acclimatize themselves to the thin air, as well as those who didn't care to venture higher into the howling ice and stone wastes above. It was also the last place climbing supplies were readily available.

That all meant the village hosted a contingent of the armed police force. The constables, Prasad had informed Annja and Pan before cutting them loose to wander on their own, were unlikely to let themselves get distracted by the current political uncertainty in Kathmandu. As cops, their first instinct would always be to preserve order. Second, no matter which party held power, the only engine that really drove Nepal's creaky two-stroke economy was tourism. So above all the armed police would be on the alert to squash behaviors that might freak out— or, worse, physically endanger—the tourists.

Apparently Bajraktari's goons were realizing

that—a beat too late. In mere minutes the police were likely to be swarming the level beneath Annja like hornets. She didn't want to hang around and deal with them any more than Bajraktari's thugs did.

Not that Bajraktari's goons were inclined to let her hang around. As she crept around the corner of the house she heard heavy footsteps pounding along the hard-packed soil behind her. Then angry shouts as she vanished from view.

Annja found herself on another terrace road. To her left a remarkably steep street climbed the mountainside, linking the levels. She decided to head around the face of the hillside to put some quick distance between herself and her pursuers. She didn't think running straight uphill was such a great idea. She was almost two miles up and feeling the strain despite having spent a week getting to this altitude. It wasn't enough time.

Quickly she walked along a street crowded close by houses on both sides. To her right stood mostly frame houses. To the left stood mostly two-story stone piles, some with a barren elevated yard surrounded by stone fences. The trim on windows, doors and pitched roofs tended either to green or blue.

To her right the houses gave way, affording her a breathtaking view of the gray terraces marching away beneath her. The buildings gleamed white beneath colorful rooftops. Outdoor markets sprouted like fields of colorful mushrooms in spaces between. It was a good day for business.

A pair of locals approached from the other direction. Annja went tense as she saw they wore green-and-brown camouflage-pattern shirts. She made herself relax. Nothing would make the local cops or military types more suspicious of you than freaking out when they got near. It tended to trip their predatory instincts.

She was just wondering where exactly these cops expected that camou pattern to help them blend in when she noticed that the two men's trousers didn't match. One pair was brown, the other faded blue, probably Western castoffs such as many folk hereabouts wore.

Annja felt her blood chill.

Guerrillas. She word thrilled down her nerves. She kept herself calm. At least they carried no visible firearms. And the bazaar town was neutral territory; Prasad had explained that, too. The guerrillas had their needs the same as any. Including, none too surprisingly, some neither Prasad nor his nephew showed any inclination to explain to her.

Something else struck her about them as they swaggered closer. They're not Jagannatha's men, she thought. They seemed both harder and softer than the men she had fought in that hill valley. Harder edged, but without the air of real physical and mental hardness. Their several-day beards looked way too deliberate, not the scruff that sprouted from the cheeks of men who were preoccupied with survival in harsh and dangerous terrain. Jagannatha's guerrillas who had attacked them consisted of recruits and veterans alike who had committed to a tough road—no matter that they had simply, and lethally, underestimated their would-be victims.

This pair struck her more as street punks. As if they expected to command fear because of their colors, not respect based on who they were.

She set her vision to soft focus, expanding her peripheral vision at the expense of detail. As they passed her they laughed with each other, probably at some sexist joke.

The second they thought they were past her field of vision they wheeled and struck like cats.

The closer one snatched at her arm. Annja back kicked him in the gut. Her heel caught his solar plexus; the air gushed out of him and he sat down hard on the bare gray dirt.

His partner came at her from straight behind. He had drawn a big *kukri* from underneath his untucked shirt. Annja's instantaneous counterattack on his partner had the same effect on him they intended to have on her. He lost focus, goggling in amazement at his buddy unexpectedly sitting, holding his belly and gasping like a landed catfish.

Annja just kept spinning. A wheeling kick of her right foot caught the inside of the wrist that held the *kukri*. He kept his grip on the hardwood hilt but the impact flung his arm wide.

Annja kept both her forward and rotational momentum, blasting her wide-open opponent with a spinning back kick. It was the most powerful blow she knew how to deliver. It caught him in the sternum with a thud like a sledgehammer hitting a fencepost and knocked him back three feet.

To both of their surprise that put him a foot past the edge of the terrace. For a moment he seemed to hang there in midair. His brown eyes, panic wide, locked with hers. He began to windmill his limbs like a cartoon character and dropped out of sight to crash through the roof of a shed six feet below.

Then a heavy weight slammed down on Annja's back.

20

Annja Creed had made the same mistake her foe had. She'd been hypnotized, however momentarily, by an unexpected twist of events. She knew she was luckier than she deserved to be that the second man hadn't recovered enough of his wits along with his wind and just plain planted the enormous angled blade of his *kukri* between her shoulder blades.

Instead he'd jumped on her. She felt his breath hot and desperate on the nape of her neck. He was strong; his arms clamped her like barrel hoops.

She slammed her head back. She felt teeth scrape the back of her skull, felt the crisp tweak of his nose breaking. He squealed. His powerful but clumsy grip slackened.

She reached back and blindly grabbed the first

purchase her fingers found. It turned out to be the guerrilla's shaggy black hair. She threw her upper torso forward, twisting her hips at the same time to add serious torque.

With a despairing wail the guerrilla flew right over her head and out into space. A hefty thump a beat later indicated he'd escaped his comrade's fate. He hadn't hit the shed. Instead he'd done a face-plant on the beaten-dirt street beyond.

For a moment she panted with hands braced on thighs. This altitude's killing me, she thought. She frowned. She made herself quit bracing like an asth-matic and breathing through her open mouth like a fish. She forced herself to stand upright and breathe from the diaphragm. She drew air deep into her lungs, causing the illusory sensation she was inhaling clear down to her pelvis. It was the quickest way she knew to reoxygenate herself.

But she could do nothing about the thinness of the air. Still woozy, she continued the way she'd been going. Though her instincts screamed at her to run she made herself stick hands in her jacket pockets and walk. Her stride length enabled her to cover ground at a pretty good clip without drawing eyes the way break-ing into a run would. This level didn't show much traffic. It seemed given exclusively to residences.

Although interrupted occasionally by seemingly random vertical jogs, probably having to do with harder veins of rock making it more difficult to cut, the terraces gave mostly good sight lines until they curved around the mountainside. Glancing back, Annja saw another pair of men appear on this level. Their height and long black leather coats, marking them distinct both from the diminutive locals and the tourists in their gaudy Alpine gear, told her more than she wanted to know about their identity. They moved purposefully after her. Too careful themselves to run, they seemed confident in their ability to chase her down.

Ahead of her another cross street took off up the steep slope. She turned rapidly into it, prepared to fly into action if any enemies lurked in ambush. No one leaped at her. The street was narrow, though, barely wider than her own arm span. Or so it seemed, any-way, so closely did the shops and hotels and tea shops and camping-gear booths impinge on the street. A man trotted by carrying a shoulder yoke with a steaming brass kettle on one end and a cluster of flagons tied to the other.

She climbed. The altitude was affecting more than her lungs. The long muscles of her thighs burned with exertion that back home in Brooklyn she'd barely have felt. Her stomach felt queasy and her head light.

She risked a quick look back. The Kosovars had followed her into the street. They swiveled their heads as if searching. Not for her, she guessed; she was in pretty plain sight, though twenty or thirty yards uphill. They must expect reinforcements, she thought.

The possibility of hollering her head off came

into her mind. Almost as quickly she dismissed it. No telling what might happen. If the police detained her, whether for her own protection or investigation, how could she know they weren't corrupted or corruptible? Bajraktari's gang appeared to have had no trouble turning cops across a quarter of the world.

And the fact that guerrillas were walking out openly suggested they had power here, too. Whether the Maoist guerrillas were actually in league with the Kosovar artifact smugglers she didn't know for sure. If both groups were after her, it hardly seemed to make much difference.

Ahead of her lines had been strung from building to gray stone building across the street. Strongly patterned carpets had been hung out on the lines for display. That they fairly obstructed the street didn't seem to bother anybody. People simply pushed through them.

Annja forged in among the carpets. They were heavy, rough, warm in high-mountain sunlight crackling with ultraviolet. They smelled of lanolin and the harsh chemical aromas of dye.

She turned back, holding up a side of a carpet with the back of a hand. The tall black-coated men following her had sunken dark eyes and olive cheeks covered with black stubble. One had a dusting of gray on his chin. Both of them were reaching inside their greatcoats with their right hands.

If she needed confirmation they were on her trail, to hunt and kill, she had it.

On she swam through heavy aromatic waves of woven wool. Glancing over the swaybacked lines she realized why nobody seemed to take much exception to the blockage of a thoroughfare. It didn't go through. A rough and ready stone wall rose abruptly a few yards past the rugs, to meet eaves that swept out as dramatically.

Annja had sought refuge in a dead end.

She pushed though the next-to-final carpet wall, mere seconds from being trapped like a rabbit.

But I'm out of sight here, she thought. That gave her options.

A quick look both ways showed recessed doorways. They weren't recessed far enough to conceal her in daylight. To her right, though, stood the four-foot-tall white shape, startling by its very familiarity in these exotic settings, of a covered metal trash bin.

It wasn't good cover. But it was better than nothing. And the alternative looked like nothing.

No sooner had she crouched down between the trash can and the wall than the first pursuer pushed between carpets not ten feet from her. She followed him with one eye peering around the side of the can. He held a Skorpion machine pistol loosely in his hand.

Apparently convinced their quarry had bolted clear to the blank stone wall that blocked the alley, the Kosovar forged straight on through the next line of carpets without glancing to either side. Can it really be this easy? Annja thought before she could stop herself.

But the next man through was clearly wary, frowning with eyebrows like smudges of coal on his dark face, his head on a swivel. He was clearly more suspicious than his comrade.

As he turned his face her way Annja melted back behind the can. She knew nothing would grab his attention like rapid motion in his peripheral vision. She might as well whistle out loud.

Boots crunched on hard-trodden soil. She could feel his presence looming, closer and closer. She smelled the sweat and harsh tobacco that permeated his clothes.

As she heard a sharp intake of breath from almost on top of her, she formed her right hand into an open fist and drove hard with her legs.

The second Kosovar held his weapon, a Beretta 92 semiautomatic, muzzle high, unusually good firearms handling for a goon. It was also, for once, lethally wrong. He opened his mouth to shout to his comrade as he tried to bring the piece down to shoot the woman springing at him like a tigress.

The sword slid into his open mouth like a ghastly parody of a tongue drawn in shining steel. He seemed to melt straight down to the street.

Some lucky combination of instincts made her simply release the sword. As soon as her fingers left the hilt, it vanished. She hurled herself backward into the recessed doorway as a burst of gunfire ripped out from up the short street. The rippling crack of the pistol rounds were oddly muted by the heavy carpets. They shook violently. Dust blossomed from them as the bullets ripped through to smash against the stone on the left side of the doorway Annja had backed into. Ricochets tumbled away.

As if of its own volition Annja's right hand found the door latch behind her. Before her conscious brain could tell it to leave off the futile effort, certain the door was locked, the latch opened. Without conscious intent she pushed the door open and half stumbled into cool darkness.

The corridor smelled of dust and varnish. Music tinkled from somewhere overhead, faint as fairy bells. She saw a set of rickety-looking wooden stairs. She bolted up them.

Behind her, footsteps hammered. Boots squeaked on boards as the Kosovar raced in pursuit. Annja's head swam. She turned, reaching behind the small of her back. Her legs buckled beneath her, landing her on the third step from the top.

The Kosovar rounded the base of the stairs and started up. He saw her and smiled. The gun in his hand was swinging toward her.

She pushed the Glock 23 out to the full extent of both arms and squeezed the trigger. The pistol bucked in her hand. The flame was pale yellow but dazzling in the gloom. The noise and muzzle-blast

reflected off the close confines was like steel trap
jaws slamming shut on her skull.

The man collapsed, tumbling back down the stairs.

Somebody shouted below, his voice harsh and
foreign. Death brushing her with its wings and her
killing her assailant face-to-face triggered a fresh
adrenaline surge. It turbocharged Annja's oxygen-
hungry system like a jolt of nitrous oxide to a racing
engine. She jumped up, took the last steps at a bound.

At the top she found a fly-specked window overlooking the street of the carpets. Turning, she saw a
hallway with doors to both sides, all closed. Another
window opened at the far end, admitting a yellowish
light.

Stuffing the stubby Glock back into the holster
inside the waistband of her pants she ran for it. As
she did someone below fired up through the floor. It
wasn't a machine pistol cycling low-powered pistol
rounds, but a full-bore Kalashnikov. The jacketed
.30-caliber bullets kicked up six-inch splinters from
the floorboards amid geysers of dust and mold.

Shooting blind, the gunman failed to lead his
target enough. That could change in a hurry if the
window wouldn't open. Annja knew better than to
try the Hollywood stunt of running into it full speed
and trusting momentum to carry her on out into the
street. Like as not, she'd bounce, leaving her stunned,
possibly broken and exposed in the middle of the
hallway when her pursuers came up the stairs. And
if she broke through, the windowpanes would turn

into numerous shards, each sharper than any scalpel, and slice her to streamers.

Holding her right hand behind her she summoned the sword. As she got in range she slashed diagonally, rising right to left. Then she cocked her sword quickly back and, barely slowing, cut forehand, from the right down to the left. Hoping the cuts had weakened the frame enough she planted her left foot, skidded slightly on the floor and thrust kicked the center of the window where the wooden struts crossed.

21

The window couldn't have flown out into the morning air neater if she'd used precision demo charges. Annja jumped to crouch on the sill as the panes crashed into the street.

Almost directly below she saw Pan Katramados battling two Kosovars. Tourists and vendors scattered like a flock of frightened ducks. The man in front of Pan ducked at the sudden unaccountable explosion right above his head, then spun at the sound of shattering glass. Pan availed himself of the man's distraction to give an elbow to the man trying to grapple him from behind. Then he whipped a front snap kick into the other man's left kidney.

The smuggler gasped and fell to his knees. Annja's weight, dropping from the floor above as bullets cracked out the gaping window frame, dropped him the rest of the way, facedown in broken glass.

Annja found herself kneeling on the prone man's back. A pool of blood spread out from beneath his head. His legs twitched.

"Sorry," she said by reflex.

Pan grabbed her hand and hauled her upright. He took off running uphill, towing her along like a tugboat. Normally she would have resented such treatment as macho condescension. This time she didn't snatch her hand away. She found Pan's strong, confident grip reassured her. And anyway, adrenaline notwithstanding, she could use the boost.

They made it up to another terrace and staggered around the corner to their left.

"How'd you find me?" Annja panted.

"Followed the crowd. Once I broke the arm of the man who had me, they lost interest in me momentarily. Especially the way Duka was clutching his knee and crying like a baby. The police took him and Bajraktari. The other gangsters took off after you."

"So…where're we going?"

Pan glanced back around the whitewashed corner of the building under whose overhang they huddled. "Right now I think, just away."

He flashed her a quick grin. She grinned back. They ran.

Around the side of the mountain ahead of them, fifty or sixty yards, a pair of men in green camouflage came trotting. One carried a black submachine gun with a curved magazine winging out to the left of the receiver. Pan spit a word Annja would bet he wouldn't translate for her.

Fortunately another street headed off up the mountainside between the guerrillas and them. We're fast running out of village, here, Annja thought. And where we're going to find safety I've no idea.

Still, Pan clearly had the right idea. With nowhere good to run to, their only real shot was to run away and trust in their resourcefulness to turn up something.

She liked that. She liked that he was resourceful. She liked that he appreciated she was, too.

As they neared the intersection a knot of tourists, chattering happily in German, spilled from a *chai* shop right into the path of the two guerrillas. The tourists shrieked like frightened cockatiels. The guerrillas got well tangled up with the panicking Germans. Annja and Pan pounded around the corner of a disreputable-looking hotel.

They ran straight into four men standing in the street arguing. Any doubt the Maoist guerrillas were working with Bajraktari's Muslim bandits vanished. Two men were tall foreigners in black leather greatcoats, while two others were camou-clad locals a whole head shorter.

Engrossed in their dispute, they were taken flat-footed by the sudden appearance of their joint quarry. Pan was under no such neurological constraints.

Brushing one guerrilla spinning, he put his head down and charged the nearer Kosovar, who turned toward him with a look of astonishment on his stubbled face.

Pan ran through him like an NFL linebacker taking down a wide receiver. His shoulder hit the man's sternum with a brutal thud and drove him into the ground. The back of the Kosovar's head smacked the ground. He lay dazed and breathless as Pan charged the next big foreigner. The man met the challenge with a very professional-looking sprawl, pushing the Greek cop down and away so he couldn't tackle him.

The local Pan had slammed out of the way was still out of the fight. His partner whipped out a *kukri* and grinned at Annja through a wispy beard. Clearly he expected his big ugly knife to scare this soft Western woman into submission.

You got the wrong girl for that, Annja thought. It registered on her that the street was empty.

The guerrilla clearly felt smug about the lack of witnesses.

The sword flashed into existence. Just that single impossible thing was enough to take the starch right out of most opponents. This Maoist was made of tougher stuff. He stood his ground, bandy legs flexed, weapon loosely gripped in a hand almost the same color as the hilt. He looked like a man who knew how to use the unwieldy-looking short sword.

Moving too fast for finesse, and fearing at any moment to feel the slam of bullets between her shoulder blades from the other guerrillas right around the corner, Annja slashed for his face. He reflexively whipped his own steel around to guard his eyes. He punched his *kukri* up and to his own right, caught the sword flat to flat, and guided it right past him, leaning slightly back. He caught Annja with her sword arm across her body and too far off balance to counter a slash at her arm or face.

She did a sort of stutter step and kicked him in the groin.

The guerrilla was quick and managed to twist his hips just enough to catch her kick on the inside of his back thigh. But so strong were Annja's legs and so great her momentum that sheer impact blasted him back three steps.

A catfight flurry in Annja's peripheral vision showed her Pan was kickboxing enthusiastically with the second Kosovar. The first lay unmoving on his face. For a few vital moments she could concentrate on her own unexpectedly formidable opponent.

They went toe to toe, trading cuts. Annja didn't try to chop off his blade again. If she got the shot she'd take it—same as any other opening. But he was smart and fast and good.

She yipped as the down-pointed tip of the *kukri* drew a line of fire down her left cheek. She thrust for her enemy's face. He had to throw himself backward way off balance to avoid taking her tip through his cheek. Catlike, he leaped away to increase engagement range and allow himself to regroup.

Then he made his first mistake. His eyes slid past her to her left. That was an old trick she'd seen before. But with her own senses keyed to sharpness, and intently focused on her foe, she saw his pupils widen, too.

It was a purely physiological response. You could fake that. Conceivably. With weeks of specialized training.

Annja spun to her left, hacking savagely with her sword.

The *kukri* the first guerrilla, whom Pan had tackled, was bringing down at the back of Annja's head was cut clean through with a musical twang.

Already chambering a kick with her right leg, she looked back over her right shoulder. The skilled swordsman closed on her, his own weapon cocked over his left shoulder for a death stroke. He'd made his second mistake. He'd focused too much on sword fighting, and not on just fighting.

Her back kick caught him square in the gut, lifted him and threw him back.

The other guerrilla stood flat-footed, staring at the mirror-surfaced end of his severed blade. Disregarding him, Annja spun and charged. The man she'd been dueling with brought up his blade. Still stunned and probably short on breath from the brutal, unexpected power of her kick, he was a beat slow.

Blood sprayed as she slashed his arm. Not waiting to see what effect that had, she brought the sword looping up to her left, around and down. Its edge bit into his neck and chest.

He fell. She opened her fist, releasing the sword, which was trapped by the severed ends of bones. It vanished.

The other guerrilla turned and ran screaming around the corner.

Annja looked quickly around. She had no clue why the guerrillas on the terrace weren't all over them by now. But she saw no sign of them.

She saw Pan buckle his opponent with a savage shin kick to the outside of his left leg. As the man bent forward Pan caught him with a beautiful uppercut on the chin that straightened him right back up. Then he drove a sideways elbow smash into his face, sprawling him on his back in a spray of blood beside his moaning comrade.

As she ran past it was Annja's turn to catch his hand. "Let's go!"

By the time they reached the next terrace, Annja was almost reeling. Her adrenaline supercharge was running out. The thin air, accelerating the draining effects of fighting for her life, had her running on fumes, and thin ones at that. Pan labored at her side. His skin was sallow and his expression grim. He wasn't in much better shape than she was.

Below them she heard shouting. A mixed group of guerrillas and Bajraktari's men rounded the corner. Whatever had held up the guerrillas, they had gotten it sorted out. The pursuers stopped to gape at the fallen bodies. Then one of the Kosovars pointed up at them.

"I'm getting so sick of these guys," Annja gasped. "What are we going to do now?"

"Down there," Pan said, pointing to their left along the new terrace. "Somebody's signaling to us."

It was another group of Gaine singers. In a doorway behind half a dozen street musicians plying their odd stringed instruments a man in a red neckerchief stood beckoning them with frantic rolling hand movements. As soon as they made eye contact he stopped, sat down and began sawing his bow across his own eviscerated fiddle.

"Could it be a trap?" Annja asked.

"At this point, how much would that matter?" Pan asked.

"Good point."

As fast as they could without calling attention to themselves they walked toward the band. A small knot of tourists had gathered about the players.

Several members of the ensemble left off playing to greet Annja and Pan with smiles, handshakes, backslaps, as if they were all lost cousins. They spoke enthusiastically in some dialect Annja thought wasn't Gorkhali but couldn't tell for sure. Their comrades redoubled their efforts, playing and singing to make up for their momentary absence.

Hands passed Pan and Annja promptly up stone steps to the red-roofed house. As the door was opened by a small wizened woman with a white cloth tied over her bun of white hair, a ripple of explosions behind them made Annja and Pan cringe and then whirl.

They saw strings of firecrackers rattling off like firefight simulators in the street, and Roman candles shooting glowing multicolored balls in the air.

Pan cursed and grabbed for his Glock in its shoulder holster. "They've betrayed us!"

Annja grabbed his arm. "Wait."

He looked at her in slack-jawed, oval-eyed amazement. "That racket will bring the bandits!"

She smiled crazily at him. "It'll bring everybody."

For a moment he stared blankly at her. Then closing his mouth, he nodded quickly and allowed the smiling old lady to escort them into the gloom of the hallway.

22

"A most fascinating ploy," Chatura murmured. He sat on a luridly colored cushion on the floor of a Party safehouse in the lower levels of the terraced bazaar town on the flanks of the Dhaulagiri Himal and sipped tea from a blue porcelain cup. "After you convince me of the value of keeping this Creed woman alive and free, that she might lead us to reclaim a great treasure in the name of the people, you strike to seize or kill her yourself. One might wonder whether you truly have the welfare of the people at heart, Enver Bajraktari."

The Kosovar paced the room. Low, square ceiling beams endangered his head. Despite the heat radiating from the iron stove in the corner of the room he wore a wool sweater. He had his hands thrust into the pockets of his black trousers.

Chatura sipped. It was an oddly delicate gesture for such a no-nonsense-seeming man. "Not to mention using men whom I had lent to you to do it."

"I saw the chance to act," rumbled the bandit chieftain. "I took it. If I acted rashly, so be it. Allah saw fit to fill my veins with the hot blood of action, not the cool blood of a snake."

Chatura's thin lips twisted in an approximation of a bloodless smile. "An odd invocation for a follower of Chairman Mao. Fortunately, I need not rely on invisible spirits for my own cool blood. Or serpent blood, if you will. I find it interferes less with my judgment. Should I for the sake of argument accept your implicit claim that you acted because you saw an opportunity worth seizing—rather than in contravention of our arrangements of cooperation—it leaves the question of why your men sought to kill this woman and her companion."

Bajraktari stopped and regarded the small man, sitting like an ungilded Buddha, with a dark scowl.

After a moment the Kosovar shook his head. "I owe the witch a debt," he said, "of blood and honor. Her Greek love-boy, as well. But my own judgment was not totally overwhelmed with my desire for vengeance, comrade. It came to me that we had a chance to capture them. Then they would lead us to the treasure. But if they died—" he shrugged "—what of that? We would have their notes, their records. We would know as much as they. If they could follow those clues to the treasure, so could we. What I fail to understand is why we're not scouring the town right now in pursuit of them, pulling down the buildings and digging up the cellars? They must be here somewhere."

"Softly, softly, comrade," Chatura said. "The police are reactionary. The recent gunfire—and fatalities—have them swarming like angry hornets. They'd be happy to fight us, and they command more force in this city of bourgeois tools than we."

Indeed, he thought, the Central Committee might deem us rogues, and decide we might make a good bone to toss the dragons of reactions in Kathmandu as a peace offering. And perhaps not without justice. For once we have secured the treasure, they shall surely be among the last to know.

From the room's corner a groan escaped from a great duffel-bag shape heaped horizontally on a pallet. Bajraktari walked over and hunkered briefly down to feel the sweat-glossed forehead of his henchman Duka. The man stirred and a peevish moan escaped bearded lips. His boss spoke a few low words in his native language. His tone was oddly soft. He swept the stiff black hair back from the fevered brow and stood.

"I hope he's ready to walk tomorrow," he said.

"We have provided him painkillers and a leg brace," Chatura said, not much interested. "Not to mention that our physicians slid his patella back into place. He looks to be a strong man. Perhaps he will keep up."

Bajraktari frowned furiously. Chatura gave him a look of studied blandness.

Bajraktari chose to let the matter drop. "And what of this Jagannatha? It is rumored he closes in on the Westerners, as well."

Chatura nodded and set down his cup. "We shall rendezvous with him north of town. I will instruct him to join his men to mine. Under my command, of course."

"But what if he makes trouble? Your men all say he's a lone wolf who hates Western decadence more than he loves the Little Red Book."

Chatura rose. "Then I shall teach him the difference between being a wolf and being a dog."

"Boo!" Pan Katramados said to the little girl in the long native-looking red dress. She giggled. Her two little friends also giggled. They ran off as an old man approached.

Annja took a sip of salty tea with yak butter. I'm afraid I'm starting to get used to this stuff, she thought.

The older man sat down cross-legged on the colorful rug across from them. Lal sat down beside him.

"Please thank Sachchit Gaine once again for us," Annja said.

Lal bobbed his head, smiled, and spoke to the elder. The old man nodded and smiled.

Once inside the red-roofed house they had been led down a dark stone stairway, and then taken by underground tunnel to a neighboring house, which on the surface was separated by almost forty yards of open gray ground with only a few sprigs of dry weeds. There they were ushered back up into a white-washed hallway, rushed out the back through a couple of what Annja could only describe as bare backyards marked by stone boundaries. Beyond them the ground dropped six or eight feet, held up by retaining walls of stone. Farther out the town petered out into a shield-like sheet of rock with gleaming ice patches.

At last they had come to this house, a pleasant three-story structure with a green roof. They'd been surprised, if pleasantly, to meet Lal. He assured them they would be safe, and that his uncle would join them shortly.

"He says the Gaine are pleased to be of help," Lal said. "These foreigners who hunt you have acted very disrespectful toward them."

"I can imagine," Annja said. "That's kind of a habit of theirs."

"What I still don't understand," Pan said, "is how you managed to locate us. Or anticipate us. As it seems you did."

Lal grinned. "My branch of the Magar clan have always maintained good relationships with the hero singers, the Gaine. Though we had business to attend to we asked their help in looking after you. Also we had some of our younger kinfolk keep an eye on you."

"That little boy in the bazaar—" Annja said.

"Hi," a voice said from the hallway. Annja saw a familiar figure in a long blue plaid shirt standing there.

"Hi, yourself," she said.

"I believe you have met my third cousin, Yuvaraj," Lal said.

Pan laughed. "We never suspected him. When he grows up he should come work for Hellenic special forces. He could be a Pathfinder, like me." A cloud passed over his face. "Or perhaps best not, after all."

"How'd you let Lal know we were coming this way?" Annja asked the boy, to end the uncomfortable silence.

Yuvaraj smiled. With an upward wrist flick he whipped open a cell phone.

Annja laughed.

"How about the police?" Pan asked Lal. "Are they looking for us?"

"Not specifically, although they would surely like to question you. I don't really advise letting them, you know? But they've got the idea the guerrillas are in with a foreign gang, probably artifact smugglers. They blame them. Although strings have been pulled from a higher level, and they haven't been able to hold anyone. Even the injured ones brought in for treatment at government clinics."

Annja set down her tea. Her stomach had suddenly turned sour. "So the Maoists are working with the smugglers," she said. "Doesn't that make the odds against us pretty bad?"

To her surprise Lal laughed. "There are Maoists

and there are Maoists. Some in the government are probably tangled up in the smuggling. But others know our country needs tourism to survive. No one knows the value of a dollar like a Communist! So while somebody used influence to get the injured bandits cut loose, the Party at the highest level isn't going to go along with anything that might scare off the tourists. Not gunplay in a tourist destination, nor wholesale looting of national treasures."

"But they seem to be willing enough to plunge the country back into civil war," Pan said, sipping his own tea.

Lal shrugged. "That is politics. When did they ever bring anything but sorrow and pain? And then again, there's Jagannatha. He's incorruptible. But he's also shadowing us. It is probably only on the orders of his own Party superiors that he hasn't yet made a major effort to wipe us out."

"Why's that?" Annja asked. She shot Pan an uneasy look. This just keeps getting better, she thought glumly.

"He hates and fears foreign influence on our country. He says that if we open ourselves to the Westerners they'll enslave us, suck us dry and discard us." Lal shook his head. "Lots of people who don't care for the Maoists or their dogmas agree with that. Even among the religious."

"What do you want to do, Annja?" Pan asked.

"I have a job," she said. "So that's what I'm going to do."

"What about the people of the countryside?" Pan

asked. With a bit of a shock Annja recalled he was a seasoned counterguerrilla fighter.

She knew how important the support of the populace—or their hostility—was to guerrillas. Although human habitation had thinned considerably in the countryside surrounding the market town, on the way in, the expedition encountered surprising numbers of homes and small farmsteads tucked among the steep-walled valleys. Surprising, at least, to a foreigner who even now, after resting for hours in the safehouse, had to struggle to pull in each breath.

"Up here most peasants are devout followers of what you'd call Tibetan Buddhism. The lamaseries have a lot of influence. That means the Communists are unpopular, the way they ridicule the people's beliefs as superstition."

"What about Jagannatha?" Annja asked.

Lal pulled down the corners of his mouth in an unhappy expression. "As I said, he does not disrespect the old beliefs. And he treats the peasants well. Not the way most of the guerrillas do, not to mention the Party men from the cities who call the shots. The people are not hostile to him, as they are the other Maoists. But not many actively assist him."

Pan had his teacup to his lips. He grunted. "It only takes one to betray us."

Lal laughed. "You're on a great spiritual quest," Lal said. "Did you really think it would be easy?"

It came to the tip of Annja's tongue to say, "No, we're on a scientific quest, not a spiritual one." But she chose not to let the words pass her teeth. Why antagonize a good friend—and invaluable ally? she thought. There was more to her reticence than that. But she didn't choose to dwell on it.

"So what's next?" she asked.

"We go high up," Lal said promptly, "though not very far as the crow flies."

"You know where there's another hidden shrine?" Pan asked in surprise.

"Oh, no, Sergeant Katramados. Since you both have shown yourselves worthy, you now must pass to the next stage of your quest."

AT FIRST IT SOUNDED like a bird cry to Annja's ears—high-pitched, with a breathless quality to it. It ran on and on from unseen heights, so that its echoes joined it even before it ceased.

Trudging along snow packed down on top of layers of older snow, the new Sherpas hired from the bazaar town—for even Magars from lower levels found the going hard this high up the flank of the mighty White Mountain—began to mutter and roll their eyes in apparent fear. Some made complicated gestures that Annja gathered were meant to avert evil.

She was glad that, once leaving the precincts of the bazaar town and the rule of law—however imperfect its coverage—they had broken out the longarms taken from Jagannatha's guerrillas. The weight of the M-16 slung over her own shoulder was comforting. The fact Pan carried a similar weapon reassured her, as did the AKM whose additional ten-pound weight Prasad added to his already heavy load without seeming to notice.

They carried a number of extra magazines and boxes of ammunition. Trinkets, spices, camping gear and hashish weren't all one could purchase in the Nepali bazaar. Lal had bought the ammunition in certain select markets. By devious means they had been paid for on one of Annja's credit cards.

"What's the matter?" she asked Prasad, who walked in front of the procession. Footprints showed others had come this way since the last snow fell the night before. Prasad still scouted to make sure the way was safe, to watch out for hidden ice or overhanging snowbanks that might drop to swallow up the travelers.

To their right the canine-tooth shape of Dhaulagiri hung over them like an alien planet. The downslope fell away to their left with what Annja understood to be deceptive gentleness. If you lost your footing and went down, you'd be lucky to stop yourself. There was the risk of causing an avalanche that would bury you. Or you might just keep going, sliding or rolling helplessly until, several hundred yards down, you shot out over a sheer five-hundred-foot drop.

The mountains were getting serious now.

"Was it the bird cry that bothered them?" she asked.

"The cry has frightened them," Prasad said. "But it was no bird."

Among the porters Annja heard a word frequently enough to pick it out of the otherwise meaningless syllable stream. It sounded to her like *"bonmanche."*

"Well, what then, my friend?" Pan said. "Don't leave us in suspense."

"Bonmanche," Prasad repeated.

Pan cocked an eyebrow. "Yeti?" he said.

Annja restrained herself from rolling her eyes. She didn't want to trample on local religious belief. "I hope it won't make them reluctant to continue," she said.

Prasad shrugged. "They knew they might encounter danger, as well as hardship. But spiritual dangers strike deeper fear than mere physical ones do."

"Spiritual?" Pan asked.

"The *bonmanche* is a highly spiritual creature as well as a physical one," Prasad said. "Did you not know?"

"Ah…no. No, I didn't," Pan said.

He looked to Annja, who shrugged.

They trudged on. The porters' body language stayed skittish.

The landscape around them turned blue as the sun declined toward the great peaks to the west along the unseen valley of the Myagdi River. There was little vegetation in evidence here; all Annja could smell was snow and chilled gray stone. Packed snow several inches deep crunched beneath her hiking boots. Lal and Prasad had assured her they would face no technical climbing. At least on the current leg of their journey.

She gave Pan a surreptitious look through her wraparound UV-blocking sunglasses. It was getting late in the day to wear them, but they were essential against the glare, practically buzzing with ultraviolet radiation, that fell like steel rain from the daytime sky and ricocheted like bullets into unprotected eyes from ice and white snow. At the moment she was glad she wore them for another reason.

By slow degrees she felt Pan withdrawing from her. She was confused. Just when they seemed to be really coming together, suddenly came an unexpected emotional retrograde.

A conflict stirred inside her. She did feel longings, and they went—except for rare, brief interludes—unrequited. The encounters she'd had mostly had the effect of whetting her appetite for some kind of deep relationship. Something that would endure.

Yet her lifestyle all but precluded that. Her only real continuing contacts were primarily professional. Her strongest continuing bonds these days were with those cranky and unpredictable ageless men the sword brought into her life: Roux, her sometime mentor, and dashing billionaire financier Garin Braden, who was sometimes her deadly enemy and sometimes her most valuable friend—depending, it seemed, on what side of the bed he'd gotten out of on any given morning. She occasionally saw her friend Bart McGilley, but things had been strained between them as he clearly sensed she was keeping secrets from him—and she was.

But Pan had the same independence of mind and spirit she rejoiced in, many of the same interests and a lively and agile mind. Although a manly man by any standard, he seemed to lack most of the ingrained male chauvinism that afflicted not just most modern Mediterranean men, but cops, soldiers and special operators—all of which he was. He showed Annja genuine respect, as well as, she thought, affection.

The fact they'd fought side by side, and saved each other's lives, may have had something to do with it.

Now she felt Pan pulling back. Her consolation, if it was that, was that he didn't seem to be drawing away from her so much as into himself. She was beginning to fear she would lose him all the same.

Possibly to madness. The dreams were coming more frequently and stronger. Lying in his pallet next to her in the Gaine safehouse the night before, he had stirred and muttered to himself in his sleep in the dialect of his Macedonian hill village. Then again in the small, cold hours before dawn, she had awakened again to find him sitting up, arms around his knees, staring fixedly at nothing in this world.

Is he in danger of losing himself to memories of someone he never was, and a place he's never been? she asked herself. Had he seen her sword? No easy answer came. Nor could she see her way to asking him.

The path veered out of sight around a fairly sheer shoulder of what seemed to be mostly granite. Another lesser peak rose ahead, across what looked like a narrow valley. Lal slipped cautiously around the boulder, then signaled the others to follow.

The procession wound around. They entered a valley slanting steeply up the mountain. The path wound up the right side. To their left a stream poured down the center of the narrow valley in gleaming, burbling zigs and zags.

The mountain the curve had put at their left blocked the lowering sun. The temperature dropped perceptibly, just from moving into the mauve shadows. Annja did up the front of her parka. A child of the hot, humid Mississippi Delta, she'd been astonished to learn that in really cold climates it wasn't keeping warm that was the real problem, unless you were just completely unprepared. It was heat management. If you bundled up too tightly you could get overheated in a frighteningly short time, exhaust yourself, fuddle your wits and finally pass out. Worse case you could die.

Beside her Pan walked along, his face thoughtful, even somewhat sad. She compressed her lips and shook her head, wishing she could reach out to him.

"How much farther?" she asked Prasad as the trail crested and wound right again.

Even as she asked she became aware of an orange glow ahead. They came around a bend and Annja's breath caught in her throat.

"We are here," he said.

Before them stood a lamasery. It was three stories of dark wood and gray stone and sweeping eaves with demon faces carved in every beam end. The faces seemed alive, from the motion of the leaping flames of the thousand torches that surrounded the place. From the middle of the roof a giant bonfire danced high against slopes covered in dark hemlock forest.

"Behold," Prasad said, "the Lamasery of Fire."

23

"Wow. So you're American," the fresh-faced young man with the saffron robe and the shaved head said. "It's good to see somebody from back home. Good to hear the accent, you know?"

Pan and Annja exchanged looks. Annja shrugged.

They stood in a sort of flamelit courtyard before the steps to the main entrance. All around them torches hissed; they sounded to Annja like the wind blowing through a stand of saplings. Slow fat flakes had begun to fall from clouds that had closed in with alarming swiftness low overhead. The smell of burning resin in the black smoke that twined like snakes from the torches was almost overpowering.

"I am," she said. "I'm Annja Creed. This is Sergeant Pantheras Katramados of the Hellenic police." She would have introduced Prasad and Lal, but they and the porters hung back by the large wooden gates as if this did not concern them. She felt strange acting like some lady of the manor with her retinue of servants. But she felt bound to respect their wishes to hang back.

"Wow," the young man said. "That's Greek? You're sure a long way from home. Pleased to meet you, Ms. Creed, Sergeant. I'm Dzogchen Rinpoche. I know that's kind of a tongue twister, so you can call me Ricky."

"Ricky," Annja echoed faintly.

Ricky smiled. "Welcome to the Lamasery of Fire. Now, if you'll all follow me, we've got rooms waiting for everybody. Once you're settled in we can eat and talk. You must be famished. I know I am."

He turned and walked back between the huge double doors of the monastery. Inside through a short foyer Annja could see a high-raftered room lit by many torches burning in sconces along dark wooden walls.

He just looked like an all-American kid to Annja. Maybe part Japanese. But all American.

She and Pan found themselves sitting in a room with a fire roaring in a great hearth and many oil lamps hung from standing black-iron candelabra. It's a relief they don't have torches in here, too, she thought.

Lama Ricky sat on a little dais facing Pan and Annja, who sat cross-legged on carpets on the floor. Silent shaved-headed acolytes in red or saffron robes laid out a variety of covered porcelain dishes between them. At their host's gesture they began to open the pots. Through curls of steam they saw heaps of rice, steamed vegetables, something in a sauce that suggested curry.

As they served themselves with copper spoons Pan said, "Forgive me, please, but Ricky seems a very strange name for a monk high up a mountain in Nepal."

The young man grinned. "You'd think so, wouldn't you? I used to be plain old Richard Yamazaki of Cleveland, Ohio, back in the day. But then I started having these strange dreams and waking visions. One day these dudes showed up at my door and claimed I was the thirty-fourth generation of the Dzogchen Rinpoche. A *tulku*."

"*Tulku?*" Annja asked between bites. It was some kind of vegetable curry, spicy and delicious. It let her know she was indeed famished.

"Yeah. The thirty-fourth reincarnation of a bodhi-sattva."

"Bodhisattva?" Annja echoed. "Sorry. I'm a bit out of my depth here."

"It's one who has attained enlightenment, and has vowed to continue returning on the wheel of reincar-nation to help enlighten all beings, isn't it?" Pan asked, raising a cup of hot buttered tea to his lips.

"Got it in one," Ricky said, bobbing his bald head. "There were these prophecies that predicted my in-carnation. The previous Dzogchen Rinpoche left behind a song that predicted where I'd be found. That is, him come back and everything. So they tracked me down and set me a series of tests. I was shown a bunch of books, prayers beads, ritual stuff like that. It turned out what I picked was what belonged to him—to me—they told me, in a former life."

He drank from his own teacup. "I see by your eyes you think it sounds crazy. Well, it seemed pretty crazy to me, at first. But it all turned out to fit. So here I am."

He shook his head. "But that's not important. It's not why *you're* here. That's all about your journey."

"You know about us?" Pan asked. Suspicion lent an edge to his voice.

But the *tulku* didn't seem offended. "Sure," he said. "Old Omprakash down south in Lumbini set Ms. Creed on a course to here. He let us know to expect you both."

"But I never told him about Pan—about Sergeant Katramados," Annja protested. "I didn't even know he'd be joining me."

Ricky laughed. "Omprakash is totally a wise old dude. Very powerful spiritually. He knows things."

Pan continued to frown. "The local population feeds the monasteries," Annja told him softly. "Don't you think the grapevine reaches here?"

Her companion's craggy face didn't exactly soften, but it did unclench a bit. His shoulders relaxed slightly. Their host ate rice from a bowl held close to his mouth with chopsticks and gave no sign of having heard the comment. But his dark eyes danced.

She was glad to see Pan coming out of his own head, even if it was to get a touch paranoid with their host. He's been brooding so much on the past, she thought. By effort she suppressed the further thought, his imagined past.

"You've got me confused," Pan said, settling back on his heels.

"Good," Ricky said. "If you think you've already got it all figured out, how can you learn anything?"

"Well, I'm willing to admit I don't know what's going on," Annja said. "Especially if it'll speed things up a bit."

Ricky's expression surprised her. He didn't look offended. Nor did he show the same easy grin he had to almost everything else. Instead he looked almost worried.

"Don't be so eager to rush into the future," he said. "You don't know what it might hold."

"We all die," Pan said, drinking. "I know that much."

"And you should know that's not necessarily a career-ending injury, Pantheras," the lama said.

Oh, great, Annja thought. Feed his obsession. Way to go. "What do you mean?" she asked.

Ricky shrugged a saffron-clad shoulder. "You know. What goes around, comes around."

"So you know what we're looking for," Annja said, hoping to derail the conversation before it vanished utterly into mystic navel gazing. "Can you help us find it?"

"I can point out signposts. But only you can find your way." He shook his head and laughed. "Sorry. Coming off all mystical and cryptic just goes with the job. Anyway, you already know that twenty-some centuries ago, this young punk came out of the West, crashing into India breaking things and killing people."

Pan exclaimed angrily in a language Annja didn't understand. It sounded Greek, most likely in the accent of his remote home village. But it sounded... *archaic,* somehow.

Ricky regarded him calmly. The Greek cop, eyes staring, face still flushed, gathered himself and said in hoarse English, "You cannot speak that way of Megas Alexandros! He was a great man. He built cities and carried civilization!"

"We *had* civilization around here already. You know what I mean?"

Pan drew in a deep, shuddering breath. "But he, he was my—" He stopped and passed a hand over his face. "Childhood idol," he finished weakly.

"Right," Ricky said.

Pan slumped. He seemed slightly abashed and mostly confused.

After a moment the lama continued. "You know how he found out about the Highest Shrine, away up the White Mountain. And he sent his most trusted general to go and grab it for him. You've been following in his footsteps. Right?"

Neither of the visitors said anything.

"So, you still are," Ricky said. "He was found worthy to come this far. Now, so have you."

Annja frowned. "You—your predecessors—found him worthy to steal your greatest treasure?"

"If that ancient warrior Pantheras had succeeded in his quest, he'd have found a treasure valuable beyond his wildest imaginings," Ricky said.

"Did he…take the treasure, then?" Pan asked, as if speaking through glass shards in his throat.

"Do the histories talk about him getting a fabulous treasure back to Alex?"

Pan shook his head. "They don't recount that he ever returned at all. He was a Macedonian. One of the elite. He would not have come slinking back a failure. As the cliché goes, he would have come back with his shield, or on it."

"But that doesn't mean he never found the treasure," Annja said. She said it softly, uncharacteristically hesitant. She felt a strong sense of intruding.

Wait, she told herself sternly. This is my quest, too. If I hadn't started out on it in the first place we wouldn't even be sitting here.

"No," Ricky said, some of his perkiness coming back. "It's not my place to tell you that, either. All I'm here for is to provide you with—"

He reached behind himself and produced a beaten-brass tray. On it rested a scroll tied with a dusty scarlet ribbon.

"This."

An exhalation came from deep within Pan. It seemed to speak of infinite weariness and sadness.

"You know the drill by now," Ricky said, rising. "General Pantheras left behind a written record of his journey up the White Mountain to find the highest treasure. The monks copied it carefully and faithfully, time and again across the centuries. And now—" he bowed "—I leave you to your studies. If you need anything, let one of the brothers know and they'll get it for you."

Annja got to her feet and started to speak. "Your men have been shown to rooms of their own and are being fed," Ricky said, reading her question correctly. "When you're finished reading, a lama will show you to your own room."

He walked out. The soft falls of his footsteps echoed in the mostly empty room. Pan still sat. His eyes were fixed on the scroll.

Although she'd eaten little, Annja forgot hunger in her eagerness to learn what was in the fragment. From her pack she produced thin disposable gloves for them both. Carefully Pan untied the ribbon. He unrolled the scroll and began to read.

For several minutes Annja sat in silence. Her eyes never left his as they tracked line by line down the yellowed, brittle parchment. Then, almost as if in a trance, he began to speak aloud in a low voice.

"Pantheras has learned that his path from here leads high up the mountain. To a place called the Lost Lamasery. It is a place even the monks speak of with trepidation. Terrible dangers guard it, natural and otherwise. He's even heard rumors it is guarded by demons."

"Demons," Annja echoed with a little laugh.

Pan didn't respond to her. "It is, he writes, a destination from which the unworthy never return.

"By the time he reached here the general had lost most of his party, the greater part to a recent avalanche. He writes of growing disillusionment. With slaughter, with Alexander, with the world. Madness and fear seem to be overcoming the few remaining members of his expedition.

"He has lost his taste for treasure. He seeks now for peace within his soul. It seems strange to him, but the teachings of this land's people offer just that—not the favor of fickle deities, but lasting serenity. Something he's never imagined before.

"But…he is a true son of Macedonia. He will carry out his orders. Whatever the danger. Whatever the cost to himself. He will deliver the treasure, as charged, to the highest and most powerful lord."

Slowly he rerolled the scroll. He tied the ribbon around it again and set it back on the tray. Then he settled back with his hands on his thighs and his chin sunk to his clavicle.

"The avalanche struck them as they were crossing the site of the present bazaar town," he said, not looking at her. "A huge snowpack slid from the great granite shield above the town. Pantheras's men called upon him to save them, called upon the gods. But he and the gods alike were powerless to help them. They were swept away down the mountain, crushed and buried."

"That's in the fragment, too?" Annja asked.

"No," Pan said. "I saw it last night in my dreams."

THE TORCHES OF THE NIGHT before were extinguished. The white light of morning shone down into the chamber from windows set high up in the rafters. Annja and Pan sat eating breakfast with Dzogchen Rinpoche, born Richard Yamazaki in Cleveland, who had resumed his earlier place on the low dais.

"You've learned what you came to learn," he said with a gentle smile. It was not a question.

Annja noticed he did not ask if they'd slept well. She got the very strong impression that he knew.

It doesn't take any kind of mystic second sight to know that, she thought. Just good enough eyesight to see the bags under our eyes.

"I suppose so," Annja said.

Although they shared a room, it hadn't been any kind of happy recreation that kept them awake. Annja was willing to maintain their relationship as strictly business until their search was settled. But if Pan had wanted to press the issue…she probably would not have said no.

She felt a strong attraction to her companion. And yet now that circumstances had conspired to bring them close together, he was receding.

Emotionally, at least. Mentally. He seemed to find

himself drawn irresistibly back into the past. For all that he seemed as solidly grounded in reality as any man she'd known, the coincidence that the general Alexander had sent to seize the treasure was also named Pantheras had caught hold of his imagination with claws of iron and would not let go.

Once more he'd spent the night tossing and turning and crying out in a strange tongue. Annja feared his fantasy of a past lifetime had trapped him and was dragging him inexorably in.

"What can you tell me of this Lost Lamasery?" Pan asked. Annja thought even his voice sounded different— deeper. Older, somehow. "Does it still exist?"

"Oh, yes," Ricky said. "Still there. Still lost."

"But surely there's no danger in trying to reach it anymore?" Annja said.

"Oh, yeah," the lama said. "Yes to the danger, that is. It's a very holy place. Its keepers can't risk allowing it to be plundered and defiled by every stray conquering thug—sorry, sergeant—bandit, or doctrinaire atheist guerrilla who wanders by. And somehow, you know, millennium in, millennium out, there's always been people like that running loose in this part of the world. Must be the air. Or maybe the height."

He shook his head. "It's a very perilous journey. And just like General Pantheras, you've got to pass through the Lost Lamasery to complete your journey."

"You've *got* to be kidding," Annja said.

The young man showed her a toothy grin. "Nope. That's karma—the real deal, not the wishy-washy watered-down New Age kind we hear about back in the States, you know? Sometimes it's your duty, sometimes it's your fate. Sometimes it just sucks."

Pan nodded as if these words held deep meaning for him. "Duty is something I can understand," he said. "Something we both understand."

Thanks for remembering I'm involved in this, too, Annja thought, a little sharply.

"So if this place is really so lost," Annja said slowly, "how are we ever going to find it?"

"I will tell you," Ricky said.

24

The sun hadn't quite reached the zenith when a cry in Gorkhali brought Annja's head whipping around.

Lal was marching just in front of her and Pan as they climbed Dhaulagiri. The dark figures winding around the mountainside half a mile behind them filled them all with dread.

"I hope they do not shoot," Prasad said from point position. He spoke softly but his words carried down the rising wind. "It could bring the mountain down on all our heads."

The slope above them was steep and white. To their left it dropped away dizzyingly into depths hidden by clouds of snow blown by a stiff wind that fortunately didn't reach this high.

"We should move," Prasad said.

Annja swallowed and nodded. The little procession began to wind its tortured way along the face of the mountain once more.

She looked at Pan. She was pretty experienced in combat herself—more so, she realized, than most men in frontline combat units. Pan had been stuck deep into the most harrowing and constant special ops in Afghanistan. And he was the professional, after all.

"Well?" she asked. "What do we do now?"

"Keep moving," he said. "That's all I can see. And the only ways to go are forward—or back."

"It does simplify our choices," Annja said.

"Lal?" Pan said. He pitched his voice low but managed to make it carry. With a cringing, contracting feeling in the pit of her belly Annja knew how dangerous it would be to shout up here with tons of snow hanging over you. "What do you think?"

For once young Lal wasn't smiling. "You're right, Sergeant," he said. "But we and they each hold a blade."

"What do you mean?" Annja asked as they studied the group pursuing them.

"They can move faster than we can," he said. "There are more of them, and they're more lightly laden."

"What about the newbies?" Annja asked. Jagannatha and his men had been following them for some time but a new and less disciplined-looking group had joined them.

Lal shrugged. "If they fall, their comrades won't even stop to watch."

"So what's our advantage?" Pan asked. "That's the part I want to hear."

"Out here on the narrow trail neither side dares shoot. Even without the avalanche threat we'd just slaughter each other out here in the open with no hiding places."

"Jagannatha might risk that," Prasad said. "He hates the Western influence. He fears what you'll do to the country and the people if you find the treasure. He'd rather die than see you turn the Highest Shrine into Disneyland."

"Like I'd do that!" Annja exclaimed indignantly.

"Voice," Pan said.

Annja put her hand to her mouth. "Sorry."

"In his way the major is a true fanatic," Prasad said.

"I thought you said he'd lapsed from his Communist faith," Pan said.

"And so he has, Sergeant. Yet what he believes, he believes in with a convert's fervor. And he believes he stands alone against the forces of what you call globalization."

"Why haven't they just opened up and finished it, then?" Annja asked.

"Because," their guide said, forging steadily along as if he hadn't a worry in the world, "he's no longer alone. Nor, it is probable, in charge. Lowlanders have recently joined them—his political officer and followers, no doubt."

"Wouldn't a devoted Maoist want to stop us at any cost, too?" Annja asked.

Prasad translated that. He and his nephew and the Sherpas all laughed. The sound was barely perceptible; Annja could mostly tell they were laughing because their smiles widened and their bodies seemed to shake. She got the idea that was, under the circumstances, their version of busting a gut.

"They want the gold, Annja Creed!" Prasad said. "No one lusts after gold like a Communist."

"They'll want to catch us and use their *kukris,*" Lal said.

"Note also the much taller figures who walk among them," Prasad said.

"Bajraktari," Pan spit.

"It would certainly appear your outlaw countrymen walk among them," Lal said.

"Not my countrymen. Once we hunted them with spears, like wild beasts…."

He broke off, noting the way Annja was staring at him.

"Pan," she said, low and urgent. "Stay in the present. We need you here and now."

For a moment his eyes blazed with anger. It was replaced quickly with confusion, then contrition. He lowered his head.

"You're right. I cannot afford to slip."

They came to a frightening choke point where they had to turn faces to the rock and inch along. Despite her precarious foothold Annja risked a look back. It seemed their pursuers had closed the distance somewhat.

"So, I still haven't heard what our advantage is," Annja said, trying not to sound too hopeful.

"The path won't stay narrow forever," Lal said. "Sooner or later, we'll reach a spot where we can leave it, fan out and find cover to shoot from."

"So it's basically a race," she said.

"Between their knives and our rifles, yes."

AS THE AFTERNOON BEGAN to wear on them, the trail never widened much beyond shoulder width, narrowing all too often to something little more than a dubious toehold. The pursuers were gaining, but glacially.

A distant cry brought Annja's head around. She saw a dark figure plummeting away from the narrow string of pursuers. She cringed in what had become reflexive fear that the man's wail of terminal despair would bring on an avalanche. She noticed she wasn't the only one. These high-mountain men were hard-core, but they were still human.

"That's two in the last hour," Pan said. "That one was a local, I think." The first pursuer to fall had been taller than most of the enemy party. They were close enough now Annja could recognize the tall gaunt shape of Bajraktari still with them, the bear-like bulk of his shadow, Duka, limping painfully and determinedly along. Apparently the kneecap she'd displaced had gotten treatment. But it had to hurt like a monster to walk on. Especially like this.

"Prasad," she said, "how much farther?"

"Not far," Prasad said. "Another hour or two."

"That may be too long," Pan said. "They're getting close. If too many of them slip and go over, they may do something desperate."

Their guide shrugged beneath the straps of his bulky pack. "What will happen, will happen. If you are worthy, nothing will stop you reaching your destination."

"What about you?" Pan asked.

Prasad grinned. "It is not our spiritual quest," he said. "What happens to us matters much to us, but little to fate."

Annja heard a whisper from Lal, out of sight around a two-story granite boulder. "Storm clouds ahead," Prasad translated. "We shall be in it soon."

Pan said something under his breath in his native tongue. Annja wasn't sure if it was a prayer, a curse or a little of both.

"Sounds like we're in trouble," she said.

But her guide shook his head. "No. It can be good for us. It will shield us from our enemies' eyes and make their hearts quail."

It's sure having that effect on my heart, she thought, but she decided not to say it.

They edged around the boulder. Annja hugged the harsh stone tightly. She felt air beneath her heels. The weight of her pack seemed to try to peel her off backward.

Then she was around. The trail widened to a luxurious five feet. Safe as the living room of her loft back in Brooklyn, it seemed.

But ahead the storm clouds piled higher than the great mountain and grayer than the rocks. Whiteness swirled no more than a quarter mile ahead, obliterating sight.

From behind Annja heard a mutter among the porters. Despite the alien intonations she caught the impression of a debate between fear and something a lot like eagerness.

"What are they saying, Prasad?"

"They say the storm is brought by the mountain spirits who protect the Lost Lamasery," he answered calmly. "Some think they're there to help us."

"And the others?" Pan asked.

Prasad shrugged. "They say the demons come to prevent us from reaching the monastery alive."

25

"How long must we wait for vengeance?"

Enver Bajraktari kept his concentration until he finished inching his way around the big rock protrusion that reduced the trail to little more than a suggestion. Then he stepped out where it widened. In front of him one of Chatura's men armed with a black British submachine gun and one of Jagannatha's with a Kalashnikov walked point, with their two leaders moving just as suspiciously behind them.

The tall Kosovar helped Duka around the last of the narrow shelf and aided him in limping to the wider area. Then he looked back and snarled an answer to his giant bodyguard. "Can't you at least wait to whine until I'm off that damned knife edge?" He was trying to keep his voice down. Their local helpers had impressed on them the necessity of keeping loud noises to a minimum up here.

Their quarry still had a good lead. They were too far away for accurate shooting. Besides, both Chatura and Jagannatha had impressed on him that gunfire was strictly a last resort up here amid the snowpack.

He assisted Duka for a few halting steps until he seemed able to proceed on his own. Normally he'd leave stragglers behind without a thought. But Duka was a special case. He was loyal as a dog to his master. That meant something in this treacherous age.

Ahead he saw Chatura and the new man, Jagannatha, trudging side by side. Speaking of unclean beasts, the major was like a dog forced to walk placidly beside a cat, Bajraktari thought. Or an old wolf. That one is dangerous, he thought.

As a matter of traditional business practice, Bajraktari had been contemplating the possibility that Chatura might not make it off the mountain alive. The little potbellied infidel was annoyingly smug and superior. His elimination would leave the more for Bajraktari and his men. And unlike his men, of course, the commissar had no extended family back in Kosovo who cherished the same blood-feud traditions as the Bajraktaris.

But Jagannatha was cut from different cloth. A highly dangerous man himself, Enver Bajraktari prided himself on his ability to read the signs. And clearly the major had no more use for the Kosovars than he did for their quarry. Nor for Chatura and his swaggering city-born political thugs, who all had their tongues hanging and their feet dragging.

The problem, Bajraktari saw, was that he and his men most clearly needed Jagannatha's help to get to the treasure—and get down with it alive.

Ah, well, he thought. It's in Allah's hands. The evil mountain would itself thin the number of hands reaching for pieces of the golden pie, he suspected. And he wasn't naive enough to believe they'd finish off the treacherous Annja Creed and her companions without getting well bloodied; the woman must be some kind of wicked sorceress.

And when at last the treasure was in their hands and the Creed woman and the policeman were dead, hopefully after a very great deal of pain, Enver Bajraktari was just the man to sort matters out. He was good at that sort of thing.

"Pasha?" Duka grunted. It was an old borrowing from Turkish, meaning "boss."

"Yes?"

The man's big shaggy head nodded. "Storm coming."

Bajraktari looked beyond the brightly colored line of the party they pursued. The thick, gray-hearted clouds that had been gathering about the mountain now swept toward them with swirling skirts of white.

Without regard to safety he began to jog forward. He had to talk to Chatura. And Jagannatha.

FROM THE BACK OF THE GROUP a Sherpa cried out in alarm. Annja tore her eyes from the snow squall flowing around the mountainside to meet them.

A large group of pursuers had separated themselves from the rest and advanced quickly in open pursuit, heedless of the treacherous and now icy trail. Heavy curved blades gleamed dully in their hands.

"Jagannatha," Pan said, a beat before Prasad confirmed it.

"He knows once we're in the snowstorm they've lost us," the guide said. "Wise old wolf that he is."

"The *kukris*—" Annja said.

"They do not wish to risk avalanche. They intend to do their work with blades."

Deal with it, she told herself. It's not as if I'm likely to survive this encounter anyway. She started determinedly toward the rear of the procession. If you want to play with sharp things, I'm your girl, she thought.

A hand caught her arm. She spun, frowning. It was Pan. He released her as if her arm had gotten hot. "Sorry. But where do you think you're going?" he said.

"Most of our Sherpas are unarmed. There's only a couple of Prasad's kinfolk left. I'm not about to ask them to fight my battle while I scuttle for safety," she said.

"Why not? They won't be alone."

She realized he had a length of steel in his right hand. Serious steel, with a wide single-edged blade a foot long tapering to a wicked point. "Where'd you get that?" she asked.

He grinned. "Afghanistan. A souvenir. It's called a Khyber knife."

"You're a man of surprises, Pan. But I can't let others fight my fights. Not even you."

He frowned. "You fight remarkably well," he said. He left the "for a woman" unsaid. It didn't sting her particularly; she knew it wasn't male chauvinism, or not purely that. A woman, a sheltered American woman at that, could rarely hope to hold her own in a face-up fight with a man. And she still couldn't explain why she was the exception....

A short, sturdy figure appeared beside them. "Prasad," she said.

"Lal will lead the men onward as fast as he dares. I will join you in the rear guard. If Lord Buddha smiles, the snow shall spare us the need to fight."

"But Annja—" Pan began.

"Do you truly not see it yet, my friend? She is a spirit warrior. If anything, it is she who will protect us. Now we must go!" Prasad said.

They paused to let the Sherpas pass them. Fortunately the porters, mountaineers by birth and bloodline, had been holding back for the benefit of their outland employers. Now they moved like eager mountain goats for what they obviously thought of as the welcoming shelter of the blizzard. Annja wished she could feel the same about it.

She, Pan and Prasad took up position at the end

of the line. The pursuers were no more than fifty
yards back. Walking backwards, trusting to the body
sense imparted by her training in martial arts, Annja
could clearly see the grizzled red face of Jagannatha
between his fur collar and his big fuzzy cap.

It chilled her in a way the rising wind couldn't
match. She realized she was looking at the face of a
man who was neither criminal nor madman, but who
had set his own interests aside to do what he believed
was right. In that seamed, stern face she read neither
anger nor hatred. Just *determination.* For whatever
reason, Jagannatha saw Annja and her mission as a
deadly threat to his homeland. And he was as unstop-
pable as a runaway train.

"Annja?" Pan said from her elbow. He was still
clearly unhappy about her being there. He was all
hard-core special-forces vet now, and wasn't buying
any "spirit warrior" nonsense. Which at least meant
he was wholly in the present.

She shook her head. How can I tell him that most
of those I've killed in the past were clearly bad men,
doing bad things? she thought. But this man—I
almost don't feel I've got the right.

She shook herself all over. Catch a grip, she
thought. If Jagannatha attacks you, you've got the
unbreakable right to defend yourself. His motives
don't matter. You can't really know them anyway;
you're not a mind reader—

A soft-voiced comment traveled back along the
line to them. "Ms. Creed," Prasad said, managing to

sound both polite and urgent, "the storm comes swiftly. Lal and the first men are already within it. We must hurry."

Annja caught Pan's eye. They turned and raced full speed behind Prasad for the storm.

Imagine thinking of a violent Himalayan snowstorm as shelter, she thought. Then she plunged into the white maelstrom.

"THEY'RE GETTING AWAY!" Bajraktari heard someone shout in his native tongue.

Though dizzy from the thin air and nervous on the slick footing, his men had begun to hurry once Jagannatha took the lead, as if unwilling to leave the pleasure of the kill to the locals. Who after all were infidels. Bajraktari hung back. Duka still found this heavy going. Chatura and most of his lowlanders stayed back of them. Content to let others do the hard part, he thought. Yet reap all the rewards afterward.

He looked up from aiding Duka past a slick stretch to see the woman and her party moving into a curtain of snow and mist so dense he couldn't see into it at all. Their curious knives in hand, Jagannatha and his men trotted after them. They were still much too far to close the gap.

Screaming in rage, one of Bajraktari's men raised his Kalashnikov and triggered a furious burst after the fleeing group.

Two of Jagannatha's men stumbled and fell. One toppled over the edge with what began as a surprised shout and ended as a despairing wail that trailed away forever. Jagannatha pirouetted. He brought up his antique Chinese-made Mauser with two gloved hands and fired a single shot at the gunman, who still blazed mindlessly away, his screams half-heard above the racket of his gun.

The man dropped the heavy rifle and fell over backward, arms outflung. His eyes stared with uncomprehending fury past the small blue hole in his forehead.

But the damage was done. Bajraktari felt a rumble that seemed to resonate in his very bones. He heard crackling and then a strange, sinuous hiss as tons of snow broke free and slid downward.

He grabbed his gigantic bodyguard and flung him against a boulder jutting from the mountainside. Then he tried to make himself very small as the avalanche roared over them.

"Oh, my God," Annja breathed as the avalanche came down. A strangely coherent mass at least a hundred yards by maybe thirty started sliding downward and outward like packed snow from a pitched roof. It hit the pursuing group of guerrillas and Kosovar bandits and washed them out of view and out of existence, right over the edge of the cliff.

But most of Jagannatha's men escaped. A few threw themselves down on the path. The major himself waved his arms for his men to run, not wanting to shout and risk dislodging more snow. Annja caught the impression that at least some of the camouflage-clad Party thugs remained on the far side of the slide, but the wave of packed snow and thrown-up powder blotted them from sight.

She felt Pan's hand clamp on her arm and tow her forcibly along the trail. The blizzard shut off her vision like a curtain falling.

26

Breathing hard, Jagannatha stood staring at the turbulent wall of white advancing toward him. The last sounds of the avalanche echoed down the blue-ice gulf between peaks. The last remnants of loose snow sifted down over the ramp of snow where the trail had been.

Although the slide's main force had missed most of them, his men had thrown themselves down against the trail's rocky inner face as its fringes swept over them. Now they picked themselves up and cleaned themselves off. Only their leader had remained standing, stubborn as a rock fixed to the White Mountain itself.

With an angry grimace he thrust his pistol back in its holster and sealed the flap. "Rope yourselves," he growled. Condensation issued from his mouth, making him look like a temple-guardian dragon.

"What about comrade Chatura?" asked his senior lieutenant, Raghu. "Shouldn't we try to help him?"

Steam puffed from the major's broad nostrils. "He knows everything. Let him fend for himself."

"What if he's dead?"

"Then we don't need to trouble ourselves over him anymore, do we? Get the men tied together. Those Western interlopers aren't getting away on *my* watch."

FOR A MOMENT Annja felt completely disoriented. She'd never encountered a snowstorm before that so abruptly cut visibility to where she couldn't see her fingers if she stretched out her arm. The wind swirled and howled. The cold cut at her exposed face like a bee swarm. She blinked ice-laden lashes to clear her eyes. Through the soles of her boots she could still feel the death rumble of the avalanche's aftermath.

"Move to the inside of the trail," she heard Prasad say urgently from nearby. His small figure appeared from the enfolding white. It had a reassuring sense of balance and solidity to it. "Pull your goggles back down. They have yellow lenses. You should still see well enough."

She nodded and obeyed, mumbling thanks. I actually lost focus there, she thought with shock. More than any other trait her ability to keep her head in a lethal crisis had kept her alive—on several occasions even before she received the unexpected and unasked-for gift of the sword of Joan of Arc.

Pan loomed up beside her, dark and solid. He put

an arm around her. It felt strong. Secure. She melted against his chest in a fervent hug.

She didn't like to think of herself—*wouldn't* think of herself—as a woman who needed a strong man's touch to pull herself together. She was not that woman.

He took his arm from around her shoulders. She felt him doing something at her waist. She realized he had her moving forward again through the blinding snow.

"Prasad wants us to rope ourselves together," Pan said. He had to bring his mouth so close to her ear his breath seared like a dragon's to make himself heard without shouting and taking the risk of dropping more packed snow on their heads. "We have to keep moving. Jagannatha will."

She gave him a little smile. "Okay."

On they pressed through the curious blizzard. It was, Annja thought, like being inside a blender making a vanilla milkshake. Indeed the snow fell so densely it felt like frigid liquid splashing against them.

Without warning the wolves were on them. Annja heard the crunch of a boot on snow behind her and spun. A figure appeared, a leathered face snarling, swinging a *kukri* at her head.

She turned away. The big curved blade whistled inches from her face. She summoned the sword and hacked the guerrilla across the face as he bent his arm across his body for a backhand return stroke. He screamed and fell out of her field of vision.

She was jerked halfway off her feet as Pan, bringing up the rear, tried to block two more attackers from getting to her. With a quick slash she cut the rope binding them together.

As one of Pan's opponents grappled with him the other darted toward Annja. She saw his eyes widen as he caught sight of the blade she held. She thrust. He ran straight onto her point. His eyes bulged and he fell out of view.

Still hoping Pan hadn't seen the weapon appear in her hand, Annja stooped to snatch up the *kukri* dropped by the man she'd just killed. Its extreme blade-heavy balance felt alien and unwieldy to her. She transferred it to her left hand and held the sword in her right.

This should give me plausible deniability with Pan, anyway, she thought.

Abruptly Pan brought a shin up between the legs of the man he grappled with. The man grunted and his grip on Pan's knife wrist slackened. Pan slammed the hilt into his attacker's face. Taking a step and driving from the hips, he hurled the man away from him—and away from the inside rock face. The man vanished into the churning whiteness. His cry as he fell was a ghostly sound.

Then he and Annja were locked in a bizarre dance as men with big curved knives swarmed them. Annja parried and slashed and thrust for fur-covered bellies and hate-twisted faces. Steel played fierce music on steel while the million voices of the wind sang haunting accompaniment.

As best they could they backed up along the trail. Prasad joined their fight without a sideways glance at Annja's unusual weapon. Lal appeared, too, Enfield slung and *kukri* drawn, to join the frenzied melee.

Although the guerrillas were determined and outnumbered the explorers they couldn't outflank them on the narrow trail, especially once Lal returned. Red slush was building around their boots and the slick-rock footing threatened to send them after so many of their enemies, screaming away in blankness.

Then a man with a ferocious scowl and eyebrows and round grizzle-bearded cheeks confronted Annja. She recognized Major Jagannatha himself. He struck at her with his *kukri*, lightning fast.

She blocked the cut with the flat of her sword. "Why are you doing this?" she demanded between crossed blades, one bent, one straight. "What have we done to you?"

"It's not what you do," he said, "it's who will follow. And then our land will no longer be ours."

Not at all fazed by her weapon, he hooked his blade over hers and pivoted hard to his left. He put his hips into it.

The swift, powerful move torqued the hilt and levered the sword right out of her hand. It seemed to vanish in the blizzard but Annja knew it had simply winked out of existence.

Jagannatha tried to whip a rising backhand hack at her face. She blocked with the *kukri* she still held in her left hand.

Jagannatha pressed her hard. He was single-mindedly trying to destroy her. With Annja fighting off-handed with an utterly strange weapon he was going to win soon, too.

Gasping for breath, forced to focus totally on his whirlwind blade to keep from having an arm hacked off or her head split by it, Annja was unable to concentrate enough to call back the sword.

Jagannatha was clearly a master of *kukri* close-in fighting. But she was strong and her reflexes were quick.

Back he pressed her, up the trail. It was mostly by luck she didn't take a wrong step and go over the edge. But suddenly her right foot slipped as she put her weight back on it. It shot forward and dropped her painfully on her rump.

Her fall allowed Jagannatha to press his advantage. It also gave Annja an eye blink's grace to curve the fingers of her right hand as if grasping a hilt and reach with her will into that unknown otherwhere. Instantly she felt the sword fill her hand.

She thrust out. The *kukri*'s weakness was that it was badly unsuited for point fighting. It had probably never faced a long sword.

But Jagannatha was a cagey and adaptable fighter. He didn't obligingly charge in to impale himself. He caught himself like a cat and leaped nimbly back from the sword's lethal point.

Despite the way her head swam and her body felt wrung out, Annja snapped herself upright with a gymnast's quickness. Seeing what he took for an opening, Jagannatha closed quickly. His *kukri* swung down for her face.

Annja had come back to her feet with her sword hand down before her hips. She whipped the blade straight up. It sheared the descending *kukri* off where its blade narrowed. By pure reflex she wheeled into a clockwise spinning back kick. Her right heel pistoned into the middle of Jagannatha's torso. Its force sent him reeling backward.

She saw his last look of angry defiance. Then he dropped over the edge in silence.

The snow was thinning, although the wind raged more furiously than ever. Annja could see back along the trail where figures continued to struggle. One held up a black submachine gun with the side-mounted magazines over his head and triggered a burst.

Lal, his *kukri* lost, had just buttstroked a guerrilla across his bearded face with the Enfield, dropping him limp to the trail, unconscious or dead. The burst of 9 mm bullets raked the young man's belly and chest. He crumpled.

His uncle barely caught him in time to keep him from falling over the cliff. Flipping his Khyber knife to his left hand, Pan grabbed the muzzle brake of his M-16 and carried it slung barrel down behind his back. He snapped up the weapon, caught the pistol grip and began to rip short bursts into the guerrillas. The *kukri*-armed men cried out hoarsely and cringed as needle-slim bullets cut them down.

With a furious howl the storm closed in again. Disregarding the risk of further avalanche Pan backed along, firing in quick, angry spurts. He tucked the knife away in his belt and held the long rifle with both hands.

With his pack still strapped to his back Prasad couldn't take up his stricken nephew into a fireman's carry. Instead he scooped Lal up in his arms and began to carry him that way. Annja willed away the sword and threw down her *kukri*. She offered to help.

He turned her down with a single emphatic head shake. A shiny tear trail ran down each leathery cheek.

Pan's magazine ran dry. He turned to climb up the trail as he changed magazines. The unarmed Sherpas had fled up the path as best they could. Annja didn't blame them. Prasad, carrying his moaning nephew, led the way, surefooted as a mountain goat.

Annja unlimbered her own rifle. If the enemy was going to shoot they couldn't afford to hold fire, avalanches or not. They'd have to take their chances. They weren't good in any case. She walked backward up the trail.

No more shots came from behind them. They rounded another bend in the trail. It offered momentary shelter from gunfire in case the pursuers opened up again.

Over the wind, or maybe lacing through it, Annja began to hear what sounded like voices. When no more sign of pursuit became evident she turned around. Before her Prasad carried his nephew as if he was an infant.

Within a couple of hundred yards they came upon the porters, huddling against the trail's inner face and moaning in apparent terror. They were already half-covered with new-fallen snow. Wondering what could possibly have frightened them more than trigger-happy guerrillas, Annja thought she heard a new sound through the wind and illusory blizzard voices.

"What's that?" she asked Pan.

For a moment he didn't answer. His head was held high, goggles still pushed up on his forehead despite the heavily falling snow. He seemed to be looking to far vistas despite the big flakes that clogged his lashes and must have been painful as they collided with his eyeballs.

Uh-oh, she thought. He's wandered off into history again.

He blinked as if rousing from sound sleep. "Sounds like a bird," he said a bit sheepishly pulling his goggles back in front of his eyes.

"That's what I thought," Annja said. "But what could a bird be doing up here in a brutal snowstorm?"

Uncharacteristically angry, Prasad kicked the Sherpas to their feet, speaking in low syllables that stung. Annja recognized one word moaned over and over by the unhappy Sherpas—*bonmanche*.

Prasad heard her question and turned his face to her. "It is the yeti," he said.

"They're afraid of it?" Pan asked.

"Yes," Prasad said. "It can be very fierce. But it is also a spirit animal. They fear it is a sign of evil coming."

Annja glanced nervously back down the trail. She could no more see through the falling snow than she could a glass of milk. Below them it seemed twice as dense as ever, although where they stood it fell relatively lightly.

"How's Lal?" she asked. Prasad only shook his head.

Struggling to his feet, one of the porters suddenly froze. He flung up his arm and screamed something so loud it made Annja cringe for fear it would bring the mountain down on their heads. Then she looked where he pointed.

27

Mist swirled like smoke around a shadowy creature. Then the snow descended again.

The Sherpas began to clamor fearfully. They repeated *"bonmanche"* over and over. Prasad had never spared an upward look. Holding his nephew's limp body in his arms, he continued to drive the men to their feet and upward along the narrow cliffside path.

"It was just a bear," Annja said, shaking her head.

"It seems pretty high up for a bear," Pan said, as the procession began to file along, bent beneath the storm as if it doubled their loads. One of the Sherpas had quietly added Prasad's pack to his own. His burden, now doubled, didn't seem to slow him any.

"We're still a couple thousand feet under the tree line," Annja said. "Or it could have been a man in a heavy coat."

"A very big man," Pan said half-dreamily.

"What else could it be? Stay with me here, Pan. We're not out of danger yet!"

He shook his head. "I'm sorry, Annja. It's…it's as if I've been awake for days, and find myself drifting off to sleep. But it's the past."

"It's a dream," she insisted. "A waking dream. I know you've snapped back when you needed to. But especially with the air so thin I'm worried you'll fall so deep in the past you won't be able to pull yourself out. Even to help us."

Speaking of thin air, she thought, the fight had winded her and her legs felt like jelly. She found she had to say the words in short bursts. She simply ran out of breath in midsentence and had to inhale before she carried on.

Pan looked at her with a strange light in his dark eyes. "I will never let you down, Annja. No matter what happens, I will stand beside you."

"Thank you," she said. She hoped it was true.

The wind swirled and lashed her with hard-driven snow. Pulling her goggles back down she walked up beside Prasad and asked if she could examine Lal. Prasad shook his head.

"We can do nothing," he said.

She sighed, felt tears start but squeezed her cheeks to keep them from squeezing out and fogging her goggles. It was just so brutal. The burst, completely unaimed and fired from the worst imaginable shooting position, shouldn't have hit anything—should have spattered across a half acre of mountainside. But somehow at least four and possibly five bullets had hit Lal solidly in the torso. There simply wasn't anything to do for him on a perilous mountain trail in a horrific blizzard, with human wolves still pressing behind in unseen pursuit.

Shrill screams rang out from somewhere behind. Pan stopped and turned, bringing up his M-16. Despite his vagueness—which Annja thought must be altitude sickness—he did come right back when danger threatened.

But whatever the danger was it didn't seem to threaten them. The wind's howling rose to a crescendo. The cries and chilling screams of men in panic and pain remained clearly audible. There were sudden, savage cracks of gunfire.

One voice rose above the rest, shrieking something Annja didn't understand but knew was in no local tongue. It trailed off into a fading wail as its owner presumably went over the cliff to his doom.

Annja had stopped. She held her rifle pointed back along the trail. She glanced at Pan, who frowned thoughtfully.

"I understand a bit of it," he said, never taking his eyes off their back trail though the snow completely blocked vision past ten feet. "The eagle's tongue, as the Albanians call their language."

"What did he say?" Annja asked.

He shook his head. "I couldn't make out all of it. But it was something about demons in the snow."

The volume of gunfire rose. There were several rifles going off, maybe many, the Kalashnikovs playing bass to a counterpoint of higher-pitched submachine guns. Then it stopped.

The clamor continued. Even through the wind's shrieking Annja could tell the voices were dwindling. Their enemies were fleeing back down the trail, faster than would have been safe even in bright sunlight with bare, dry rock underfoot.

"There's no such thing as demons," Annja said firmly. "The altitude must be affecting them, too, especially Bajraktari's gang. They got jumbled up in the storm and started fighting each other. That's all."

Pan said nothing.

"Hurry, please," Prasad called back to them. Urgency rang clearly in his voice.

Annja didn't ask why. She and Pan just turned wordlessly and moved out again. Both still held their rifles. Annja truly didn't think the pursuit party was going to be catching up to them any time soon. But even the relatively light weight of the weapon reassured her.

Almost at once the cliffside path ended. Prasad led them right, up into a cleft in the rock that might have been made by a cleaver. After a sharp climb of maybe fifty yards they came out between two big rocks to find themselves walking up an easy slope.

Annja didn't know how much farther they walked. The wind had lost its edge of fury, as if it had spent itself in the squall that caused the guerrillas and bandits to accidentally go for each others' throats. The snowfall gradually diminished. The surroundings became clear slowly. They were in a valley with big rocks interspersed with stands of hemlocks, so coated in snow they might have been snow sculptures except for the occasional dark branch peeking out.

They crossed a saddle of land. Before them a crevasse thirty yards wide plunged down into the earth as if it wouldn't stop short of the core. A plank bridge hung from thick, hairy ropes crossed it. On the other side the high stone walls soared and the steeply pitched, sweeping-eaved roofs of a great monastery were visible, perched like a castle on a crag that stood up out of a cloudbank as if floating.

"I AM SO SORRY," the lama in the red robe said. "There was nothing we could do for your friend. As learned as our healers are, we have limited resources."

Annja sighed and shook her head. Sorrow for the brave and cheerful young man who had done so much to help her would haunt her for a long time.

As always, Prasad had refused to accompany them to their interview with the head lama. They left him grieving over his nephew's body. The lamas led the Sherpas to a dormitory to eat and rest.

"I don't think he could have survived those wounds no matter what treatment he got, nor how quickly," Pan said. He knelt beside her sipping salty buttered tea.

"Nonetheless, we share your sorrow for the loss of your friend," the monk said.

For a few moments they sat in silence. Like some of the shrines she had discovered, the room was startlingly colorful. The walls were carved with shapes from Tibetan Buddhist mythology. These were all brightly painted, in crimson and cerulean, forest green, chrome yellow.

Halfway up one high wall ran a balcony. Its thick wooden rails were painted in different colors by one-yard sections—red, green, yellow, blue. Melted-butter lamps on twisted black iron stands sent yellow light dancing over all that color. A bell-shaped iron stove sat in one corner, its rusty sides seemingly on the verge of glowing red-hot. The wind moaned constantly and softly in the background.

Looking like a Buddha, with his clean-shaved head and his cheeks spilling straight onto the crimson shoulders of his robe without any sign of a neck, the lama nodded to indicate the moment of silence was over.

"I am Toshan," he said, a smile coming back. "I bid you welcome to the Lamasery of the Winds."

Annja sighed. Business pressed. She felt almost as reluctant to turn to it as to let go of mourning for Lal. There's always time for grief later, she reminded herself.

"You speak English very well, Toshan," she said.

"I did not always live on a remote mountaintop, my friends. When I was young I, too, traveled the world. Once, I visited America. I spent time with relatives who lived in a most magical city."

"Which one?"

He beamed. "Pittsburgh. Also," he said, "we have a satellite dish."

For a moment Annja was unable to do anything more than gape at him, dumbfounded.

"I thought this was called the Lost Lamasery?" Pan said.

Toshan laughed. "But it is not lost!" he exclaimed. "We know right where it is. You are here, are you not? No, the proper translation, taking mind of the difference, is Lamasery of the Lost."

"Wait," Annja said. "What does that mean, exactly? Lost souls?"

The lama laughed some more. "Perhaps 'found souls' would be better. No, not of lost souls. It is a gathering place for those who are lost to this world."

Annja glanced at Pan. He looked distant again, almost as if in a trance. She halfway hoped he was still altitude sick.

"But I'm not lost to the world," she said.

"Are you not, Annja Creed? You, who carry the burden you do? Can you truly belong to the world you knew, the material world of ready explanations it pleases you to call 'scientific'? Or do you merely cling to that which you have already lost beyond recovery?"

She said nothing.

Toshan clapped his hands. Lamas in both saffron and red robes entered bearing beaten-brass trays with colorful covered ceramic bowls on them.

"Now you must sustain your bodies, my friends,

that they may adequately house your spirits. That's very important, you know!"

The lamas set the bowls between the visitors and Toshan. There were a variety of vegetables in various sauces, and white sticky rice. Toshan beckoned his guests to serve themselves. Moving almost like an automaton Pan served Annja and then himself healthy quantities on oblong plates of scarlet ceramic, painted with mythological beings.

Annja began to eat, the sudden awareness of how ravenously hungry she was driving almost everything else from her mind. Beside her Pan ate as wolfishly. She had thought the nausea that had roiled incessantly in her stomach all day, another reaction to higher altitude than her system was prepared to handle, would keep her appetite at a minimum. But it made no difference.

Toshan watched with apparent satisfaction as his guests ate. Then with a nod he graciously permitted red-robed acolytes to heap his own plate high with food.

"You are to be congratulated, my friends," he said at last. "You have passed through the four previous lamaseries—earth, stone, water, fire, each named for the element which dominates it. To reach each one you have faced trials. At each, you received further guidance on your path. We are, as I have told you, wind. Here you shall receive the final guidance. I warn you, though, that your greatest trials, physical and spiritual, await."

"You should know, Toshan," Pan said, pausing between spoonfuls of rice, "we're being chased by a combination of Maoist guerrillas and bandits from Kosovo."

Toshan's laugh boomed off the walls. "Do you think us unaware of this? Ah, my foreign friends, do you think anything passes in this land without our knowing? We have abided here many centuries, while enemies and kingdoms and parties came and went. Do you think isolation alone has served to protect us? Forbidding walls of stone?"

He shook his head. "Those of whom you speak do not threaten us. Only those whom we allow can find this place."

"What will keep them out?" Pan challenged. "The demons they claimed attacked them in the snow?"

Annja felt a twinge. Is this the real Pan asking the question? She could as easily imagine his fantasy persona of an ancient general speaking those words in just that imperious tone.

"That's all just suggestibility and altitude sickness," she found herself saying.

Toshan smiled. "Perhaps. Perhaps indeed. Maybe we did send demons—maybe we sent the storm that shielded you and perplexed your foes. Or maybe those impure ones who follow you summoned up demons from within their souls to torment themselves. Perhaps it is all those things, and none." He laughed again.

Annja could only shake her head. She decided to eat more.

When she and Pan sat back, their hunger fed at last, Toshan said, "As you see, I know about your quests, my friends." Annja noted his use of the plural. "General Pantheras came here on a quest, too. He neared his goals. The one he had set out to reach. And the true, greater one."

"Will you answer a question for me, Master Toshan?" Annja said.

He laughed yet again. "Please. Just Toshan. Spare me the burden of titles."

"All right—Toshan. Why have we found all these clues? Every lamasery we've stopped at has presented us with scraps of transcriptions of a journal written over two thousand years ago. Hasn't that been awfully convenient?"

"It is because you were fated to come here," Toshan said.

Annja thought she showed no reaction. But the monk chuckled.

"Oh, I know that you do not believe in *fate,* Annja Creed. Any more than you believe in demons. Despite the secret burden you carry. You are simply too polite to tell a fat old man to his face that you believe he is, as you might say, full of it.

"You believe that only you, and those who think as you do, see the true face of reality. I can only shake my head sadly, and hope that someday you might see that this universe of shining gears and ratchets you have constructed to believe in is itself merely a glittering toy, an illusion by which you hide the truth from your eyes."

She started to say something. Whether to dispute him or make some polite evasion she didn't know. But he held up a chubby finger.

"No need exists for us to debate. My universe, like your unseeing, unfeeling, uncaring machine, shall carry on regardless of whether either of us believes or disbelieves. I only caution you, for your sake— do not be too hasty to disbelieve in the help that comes to you in your direst need. You can explain it away later. What is vital to your quest, and possibly your survival, is that you not fight it."

She nodded. "I'll do my best."

"Of course you will, child. The clues you speak of were given so that you might be tested. As I say, you have proved worthy. Of course, what you have proved worthy of is nothing more than a final test. Is that not the way of quests?"

He rang a small brass bell with a blue-painted por- celain handle. A yellow-robed lama entered carrying a scroll on a tray.

"As you no doubt guess," Toshan said, "this is yet another transcription from General Pantheras's journal."

Pan accepted and carefully unwrapped it. Annja saw with relieved approval that he had pulled on a pair of thin gloves before handling the age-yellowed document. Either he had returned fully to the present or the habits ingrained by archaeological training and fieldwork transcended space and time. Whatever works, she decided.

His handsome face grew craggier in his concentration, despite the softening effect of the butter-bowl light. "It's short," he said. "He says he has been given directions to the cave shrine. He also mentions that the lamas say it is guarded by a hairy man-like creature."

He looked up blinking. "That's all. He doesn't actually repeat the directions."

Annja felt as if her heart had entered free fall. Stricken, she looked to Toshan.

He smiled beneficently. "Open your hearts, children, and you shall not leave this lamasery without the knowledge you need to complete your quest."

Before either could say anything he clapped his hands. A young lama in a crimson robe entered and bowed.

"You are tired from your travails," Toshan said. "Now you will sleep. Zonpa will see you to your chamber. Your possessions have been carried there for you."

Throughout, he never stopped beaming at them as if they were his very favorite niece and nephew. Nonetheless, his tone was as final as the closing of the immense iron-bound gates of the lamasery itself.

Annja and Pan rose and followed the silent Zonpa. He led them out of the chamber, down stone hallways lit by torches, up several flights of stairs and along another corridor. This one had unadorned walls and was lit dimly by butter lamps guttering in infrequent niches.

Zonpa stopped and bowed them through an open doorway. They entered. It was a simple chamber with windows set high in the walls, illuminated by the inevitable butter lamps. Two pallets had been laid out side by side. Annja's and Pan's gear, rifles included, was stacked to either side.

Clearly the lamas didn't care much about maintaining the appearance of propriety between their guests. Or its actuality. Annja glanced at Pan.

Kneeling, Pan went through his gear. "So our yeti guards the highest shrine," he said thoughtfully.

She looked at him sharply. "What happened to your earlier hardheaded skepticism about yetis?"

He chuckled. "I saw one, to start with. So did you."

"The visibility was bad. And we were fighting for our lives. It was just a bear, Pan," she said.

"It didn't look like any bear I've ever seen."

She shook her head in annoyance.

"It didn't really look like a man to me, either, Annja. Manlike, but not a man. And why do the natives all say the creature exists? They live here."

She drew a deep breath and sighed it out. "This altitude is getting to both of us," she said, shaking her head. "There's no point debating this."

"No doubt you're right, Annja."

She knelt with hands on knees, looking at the bones of her hands where they stood out against the skin. The wind sighed and cried faintly. There seemed no place in the vast fortress-like lamasery where she didn't hear the wind.

There was so much she longed to discuss with

Pan. But suddenly the whole weight of the day's events seemed to land on her at once.

She barely had the energy to unlace and remove her boots and crawl beneath the waiting blankets and furs before she dropped into a deep sleep.

28

Dressed in his black leather greatcoat, despite the fact it wasn't as well insulated as the puffy, brightly hued jackets that tourists and even many locals wore, Enver Bajraktari stood with his arms folded as his enormous henchman, Duka, plunged an arm into the drift of snow the guerrillas had been excavating. The bodyguard was roped to another Kosovar who sat on the trail several yards above with feet braced against a rock, belaying him. A few yards farther down, past a rugged gray rock, was nothing but air.

Pushing with his uninjured leg, Duka grunted mightily and heaved. Up came a dark shape encrusted in snow. It was the hood of a furry mountain coat, with a man's head inside.

Several of the up-country guerrillas—a different breed, Bajraktari knew, from the city-bred barroom commandos who accompanied Chatura—slid down the short slope, their legs raising white swells of snow. They pulled the man Duka had found the rest of the way from the snowbank and laid him carefully out on the slope. One held a canteen to the badly chapped lips surrounded by a fringe of grizzled stubble and dribbled water between them. The man sat up coughing. The hood fell back from his head.

"Why did you disturb me?" Major Jagannatha demanded.

"Left to my own devices," Chatura said, "I wouldn't have. But, it seems, you are too much the legend to be allowed to slip peacefully into oblivion. Even by my own men."

"If it's any consolation, Major," Bajraktari called to him, "we thought we were recovering your corpse."

Jagannatha looked up at him with red eyes and spit. His men helped him to his feet. He shook them off and trudged up to the trail unaided. At once he was surrounded by his own troops and men in green-and-black camouflage, cheering and clapping him on the back. Chatura stood to one side looking sour.

Bajraktari moved over beside the commissar. "Don't be downcast, comrade," he said. "We lost many men to the avalanche and the storm. Many of Jagannatha's wolves died fighting the outlanders. This man is a seasoned warrior. I know the breed. We need his courage and his cunning. And afterward, when the treasure is ours, we can give him his desire to rest—is it not so?"

"I REGRET TO SAY that the Sherpas you brought with you have refused to proceed any further," Toshan said over a plentiful breakfast. "They have opted to return to their villages."

Sunshine shot into Toshan's audience chamber through high windows. Its brightness bleached the colorful carved walls where it touched them. The iron stove cast its warmth. The wind muttered and occasionally boomed.

Annja paused long enough to swallow her mouthful of food. "I don't blame them. We'll carry on as best we can," she said.

"Oh, you're not to be left in the lurch, my young friends. No worries. Prasad has elected to remain with you. He is a good man."

"He is," Pan said.

"We have told him we will keep the body of his nephew until his return. Should he not return, we will give the body to you to deliver to his relatives in Baglung. If you do not return, we shall see him home ourselves."

Annja nodded.

"As for Sherpas, we have arranged for men from the vicinity to carry such supplies as you will need."

Annja looked at him in surprise. "I didn't think there'd be many people up here."

Toshan smiled his world-encompassing smile. "The White Mountain holds many surprises, my friends."

OUT IN THE YARD they found a glum Prasad awaiting them. Annja went to him and hugged him briefly.

He endured it stolidly. Pan gripped him on the shoulder.

They turned to look over their porters. A half dozen small sturdy men in heavy, fur-lined coats with big fur caps looked back at them curiously. To Annja's surprise each man carried a bolt-action Enfield rifle slung over his shoulder.

Toshan came down the monastery steps behind them.

"Guns?" Annja asked.

He smiled. "Some of the bloodier episodes of the history of Tibetan Buddhism might surprise you, Annja Creed. We are not always men of peace. When pilgrims face peril from the unrighteous, it is certainly permitted that they defend themselves."

"Pilgrims?" Annja said.

"I think he means us," Pan said.

She glanced up at him. He had his head up and was looking at the great mountain looming above them. In the early-morning sun his expression seemed composed and determined.

She looked back at Toshan. The fat monk stood with his plump, bare legs splayed wide and the wind whipping his scarlet robe around his calves.

"The shrine lies higher up the mountain, above the tree line," he told them. "In your hearts you know where to find it."

Annja looked at him in puzzlement. But Pan nodded. "I can find it."

"Go with my blessings, then. And an old man's

wishes that you both attain that which your hearts truly desire."

"Thank you, Toshan," Annja said.

"You do us a great service," he told her. "What we have done is the least we can do."

She kissed him on his cheek. His skin felt smooth as a baby's. Then she turned and led the way out of the Lost Lamasery and off across the swaying rope bridge.

THEY FOUND TRAILS along and up the mountainside. They were steep, and snow and ice made the footing treacherous, but the only real difficulty was the thinness of the air.

General Pantheras didn't have oxygen bottles, either, Annja told herself grimly as they trudged up a broad rocky chute. The early-spring Himalayan sky, when she paused and pushed her goggles up her forehead, was clear. But she knew that everything could change in an eye blink at this time of year.

The trail led around the mountain's flank. The path was relatively broad, the slope to their left relatively gentle. She knew that was deceptive; beyond the edge it was a long way down. The trail wasn't as gut-churningly terrifying as the ones they'd threaded yesterday. But a moment's inattention as her boots crunched through the snow could kill her just as dead.

Although she felt rested and fit, she knew that was partly illusion. The high-altitude climber's rule was to sleep below ten thousand feet whenever possible.

Above that the air's meager oxygen density challenged the system and made it hard for the body to recover even with rest. The Lamasery of the Winds was at twelve thousand feet. She wished they could have overnighted in the old Italian base camp north of Pakabon, currently visible beside the riverbed almost directly below them.

And if wishes were wings we'd just fly there, she reminded herself.

She was seeing phantoms. Strange shadow shapes lurked at the corners of her vision. Twice already she had started, turning and preparing to call the sword into her hand, before realizing they were figments cast up by a brain whose oxygen hunger her deepest breath couldn't fully assuage.

This was a usually well-traveled part of Dhaulagiri. Yet they'd seen no one the past two days but themselves, their pursuers and the monks. Toshan had told them over breakfast that word of an increase in the violence of the civil unrest was driving tourists off the mountain and indeed, many out of Nepal itself.

As the sun neared the zenith a cry floated back from the leading Sherpa, who walked well in advance with his Enfield in his thickly gloved hands. Standing on a trail that switched back above their heads he waved and pointed.

"He says he sees the cave," Prasad said, trudging toward Annja and Pan.

He walked bent over, as if he still carried the dead-weight of his beloved nephew. Which in a sense he does, I guess, Annja thought. Her heart went out to him.

Pan straightened. His gaze was clear as he turned his face up the snow-bright slope toward the non-descript jumble of rocks the excited guide pointed at. But was it the clarity of sanity, she wondered, of being fully present in today and his real self?

A sound, shocking and bright as a raw red wound, snapped out from below. Spinning around with her heart hammering, Annja saw, strung out along the slope below, the dark sinister shapes of the hunters.

29

Echoes of the gunshot seemed to rush over them like smoke. Prasad shouted instructions to the men. Although strangers to him, they obeyed unhesitatingly. The monks had chosen well. As Pan unlimbered his own slung Kalashnikov, several Sherpas shed their packs and started fanning out to seek cover with their bolt guns.

As more gunfire crackled from below, Annja realized both Pan and Prasad were looking toward her. Prasad had also dropped his pack. She knew immediately what that signified—this would be the fight that decided all.

No bullets came near them. But Annja could see puffs in the snow below them where they fell short.

"We should press on," she said. "The cave has to

be more defensible than being out here on the trail like this."

Prasad nodded instantly. Pan looked at her for a moment.

She remembered his promise to fight beside her. She didn't know who had delivered that promise— Sergeant Pan or General Pantheras.

Pan nodded crisply. Gunshots began to thud from the men who had taken up blocking positions on their back trail. Annja led the rest up as fast as she dared go.

"Look," Prasad called, pointing, just as they reached the switchback. Following his outstretched hand, Annja looked up the valley. Her heart sank.

Like a volcano's deadly flow, a white mass streamed down the glacier.

"The storm will be on us in minutes," Prasad said.

"It will help us," Pan said, his voice seeming to come from unusually deep in his chest. "In the snow they cannot shoot at a distance. If we have a good defensive position, they will lose the advantage of numbers."

Head around a switchback, Annja nodded. She was pleased to have a seasoned veteran—whichever one he was at the moment—second her own flash assessment of the situation. She knew her judgment was good. But it never hurt to have confirmation.

As she started up the next stage Annja heard the gunfire increase. She couldn't see whom her men were shooting at.

Pan touched her arm. "There it is."

She looked up the slope. Forty yards above and to their left a sliver of shadow showed dark beneath the slab that crowned the rock outcrop their point man had indicated. Without waiting for instructions, Prasad began to forge straight toward it, angling to avoid the sheer drop that fell from a little ledge before the cave. Annja and Pan followed, plunging instantly into snow up to their thighs.

She heard the crack of bullets passing. Five yards to her left a Sherpa grunted and dropped forward. The snow swallowed him, leaving only a hole to mark the spot where he fell.

Annja's heart was already laboring. She looked back. The four men who had positioned themselves as rear guard suddenly shouted in alarm. Two of them leaped to their feet, spinning to point their rifles uphill. A shattering burst of Kalashnikov fire from above knocked them both down. The one positioned outside the trail fell down the slope, rolling over and over until he became cocooned in snow.

A hand clamped her arm. "Come on!" Pan shouted, pulling her toward the cave.

She hung back. "But we have to help them!" she shouted.

"We cannot. Jagannatha has flanked them. They're caught in the kill zone."

As Pan spoke the words, the other two men jerked and fell as bullets found them. One lay utterly still. The other continued to kick until a single shot cracked out. He spasmed and then he also stopped moving.

Annja turned and raced for the cave, churning through deep snow. It was like trying to run along the bottom of a swimming pool but even harder. She forced her way onward against weight and resistance.

As she neared the beckoning darkness of the cave mouth, Annja's legs gave way beneath her. Pan seized her from the left, Prasad from the right. The two men hauled her up and carried her the last few yards with her legs dragging trails in the snow. When they reached the snow-covered stone ledge in front of the cave they laid her down carefully. Then they dropped to their knees, panting.

Without being fully aware of doing it, Annja found the metal-shod plastic butt of her rifle, pulled it tightly to her shoulder, the iron sights swimming before her eyes. Figures trudged up the mountain toward her, shockingly close. Some were small and carried submachine guns. Others carried broken-nosed AKs.

Annja laid the front sight on one of the taller forms and pulled the trigger. The man slumped. She drew another breath deep to her belly, let some out, held it as she switched to the nearest target to her left. It was one of the Maoists. She squeezed the trigger and he fell.

She was sitting but not in anything that could be called a proper shooting posture. It didn't matter, especially with the weapon's weight and recoil as light as an M-16's. Her world had narrowed to a sort of white tunnel with out-of-focus figures beyond. Only vague stirrings of motions at the fringes of her tunnel vision alerted her to more targets. She felt neither fear nor fatigue. She felt nothing at all. There was only deep-breathing meditation.

The meditation of death.

She shot two more attackers. Another two fell from shots that thundered from somewhere outside her narrow field of vision. Hands hauled her up until she got her boots beneath her. She stood and spun, then staggered into the cave under her own power as another burst of Kalashnikov fire cracked off the rock around her.

Above her, someone screamed. Her small brave party was already mostly gone.

Inside, the cave was still cold, but felt almost hot after the chill of the wind outside. It was dark. A greenish glow sprang up to fill the space as Pan cracked a light-stick.

The cave was smaller than Annja expected. There was no question it was artificial—the walls were flush, polished smooth and shiny.

It was also empty. Annja felt herself sag.

She heard harsh voices outside the cave. Dropping his light-stick, Pan spun and fired a burst from his hip. The muzzle-flash filled the tiny cave with angry, jittering orange glare. The sound in the tight confines was like jackhammers pounding not just Annja's eardrums but her very skull. In the irregular glow of snow-whitened daylight that was the cave entrance, furry figures danced and fell as copper-jacketed slugs peppered them.

A waist-high bank of blue smoke, stinking of burned propellants and lubricants, filled the cave. So did the copper smell of blood. Prasad darted to the entrance and fired his own Kalashnikov until the heavy bolt locked back over an empty magazine.

She heard another sound, like fat raindrops spattering a cardboard box. Prasad grunted. Dropping his heavy rifle with a clatter, he reeled back into the cave. Annja saw small holes, deceptively neat, in the front of his coat.

Something clanked on the smooth stone floor. A metal egg was bouncing toward Annja. She stared at it as if it was a serpent in midstrike. For once she was frozen in indecision.

Prasad fielded it one-handed like a major-league shortstop bare-handing a bouncer up the middle. He jammed it to his chest, folded his arms over it and rushed outside.

Annja heard the thump of bodies colliding. The grenade went off, its explosion muffled by human flesh.

It was followed at once by a whole series of explosions like a firecracker string going off, but magnified a hundredfold. Brilliant hellfire flashes danced in the cave mouth as Pan's body hit hers, slammed her to the cave's back wall and pressed her down to the floor.

The blasts and blue-white flashes seemed to go on and on. The flashes ceased, and Annja realized she was hearing the echoes in her own head. Her ears rang with a high keening note.

Pan climbed painfully to his feet. Picking up his rifle from where he'd dropped it, he went cautiously to the cave entrance and stuck his head out for a three-second look. Then he stepped outside.

Annja sat up. Her head spun. She felt numbed horror at Prasad's self-sacrifice. For a moment she couldn't bring herself to budge.

To her enormous relief, Pan quickly returned to kneel at her side. "They've pulled back," he shouted. "We should check out the cave."

She nodded. He rose and extended a hand to help her. She shook her head and pushed off with her hands. She swayed, had to get a knee beneath her. Finally, with a heave of her will, she got upright and shook her head. Her hood had fallen back.

Since Pan had stuck his head out into the daylight, Annja's eyes were better adjusted to the dark than his. She quickly found a second crack that, from the proper angle, turned out to be a four-foot-wide tunnel angling into the rock of the mountain. From where they had been it was completely invisible.

They shared a look, then cautiously entered the passageway. Annja held her M-16 in one hand and a small flashlight in the other. Ahead of them the tunnel, which like the cave was either wholly artificial or natural but improved, curved right. As they crept around the bend they saw a yellow glow.

Pan moved in front of Annja, rifle at the ready. She followed close behind, holding the flashlight up over his shoulder and making sure to keep the muzzle of her weapon covering his back.

A few feet beyond the tunnel a wide, smooth-walled chamber opened. Pan advanced into it. At once he sidestepped left, by policeman's reflex clearing the area where any hypothetical waiting enemy would have a perfect shot at him. Annja followed, quickly stepping right. Then she let herself take in her surroundings, and inhaled sharply.

By the light of butter lamps she saw treasure. Gold coins, silver ingots, jewels, glittering idols, covered the floor. Overflowing crates were stacked high up the walls. A path through the center of the room led to a jovial golden Buddha statue, at least twice life-size, sitting in lotus position in an alcove in the far wall.

Before his crossed legs rose a stone catafalque. Upon it rested the perfectly preserved body of a man in full Macedonian armor.

"Oh, my God," Annja breathed.

Aside from his full beard, which was black lined with silver, he was a perfect match for the man who stood beside her.

30

As if in a trance, Pan walked slowly forward. A sword in a scabbard of what appeared to be leather as well preserved as the dead man lay across a bronze breast-plate molded to resemble a heavily muscled torso. The bronze itself was still a deep yellow-red color, not the green of verdigris. A large oval shield stood propped against the stone bier by his feet. Its polished face was silver, its sheen dulled but not discolored or severely tarnished.

Pan picked up the sword and drew it from the sheath by its gilded hilt. It was a *xiphos*, the characteristic Macedonian sword, with a straight, double-edged blade about two feet long.

Yellow light from the improbably burning lamps reflected across Pan's face from the shining blade, illuminating a look of sheer reverence as he turned it in his hands. He spoke words Annja could not hear. She knew she would not have understood them if she had.

A shot shattered the cavern's silence and her world. Pan pitched forward across the corpse.

Too shocked to feel, Annja spun. A man built like a short bear with a tattered and bloody coat stood at the treasure chamber's entrance. Half his face was burned black, and his left eye was invisible behind a crust of baked and congealed blood. His unscorched cheek bristled with a graying stubble of beard. In his right hand he held an ungainly pistol with a short box magazine in front of the trigger and a long slender barrel.

It was Major Jagannatha. His terribly disfigured face was a mask of conflicting passions. Annja was astonished to see what she could only take for grief predominate.

"I'm sorry," he said. "It must be this way. I cannot let you tell the world of this."

She felt as cold as the glacier in the valley below. "So you'll let Chatura plunder it instead," she said angrily.

He frowned, mulling that over. "No," he said slowly. "I'll die first. But before that I shall kill him."

The numbness of seeing her companion, her friend, unexpectedly gunned down before her began to fade. Emotion began to seep in around the edges of Annja's being. She felt *rage*.

"You're right about one thing," she said. "You will die."

The sword appeared in her hand. She lunged to impale the guerrilla chieftain. His gun roared again. The sword's sudden apparition and the ferocity of Annja's assault made Jagannatha flinch. It threw off his aim.

Pain lanced through Annja's left thigh like a white-hot iron. The leg gave way beneath her. Jagannatha danced back.

The pain was literally breathtaking. Each move seemed to tear her muscles apart. But the anger kept growing, driving her on. She forced the leg to work, to launch herself at him again. His next shot missed her clean. He evaded a clumsy swipe of her sword.

She ran into him. They grappled as her momentum pushed him back. She bounced him backward off the walls of the passageway as they battered and clawed ineffectually at one another. He held her too tight for her to wield the sword. She had his gun wrist in an unbreakable grip, and its long barrel worked against him as the sword's length did her.

Their wild pinball battle carried them into the cave's outer chamber. By a random shift of their writhing Jagannatha managed to bring a knee up hard into Annja's stomach. The breath rushed out of her and her grip weakened.

He pulled away and raised the handgun. His muscles trembled with exhaustion and oxygen star-vation. He fought to control the swinging of the muzzle enough to get a shot into Annja.

Taking a two-handed grip on her sword, she wound up and swung with all her might. They both screamed as the mystic blade struck his gun arm two inches above the wrist. As he raised the bleeding arm before his face in horrified disbelief she side kicked him out the cave mouth. His head struck a rock as he fell.

In grief and pain and fury, Annja collapsed on the cave floor. The cold stone sucked the warmth from her body. Somehow that felt seductive. She felt as if she should just let go, allow her life to flow from her and merge with the stone of the great White Mountain, to make an end of strife and pain.

But that was not her way. She refused to give in or give up.

Full of pain, she crawled forward and disengaged the autopistol from Jagannatha's still-twitching fingers. I'll need all the firepower I can get, she thought.

She no longer had any reasonable hope of escape. She was alone on the mountain. All her friends and allies were dead. But she was coldly determined to take as many of her tormentors with her as possible.

"SO," CHATURA SAID, standing on the trail with hands on hips. "The mighty Jagannatha still lives."

Enver Bajraktari and Duka stood right behind him. The guerrilla chieftain lay bent across a boulder ten feet beneath the ledge of the cave, his arm bleeding in fitful pulses. Though his chest continued to rise and fall, his spine was clearly broken. The storm had subsided for the moment; the wind was almost still, and only flat flakes fell slowly upon his shattered body.

"We'll have to remedy that," the commissar said.

Bajraktari was woozy with more than altitude and exertion. They were down to fewer than twenty men. Almost as many lay strewed along the trail and especially around the cave mouth.

The pursuit had been nothing but disaster piling upon disaster. Only a mad rage for revenge combined with an even more insane lust for the gold that must await them within that cave had kept the mixed group from breaking and fleeing back down the mountain.

There couldn't be many living enemies inside the cave with that terrible witch woman. She might even be alone. All the same, by now Bajraktari felt they'd need every man they had to force their way inside and overcome her.

Duka looked at him. Jagannatha had fought like a hero. But he was no use to them now. Bajraktari looked his henchman in the eye and shrugged.

Although he still favored his right leg in its brace, Duka disregarded the sheer drop. He slithered out toward Jagannatha. When he reached the guerrilla leader he picked him up and flung him unceremoniously over the cliff.

Bajraktari stood watching the dark, spread-eagled shape dwindle beneath them. When it fell out of sight he turned his dark eyes up to the mouth of the cave.

Chatura brandished his autopistol. "What are you waiting for?" he shouted as the wind again began to rise to a howl. "Seize the cave, in the people's name!"

Reluctantly the men began to advance along the barely visible wisp of trail toward the cave's dark mouth.

Blasts of gunfire met them.

ANNJA FIRED her M-16 until it ran dry. That made her enemies fall back from the entrance. Throwing aside the rifle, she pulled Jagannatha's gun from her belt and went to the entrance.

A Kosovar loomed in front of her. She shot him in the chest and he went backward over the ledge. Leaning around the entrance, she aimed shots at her attackers. At least two went down before a wild fusillade from a half-dozen automatic weapons drove her back into the cave.

She shot the first two men who came in after her. The pistol's bolt locked back. Its magazine was empty. Any spare magazines had gone down the mountain with Jagannatha.

Falling back, she dropped the useless weapon. A shadow blocked the entrance. She recognized the vast ungainly shape of Duka. He entered with Bajraktari right behind him.

The Kosovar chieftain looked at her with his living eye as cold as his dead one. "Take her," he commanded.

The sword flashed into Annja's hand.

Bajraktari shrugged. "Very well, then. Shoot her."

Laughing uproariously, Duka raised a Skorpion machine pistol. His laughter boomed off the walls of the cave. Something spun past Annja, moaning. She felt its breeze of passage puff against her sweat-drenched cheek.

In wonder Duka looked down at the golden hilt of the ancient *xiphos* buried in his chest. Then he toppled forward.

Bajraktari gaped at his henchman's fall. He tried to raise his gun.

Annja was already gliding toward him like an avenging Fury. "You lose," she said, and slid the sword into his belly until the cross-shaped hilt stopped against his torso.

Bajraktari's dark eye stood out from his head, staring at her in agonized disbelief. Savagely she twisted the sword. His lips worked beneath his mustache as he tried to force out words. All that came forth was a flood of bright blood.

She yanked the heavy autopistol from his hand. Despite the pain she raised her wounded leg—she didn't trust it to bear her weight unaided. Putting the sole of her boot against his chest she pushed hard. The sword tore free.

Bajraktari tottered backward. Shrieking, he went over the edge, to free fall a thousand feet with his guts streaming from his body.

The pain the exertion shot through her leg brought

Annja to tears and robbed her of her strength. Her legs buckled beneath her.

A strong arm caught her from behind as she fell.

She looked up. Pan held her. He was dressed in the full armor from the dead man on the bier. Still supporting her, he stooped to yank his sword out of the dead Kosovar's chest.

She stared at him. "How?"

He only smiled down at her.

Her vision faded. She sagged. He steadied her until she could stand on her own again. Then he took up the silver shield he had carried in with him.

In a moment the enemy was on them again. Side by side they fought. The three surviving Kosovars charged in and were cut down before their eyes adjusted to the cave gloom.

Annja and Pan moved to stand to either side of the entrance. Guerrillas rushed in blazing wildly with submachine guns. The defenders slashed them down from behind. Then came four of Jagannatha's men, *kukris* in their hands and vengeance in their eyes.

Ignoring the shortness of breath that seemed to tear at her chest at every inhalation, ignoring the agony of her wounded leg, Annja fought in a whirlwind. Pan fought with controlled fury, blocking deftly with his shield. His *xiphos* licked out like a frozen steel flame.

Silence descended. The sound of the rising storm rushed in to fill it. Dead men lay heaped at their feet. The floor ran slick with blood.

Strength deserted Annja. Sheathing his sword, Pan caught her again. He pressed his mouth to hers. They shared a passionate kiss.

Then consciousness left her, and Annja slid into black.

WHEN SHE AWOKE, Annja was alone. Except for the dead.

Using her elbows, she dragged herself to the cave entrance. The storm was about to hit again. The first hard-driven flakes of snow struck Annja's cheek like grit.

Coming up the path below she saw a fresh squad of Maoist guerrillas, trudging bent over into the wind with their submachine guns held across their chests. A small figure slipped from hiding among the rocks to join them.

Annja was flooded with anger. The man was Chatura, the district commissioner for antiquities division.

He was the one behind all her troubles. The man guilty of the deaths of her friends. He had set her up from the very outset.

Chatura gestured up at the cave.

She grabbed a submachine gun dropped by a fallen foe and sprayed the advancing men with bullets. Two of them went down, one dropping on the narrow trail, the other tumbling down a few yards before going over the cliff.

The others went to their bellies and fired back.

The flames from their muzzles were like small bonfires in the fading light. She lashed the flame sources with bullets until the curved magazine emptied. Then she slithered back far enough to find another weapon and fight on.

The snow closed in like a white wave sweeping over the face of the mountain. The last weapon Annja could reach without going back into the cave and giving her enemies a chance to rush her ran dry.

Frustrated and filled with fury she retreated. Exhausted by blood loss and altitude, she collapsed against a wall of the small cave. It's not fair, she thought. We won. How can more enemies turn up now to make a mockery of it all? Of Pan's sacrifice?

But Pan's still alive…isn't he?

She might have retired to the treasure room and made a last stand there. But she didn't have the strength anymore. It felt as if her bones were melting within her.

The wind began to keen as if in mourning for the day's dead. Through the white blizzard curtain that covered the cave mouth Chatura stepped, grinning. He aimed his handgun at her.

"You have given me a very great deal of trouble, Ms. Creed," he said. "I am about to shoot you in the belly. I don't want to kill you right away, you see. I mean to disable you, and allow my men to take their revenge on you for the deaths of their comrades."

Annja gathered the last threads of her strength for a death leap. As she curled her hand to summon the sword she heard shouts from outside the cave. They quickly turned to screams.

Frowning in puzzlement, Chatura started to turn. He was yanked backward out into the storm. Through a scrim of falling snow, Annja saw in silhouette a huge form holding the struggling man aloft. Chatura was tossed to his death.

Roaring, the creature turned on the other gunman. It moved out of sight. A heartbeat later Annja saw guerrillas hurled past the cave mouth and over the cliff, following their treacherous leader to destruction.

She could hold on no more. Oblivion claimed her.

"IT WAS A BEAR," she insisted. "What else could it possibly have been?"

Annja sat with Roux at a sidewalk café. It was three weeks after the desperate fight for the cave shrine, and her wounds had mostly healed. A gentle spring-morning breeze made the streets of downtown Delhi almost bearable.

Uncharacteristically, Roux said nothing. He merely sat and sipped his coffee, well dosed with cream and sugar.

"Next thing I knew I woke up in the treasure room next to Pan," she told him, "with my wounds all bandaged. I got lucky. The Mauser bullet was copper-jacketed, not pure lead, so it didn't deform much when it hit me. It passed through my leg cleanly. Missed the bone. The doctors here say it didn't do any lasting muscle or nerve damage."

"Which Pan?" Roux asked with his usual lack of sensitivity. "I or II?"

Annja fought back tears. She was determined not to let her guard down with her sometime mentor.

"I don't know," she said.

He sipped coffee and gazed at her with impassive eyes.

"Even though it's up above the tree line, *somebody* must live up there," she went on, trying to steer him back to the main line of her narrative. "Or at least, somebody visits the shrine regularly, tends it. Somebody has to keep those butter lamps filled and burning. They must have found me and bandaged me."

"Indeed."

She drew in a deep breath, then let it out, shaking her head. "I didn't hang around after I woke up. For one thing, I was still desperately weak. For another, I was half-crazy from hunger. I used an M-16 as a crutch and somehow made my way back down to the Lamasery of the Winds. I have no idea how long it took—I really don't remember anything about the trip. Which is probably for the best.

"The lamas helped patch me back together. Whatever treatment they gave me seems to have worked really well. They also got a message out by satellite link to the Japan Buddhist Federation. It took a whole week before I was back on my feet."

For a moment they sat while the traffic growled and honked around them. Pedicabs jingled impatiently at one another. Roux looked indecently cool, composed and somehow superior. He said nothing. A hint of a knowing smile played around his full lips.

She practically felt his unspoken question. It had nagged her, too. "I don't have any idea how Pan did it," she said. "He must not have died at once from Jagannatha's gunshot after all. He somehow got the armor off his…his counterpart…put it on and came to help me fight one last time."

The look on Roux's face was almost pitying. "The truth is so plain," he said, "yet you refuse even to consider it."

"And that would be what?" she asked, daring him to continue.

He set down his cup and sat back, gesturing grandly. "Why, what else? That your savior was the long dead General Pantheras himself. The great champion, the hero who chose to become eternal guardian to the treasure he had been sent to steal. In the last extremity he rose up from his sleep of millennia to carry out his task. Your Pan's sacrifice must have given him the strength."

"You're right," she said quietly.

He blinked at her. "You mean, for once you agree with me?"

"Not about Pan. I mean, you're right, I *won't* consider that."

He sighed peevishly. "And I suppose you're also in denial that the one who finished off your attackers in the storm and the one who ministered to you and laid you beside your Pan were one and the same.

Who but the famous yeti, the *other* guardian of the Golden Buddha?"

"Yep," she said. "I sure do deny that. It was obviously an angry bear that killed Chatura and the rest. And it was pilgrims who tended to me. Nothing else makes sense."

"Ah. Your precious rationality, which means so much more to you than *truth*."

He picked up his cup on its saucer again and drank. "Well, I hate to add to your sorrows by bearing bad news. But I must."

She frowned and leaned forward. "What bad news?"

"The team the Japan Buddhist Federation sent to secure the Highest Shrine claims they found no cave."

"But I gave them the GPS coordinates! It kept track of every step we took."

Roux shrugged. "Nevertheless. That is what they claim."

She fell back against the uncomfortable back of her white-painted metal chair. Her whole world had suddenly imploded.

All that sacrifice and sorrow and loss, she thought. All for nothing. I've totally failed.

To make matters worse, she had undoubtedly deep-sixed her own credibility. If the JBF claims my story is false, I'll be lucky to hang on to my job at *Chasing History's Monsters,* she thought. To say nothing of the grim fact that she would certainly lose both her standing in the academic community and even the chance of continuing employment as an undercover archaeologist.

Roux sat studying her face. Then he smiled.

"While it's a shocking, cynical lie that every cloud possesses a silver lining," he said, reaching inside his coat, "this one, as it happens, does."

He produced an envelope. He handed it over. After a quizzical look at him she tore it open.

Inside was a check. From the Japan Buddhist Federation. The amount made her suck in her breath sharply.

"Not only are the JBF paying off on your full contract," Roux said, "they've thrown in a healthy bonus. They also prefer to maintain complete discretion about the whole affair. Insofar as they are concerned, you have successfully carried out your assignment of surveying and cataloging a number of historical shrines in Nepal. Nothing else happened."

She stared at him. "Why?"

He shrugged. "How would I know? Am I a Buddhist? Or Japanese?"

He held up a hand to forestall an angry verbal onslaught. "Peace, woman. If I had to form a guess, and no doubt I do to keep you from flying at my eyes like a Harpy, I should guess that a guilty conscience can sometimes pry open the tightest purse."

Annja's shoulders slumped. "And in the end," she half whispered, "it was still all for nothing."

She drew in a sharp breath. "Except maybe—"

"Except?" Roux asked.

She raised her face hopefully. "Maybe Pan found the prize he was really seeking all his life. As his namesake before him did. Peace?"

Without much interest, Roux shrugged. "As to that, you and I will never know." He leaned forward with elbows on the table and a gleam in his blue eyes. "But come, you must still have your GPS unit, with the coordinates saved. As the saying goes, the ball is in your court, yes?"

Annja leaned back. From an inside pocket of the light cream jacket she wore, she took her GPS. She recalled the cave's coordinates.

For a moment she sat looking at the display. Tears fuzzed out her vision. She blinked them away.

"Farewell, Pantheras Katramados," she whispered.

She pressed Clear.

TAKE 'EM FREE

2 action-packed novels plus a mystery bonus

NO RISK

NO OBLIGATION TO BUY

  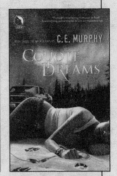